222z

The Untold Stories

Lawrence Katz & Cybill Validum

Copyright © 2024 Lawrence Katz & Cybill Validum. All rights reserved.

2222: The Untold Stories
ISBN 979-8-9883714-0-3 (Paperback)
ISBN 979-8-9883714-2-7 (eBook)

Editor: Carissa Barker-Stucky
Cover: Books and Moods

No part of this publication may be reproduced, distributed, or transmitted in any form or by any means, including photocopying, recording, or other electronic or mechanical methods, without the prior written permission of the author, except in the case of brief quotations embodied in critical reviews and certain other non-commercial uses permitted by copyright law.

The following content is a work of fiction. Any likeness to actual people or events is purely coincidental.

This book is dedicated to our three amazing daughters, Jadyn, Julie, and Abby, and our newborn son, Noah.

And to all the people who are tired of being in the dark and are searching for some light.

Table of Contents

Introduction iii
Chapter 1 1
Chapter 2 11
Chapter 3 21
Chapter 4 31
Chapter 5 41
Chapter 6 53
Chapter 7 61
Chapter 8 73
Chapter 9 79
Chapter 10 91
Chapter 11 103
Chapter 12 115
Chapter 13 125
Chapter 14 133
Chapter 15 143
Chapter 16 149
Chapter 17 157
Chapter 18 171
Chapter 19 183
Chapter 20 193
Chapter 21 205
Chapter 22 215
Chapter 23 225
Chapter 24 237
Chapter 25 247
Chapter 26 259
Chapter 27 273
Chapter 28 287
Chapter 29 297
Chapter 30 305
Author's Notes 309

Table of Contents

Introduction ii
Chapter 1 1
Chapter 2 11
Chapter 3 21
Chapter 4 31
Chapter 5 43
Chapter 6 53
Chapter 7 63
Chapter 8 73
Chapter 9 79
Chapter 10 93
Chapter 11 103
Chapter 12 115
Chapter 13 125
Chapter 14 135
Chapter 15 145
Chapter 16 155
Chapter 17 165
Chapter 18 175
Chapter 19 185
Chapter 20 195
Chapter 21 205
Chapter 22 215
Chapter 23 225
Chapter 24 237
Chapter 25 247
Chapter 26 263
Chapter 27 273
Chapter 28 287
Chapter 29 297
Chapter 30 305
Author's Notes 309

Introduction

We encountered unbearable daily challenges while writing this book, which led us to believe we were on the right path. Then we realized angel numbers were following us. That's where the title came from: 2222 perfectly describes some of the themes we touch on in this piece.

It was subtle at first. A number here and there. But they grew in occurrence. If we sat down to discuss the sale of our book or how it may help others, we would immediately see three or four consecutive sets. We saw them everywhere: shirts, hats, license plates, billboards—even some graffiti splashed across the walls throughout New York City. Then we noticed they were multiplying into sequences of four, five, six of the same numbers. Our spirit guides were supporting us, guiding us to continue.

So what did we find that led to these challenges and blessings? We chose to shine light one some of the darker aspects of our society. Deception. Lust. Unfaithfulness. The lack of true connection.

Marriages fall apart, sex becomes a hobby. Friendships and relationships are spurned for a follower count and internet fame. The person you lay beside at night should be your person; your deepest connection. Society has become a slave to lust, and faithful marriages are martyred. Cheaters deprive their family of time, expect their dirty little secrets to stay hidden in the dark.

Perhaps it's the rush of dopamine. Perhaps it is something we can't see. But humanity has developed a recurring need to please and be pleased. They'll get on their knees to worship anyone but the Holy Father.

It's time to find repentance before all that's left is regret. Let's stop living in hell and face the light.

Liar, liar, your lives are on fire...

Chapter 1

It was a crisp winter morning when Abraham Alvarez made his first big mistake.

The roads were surprisingly clear, of snow and people. Sure, it was Sunday morning, but how many people in New York really went to church? Particularly when all the good Christmas sales were just getting started. Perhaps he really had chosen the best time, a nice early start.

"Where are you going this early?" Maria had asked. "Can't you help me with the kids?"

"I got breakfast ready, what more do you want?" he had groused. She fell silent after that, just shaking her head and going to answer the cries of their youngest. He was still in a foul mood. Why did she have to question every little thing he did?

"I just wish you would dedicate as much time to your family as you do..."

He had heard the line time and again. The object of her ire changed constantly— tutoring his students, hanging out with his friends, running errands. It didn't matter. He shook his head to clear it, glancing out the window of his truck. Another drone in the sky. It wasn't Christmas yet, but they kept peppering the air. Kids, young and old, celebrating early, probably. Testing gifts before giving. Spying on their neighbors. He couldn't help thinking this one was flying surprisingly high. Weren't there rules or something? Not that it affected him. If some kid lost their shiny new toy to an airplane, it was their own fault.

Still. He really was seeing them constantly. Sometimes he wondered if he was really seeing multiple or just the same one throughout the day, but then he would remind himself that was paranoid thinking and briefly entertain the idea of getting sober.

Even now, as he pulled into the parking lot at Jinx's Sporting Goods, he questioned if he was hallucinating. There it was, in the sky yet again, just below cloud cover. And then up it went.

"You're going crazy, bro," he muttered to himself. Luckily he was early. He slipped out of the cab and reached into the container in the back of his truck, slipping out his stash of Hennessy and returning to the cab for a couple of shots. Now that he was here, he felt a little nervous. Meeting new people always spiked his anxiety, ever since he was a kid. As he slid his shot glass back into his dash, the winter light caught his heirloom ring. The diamond and ruby set in gold sparkled to life, looking alive, magical. The sight gave him confidence. Things always went well for Abraham. Today would be no different.

But a little blow never hurt when he was anxious. He reached for the secret compartment in his dashboard and pulled out the snow-white powder. He had a handkerchief ready in case he got another nosebleed. It was always more likely in the winter, with the cold dry air. This time, however, a slight shot of pain was the only effect as he slid the baggie back in place.

The perks of having money— car companies never questioned secrets. If Mr. A wanted secret compartments built into his dash, Mr. A got it. It was no business of theirs what he used them for, though that never stopped the people building the truck from speculating.

As Abraham slipped from the truck, he took a moment to re-tuck his shirt. It fit tight across his rotund shape; he had chosen one that was a little small as if that would translate to his looking smaller, too. He checked his messages and smirked.

> *I really appreciate this, A.*
> *I'm heading out.*

> *Of course, Joseph. Anything to help.*
> *I'll see you soon.*

He tucked the cell back in his pants pocket and started walking towards the store. Though they had been talking for a few months now, this was his first time meeting Joseph in person. Despite the mostly empty streets, Jinx's was packed. Luckily he had a photo to the name, so he wasn't worried about picking him from the crowd. He pushed his way through the front doors and glanced around for the shoes. No one paid him any mind— it was close to Christmas, who cared if a big guy went shopping in an athletic store? It wouldn't be until after Christmas, closer to New Year's, when the sales people would make nuisances of themselves.

Abraham poked through the aisles, trying to avoid feeling claustrophobic. The concrete floors were a bit slick despite the workers' best efforts, the building filled with the sound of voices and squeaking shoes. There was a nice clear area near six benches, with only a few people sitting to try on new shoes. The upholstery used to stick up a good six inches, but years of business had seen it slowly flatten over time. The wooden frames still shined from the clear lacquer protecting them.

People kept pushing past Abraham, and he could swear there were eyes on him. He didn't catch anyone staring, but he just knew they were. Still, he pressed himself back into the crowd and hunted down Joseph's shoe size. Aisle six. He could go ahead and do some browsing before Joseph got there, have a few pairs ready for him to try on.

Once he actually started looking at the shoes, picking up a few boxes to look at information, he saw someone pushing through the crowd towards him. The lighter skin told him it wasn't Joseph, so it was probably an employee making the rounds. Then he frowned. No, the employees had a uniform and this guy wasn't in it. He did have a name badge, though. Management, maybe? As the tall man cleared the crowd and approached Abraham, he smiled. He was dressed in khakis and a button up, with a name tag reading *Javier* and a logo Abraham didn't recognize.

"Can I help you find anything?"

Management, then. Regional maybe. Or a vendor?

"Nah, bro, I'm just browsing for now. Thanks, though." He didn't want to be too abrasive. The guy was just doing his job. But Abraham really wanted him to leave before Joseph showed up. He didn't want to scare him off after going through all the trouble to convince him to meet.

"Browsing for shoes or browsing for 'Joseph'?"

Fuck. Not management. Abraham was sweating a little, but he convinced himself it was the heat from the crowd.

"Who the hell is Joseph? I'm just Christmas shopping, man."

"Sure you are." Javier reached into his pocket, pulling out a cell phone. "'I don't know about this, A,'" he read. "'My parents might not like me heading out so early on a Sunday. What am I supposed to tell them?'" He glanced at Abraham to make sure he was listening. "'Don't worry. Just tell them you're going Christmas shopping with your friends from school. That there's a really good sale, but you don't want them to know what you're getting them.'" Abraham was sweating a little harder now. "'Why can't I just tell them about you?' 'Because adults get weird ideas when other adults want to help out. They don't like charity. And you need these shoes, right?'"

"So what?" Abraham snapped.

"So what?" Javier moved to push a button on his phone. "My name is Javier, and I'm now recording this conversation for my safety. Abraham, I'm Joseph. I set up a fake social media profile, acted like I knew shit about privacy and security. When you messaged, I told you I was a twelve-year-old kid, and you wanted me to lie to my parents about meeting you. And that's pretty damn innocent compared to some of the other things you've said. And you're gonna ask 'so what'? You really don't see a problem here?"

Fuck. *Fuck.*

"I just offered to buy him some shoes. That's not a crime."

"I have 66 pages of conversation saved on a secured hard drive. I just told you, *I'm* Joseph. You can't bluff your way out of this one, Mr. Philanthropist."

Abraham's mind was racing, but he forced himself to look calm. He was a master of secrets. Everything always worked out in the end. He just needed to buy some time, get away from the scene, and have matters dealt with. He had money— these things always went away. Right?

"The fuck do you want, bro?" he growled, eyes intent on the shoes. The crowd swelled around them, absorbed in their own tasks and lives.

"I want to get freaks like you away from kids."

"Then call the damn cops. I don't care about your doctored messages. I'm out of here."

He started to walk away, but Javier caught his arm. "You know damn well they're legit. And forensics will say the same thing. Besides, what's your wife gonna think when you get arrested while they figure it out?" Abraham paused, glancing back at him. His eyes narrowed. Javier wasn't done. "If you try to run, I'm going to let everyone here know what an asshole you are. Or you can stay, and we can talk."

"I have no interest in talking to you. Who the fuck do you think you are, Batman? Swinging your camera around, making up a bunch of shit? And then not calling the cops?" He scowled. "You don't give a damn, do you? No one does." He yanked his arm free. "Trying to take on all the sins of the world? Good luck." He then made another mistake: he tried to leave.

Javier reached out to snatch a megaphone from a nearby employee who had been hawking the wheel of prizes corporate used to trick people into making larger purchases.

"Everyone say 'hi' to Abraham! He came here to meet a twelve-year-old boy and met me instead! Now he's running!"

Curious heads turned; cell phones came out. Everyone loved the drama, it always led to views. Abraham wasn't going to give them a show.

He wasn't the most in shape man, but he managed to get out of that shop faster than he liked to move. By the time he reached his truck, he was huffing, puffing, and in pain. But he whipped open the door, climbed in, and took off as fast as the ice allowed.

He didn't see Javier push out after him, snap photos of his truck and license plate. He didn't even notice the drone. For now, he was more focused on making a phone call.

While Bluetooth picked up the call, he reached for one of the remaining bacon and egg sandwiches he had grabbed from a drive-through. He'd eaten the first two before getting to the store, and now he devoured the third ravenously. This would blow over. The place had been too damn crowded for good video, and Abraham had kept his cool. People would think it was staged, if they even remembered it happened past their fifteen minutes of social media attention.

Everything would be fine, just like it always was. But Javier was going to be a problem.

And now he saw that damn drone again.

"Yo, cariño, shouldn't you be at the church?"

"I got time. Even more, I got a problem." He glanced in his rear-view to check for any cars following him. Jose laughed.

"When don't you have a problem? What is it this time?"

"For one it feels like this damn drone is following me."

Jose laughed harder. "Damn, man, you gotta lay off that powder. You're gonna give yourself a heart attack."

Abraham snorted. "If that's how I go, that's how I go. No point in not enjoying ourselves while we're here, eh?"

"What other problem you got, then?"

"Some asshole named Javier is trying to shake me down for cash. Making up some pretty outrageous shit about sexting kids."

"Holy shit. You call the cops?"

"The fuck they gonna do? Cops are worse than these scammers."

"Eh, I guess that's true. So what you want from me?"

"What you do best. Find wherever he's posted this shit from meeting me at the store, find anyone else who posted it, and get rid of it. See if you can hit those fake texts, too."

"You know that ain't cheap, mijo."

"Since when do I care about cheap? Just let me know when it's done."

"True, true, one of the reasons I love ya. So why did you go meet some scammer, anyway?"

"Fed me a sob story. You know me, man, kids with daddy issues hit where it hurts. I just wanted to get the kid a pair of shoes."

Jose was quiet for a minute, and Abraham could hear him moving around. "You're too good, man. And too gullible. Don't worry about this guy, I'll get it done."

"You're the best, Jose."

"Tell that to your wife. She gotta be a saint with you running off to buy some kid shoes today of all days."

Abraham was pulling into the church parking lot. "I'm here in plenty of time, it's fine. I'll talk to you later, bro. Let me know when it's done."

"Alright, man. I'll talk to you later. Give Jesús a kiss from his favorite cousin. You remembered his ring, right?"

"Course, man. Got it right here." Once Jose was off the line, Abraham pulled up his phone and started deleting certain messages with 'Joseph'. He should have used a burner. Luckily he could just claim AI made those damn photos. Next time, he would make the kid send nudes first before he trusted them.

Chapter 2

"Forgive me, Father, for I have sinned."

"Tell me, child."

"I grow jealous and distrustful of my husband. I question his every move. I worry about where he is, what he is doing."

"Has he given you reason to distrust him?"

"He has, in the past. But he swears he's a better man."

"Trust must be earned, child. But you mustn't let bitterness guide your heart. Leave vengeance to the Lord, and let your heart be vulnerable."

"I also worry about our wealth. My husband tells me nothing of our finances, and yet I know we have much. His family is rich, has always been rich, but no one knows why. Only those related by blood are let in on the secret."

"Do you have reason to be concerned?"

"I don't know. I don't know why it's such a closely guarded secret, yet they flaunt their wealth so openly."

"Is the wealth used wisely, in the Lord's name?"

"In some manners. I know he helps his students and their families when they struggle. And we donate a lot of money to a lot of places. But then in other ways, it just seems squandered. Every boy in the family gets this weird ring. There's a whole damn trust to ensure they have them." Maria hesitated. "Pardon my language, Father."

"The tongue is as hard to tame as the heart, but we must try, child." Father Peter paused to scroll down his phone, though Maria thought he was simply considering her words. "Do not be so disheartened. Likely these stipulations are embedded in tradition and paranoia, but this does not reflect on your heart. You must not concern yourself over everything you do not know, lest the darkness take over your heart. Trust that the Lord will make good use of the money, and if it is gained illicitly, will deal with the family in His own time."

"Yes, Father."

He heard the hesitation in her voice, pausing the current video. "Is there more, child?"

"My own sin, Father. Beyond being anxious and judgmental."

"Go on."

"I have been tempted, Father. To cheat on my husband. He is always so distant, so distracted. He never has time for me or...drive for intimacy. My heart has started seeking, and the temptation only grows."

"And have you acted on this temptation?"

She was silent.

"Child, you cannot judge your husband so harshly with distrust only to commit his sins in turn."

"Yes, Father."

"You need to end whatever tryst you are in. You should say 5 Hail Mary's and 5 Our Father's."

"Yes, Father. What else can I do to make things right?"

"Speak with your husband." She started to speak, but he gently hushed her. "Not of the affair, but of your heart. See if he will work with you, whether alone or with the help of a counselor. Build a strong foundation for your children."

"Yes, Father."

"Go, and be at peace."

Maria slid from the confession booth, slipping out her phone and frowning. She hadn't heard from Abraham yet, and mass would start soon. Surely he wasn't going to bail again? Not today... She put the phone away and forced a smile when she heard their oldest son call for her. She opened her arms as James ran from Esmeralda's grasp to hug her. She noted with some concern that he was struggling to run now.

James had the unfortunate luck to take after his father. He was only six years old, and the pediatrician was advising a diet. Maria did her best, but the boy was strong-willed and Abraham never listened. He gave their son whatever his little six-year-old heart desired, doctor's advice be damned. And his father's leniency was making it harder for Maria to set boundaries. She stood, taking James's hand and heading back to Esmeralda. "Thanks for holding them, Esme."

"It's no trouble, Mrs. A," the twenty-two year old assured her. "Jesús really loves the windows." She smiled as she carefully handed over the surprisingly small six-month old. "He knows who saved him, I think." The bright-eyed boy was staring up at the stained glass, but he turned to his mother and gurgled happily.

"And Praise Him for such a miracle," Maria murmured, kissing Jesús's temple. "And no major consequences from being so premature. At least that we know." Esmeralda had been the family's nanny since James was born. Six years of service so far, and six months of help while Maria was ferrying Jesús between doctor's appointments. "Have you heard from Abraham?"

"No, but maybe he's out in the parking lot? You know how he is about coming in here."

Maria rolled her eyes, muttering a 'yeah' under her breath. "I'll go check the parking lot and maybe give him a call. Can you get Jesús changed?"

"Of course!"

Maria dug out her keys. "His gown is airing out in the car. Thanks." The pair walked out to the parking lot together. This close to mass, there were several cars— and even more since families were attending the christenings. Most of the kids being dolled up for the day were far younger than Jesús, but they had been worried for his health. He had been baptized while he was in the NICU, but the actual christening was such an important milestone for their families that they had worked with the priest to have another baptism, this one for show.

Maria shielded her eyes from the winter sun; it wasn't very bright, but she had just been inside. She sighed when she saw Abraham's truck near the back. What the hell was he doing just sitting there? She started stalking that way, scowling when she noticed he was sleeping. *Sleeping.* He should be inside, helping her with their sons. She shook her head before walking up and knocking sharply on the window. Abraham jerked awake, looked at her, looked at his phone, and then opened the door. His clothing was rumpled from being in the car, but he had changed into something nicer than what he left the house in. It still didn't fit him, but Maria had given up on getting the man to buy clothes his size. She had been choosing fewer and fewer battles lately.

She braced herself for whatever story he was about to feed her, but he jumped out of the car and hugged her. Maria stood frozen for a second before hugging back.

"Sorry, baby, that early morning caught up." As he pulled out of the hug, he frowned at her expression. "What?"

"What did you do?"

"What?"

"Have you been drinking?"

"Am I not allowed to hug my wife? Jesus, Maria, you were just telling me I don't do enough for you. Why the hell should I if you instantly start accusing me of shit?"

Maria sighed. There was the old song and dance. Blaming her. "Fine. Ok. We don't have time right now. Let's just get inside."

"Where are the kids?"

"With Esme." Maria reached up and started straightening Abraham's hair. "If you hurry, you've got time for confession with Father Peter."

"I met with him earlier in the week."

Yeah, and what have you done since then? Maria bit her tongue. "Fine, let's get inside." She glanced at his ring when the light hit it and danced within the diamond and ruby's facets, making it seem magical and alive.

"I've got his," Abraham assured her, misinterpreting the look as he tapped his suit pocket. He offered his arm and she took it as they walked back towards the church.

Maria was quiet for a moment before asking, "When was the last time we walked into church together?"

"Ma, don't start. I'm not interested in coming with you. Today's just special. You know these motherfuckers are only interested in money. How many times do they pass around those baskets while others are broke as fuck? I met with the priest so he would let you bring Jesús in, that's it."

Maria snorted. "We're not broke," she pointed out flatly. "Though I've never seen you give them a dime, let alone anyone broke outside of your circle. Why the fuck are you complaining when you don't put your money where your mouth is?"

"I put my money plenty of places. I'm not gonna give to every bum and scammer with a sob story. I give to the kids at school 'cause I know 'em and their parents. I don't know that random bum on the street. Otherwise we would be broke before you know it. My father and his father before him didn't get here by giving everything away, and I'll be damned if I lose it all."

You're already damned. Again, she bit her tongue. The pair fell silent as they reached the doors, but it was easy to see they were tense.

***

See? Look what a good father I am. My family is provided for, and we are blessed, Abraham thought to himself as they sat through mass. Whatever the priest was saying went in one ear and out the other. He hadn't heard back from Jose yet. How long would it take to be sure all those videos were gone? All because he hadn't been careful. Abraham was the master of secrets, but in this, he had slipped. He was mostly worried about Maria finding out. She already suspected his every move, she would never believe he was innocent no matter what he could tell her. She was too sharp for him. He didn't want another thing to argue about, but at least he could throw her own affair in her face if she tried to accuse him of cheating.

After all, Abraham was a master of secrets, even those that weren't his to keep.

There had only been one close call before, with one of his students. It was the first time he had ever been worried about consequences, but like all things, the problem went away. The dad gave his threats, the student was moved to another class, and that was it. There was no evidence, no investigation. Abraham argued his innocence, and the dean believed him. Everything always turned out in his favor.

Abraham glanced down at James and smirked. The kid had given up on mass and was playing a game on his tablet. Esmeralda had gotten him to put one earbud in and leave the other ear open so he would at least notice when he needed to stand. Only six and already starting to share his father's concern for church.

And yet, that small voice in the back of his mind chided him. *Your family is blessed. Your son is alive. And what have you done besides pay to make your problems go away? Where has that gotten you?*

Abraham checked his phone. He was getting several texts, but none were from Jose. Some were family business, however, and he never left family on read. Maria's sharp elbow let him know when mass was over and the christenings had begun. The Alvarezes weren't the only family, so he kept to his messages until she elbowed him again. Then he put on his public-facing smile and walked the six rows to where Father Peter waited. The priest gave Abraham an enduring smile when he caught the man's eyes drift to his phone again, and Abraham sheepishly put it away.

"Sorry, lots going on with work."

Father Peter frowned; he knew Abraham was a teacher. He thought back to what Maria had said in confession, but he said nothing. After all, liars know liars, and liars keep each others' secrets.

After Jesús had been baptized, Abraham pulled out the ring. Most people took this time to choose godparents before the church, but Abraham's family had their own tradition. The ring was a match to his, diamond and ruby set in gold. Like his, it seemed alive under the light. Jesús gurgled curiously as Abraham placed the ring on his finger. It was perfectly fitted so that while the boy was able to twirl and play with it, he couldn't get it off alone.

Chapter 3

Monday morning found Abraham at the school, waiting patiently as his kids filed in for homeroom. At his school, classes had the same homeroom teacher through the grades. The idea was to let kids have a stable mentor, someone who could always be there for them. The current class had been with Abraham for a while now; spring would be their last semester before graduating to high school.

Abraham never rushed his kids in the morning. He let them take their time waking up, and they loved him all the more for it. To the kids, Abraham was a dream teacher. He was kind, compassionate, and genuinely seemed concerned for their well-being. They could come to him for anything, from help with math to other classes, to help paying their school lunches off. There were rumors that he had given some families bigger gifts, but he would never confirm them.

It wasn't a secret to his students— or the school —that Abraham came from a wealthy family. Just how much wealth was always a matter of speculation, but the kids tended to focus more on the idea that he didn't need to work such a thankless job.

To the unknowing eye, Abraham was a saint of a teacher, and he had every intention to keep up that persona— even with the devil whispering in his ear.

Working in a school was the perfect job for him. He had always played his cards carefully, and he rarely risked revealing his attention to his students. He had mastered the subtle glance, the denial and perfect excuse. No one ever suspected the thoughts running through his mind surrounded by the vulnerable young.

Only once had he misjudged a student, and nothing had come from the confrontation that followed. Rumors swirled, as they always did, but his reputation outweighed them. The instance had taught him to be more careful around his students— after the 'Joseph' incident, he would need to be more careful about kids not from his school, too.

God, I don't know if you're real. But I'll try anything right now.

He still had not heard from Jose. In one breath he would tell himself it had only been a day, give him time; in the next, he had taken to praying of all things. He couldn't let that rumor mill start. It would just give Levi's dad and his own wife more firepower against him. His life was easy, perfect, and it was going to stay that way. Everything always turned out well for him.

I couldn't sleep last night. Can't concentrate. I almost didn't eat.

Despite his personal affirmations, reaffirmations, and prayers, he had started the school day in the teacher's restroom, bolstering himself for the day with a bump. He hadn't started a school day high in a while, but his nerves were getting the best of him. Now he was calm, surely. The dark movement outside the window was just a bird. The other teachers' smiles were genuine as they greeted each other and dispersed to their classrooms.

Please don't let that video spread. Let this go away, as it always has.

As Abraham's homeroom class filed in, he was subtly checking his social media feed for any signs of Javier's video, or videos from the crowd.

I'm begging, please, if You're listening. Hey. I'm talking to You, can't You hear me? If You're real, help me. Let me know. Give me some kinda sign or something. I'll start giving to the church or whatever. It's a win-win, so long as you excuse my sin.

Never mind he had made some of those promises before. To God, to Maria.

Abraham slid his phone away as 7:00 am rolled around. All thirty-three of his students had arrived, the last six scrambling to reach their desks. He didn't call them out for almost being late; the halls were always packed between classes, and sometimes they just couldn't help it. He gave them another six minutes to get their bags away and greet their friends before clearing his throat.

"Good morning, everyone. I know I normally give you a bit more time, but there's something I'd like to discuss with you. Please finish putting your things away and let me have your attention."

A few of his students glanced at each other in confusion, but they all complied. Abraham scanned the room.

"I know you're excited for winter break, and even more excited to finish grade 8 next year and move on to high school. But you still have finals for this semester, and then six whole months for the next."

He noticed one of his students, Jenna Bowman, had her face buried in her lap.

"Please put your cellphones away for this. Take out your AirPods. Let me speak to you without the usual distractions. I always give you the courtesy of my undivided attention, so today I'm asking for the same." Jenna sheepishly met his gaze, and he just smiled. She had beautiful eyes, but they paled to some of the others in class. He didn't pull attention to the others he saw subtly tucking away their electronics.

"A lot can happen in six months. And it's easy to forget matters during the holidays." He met each student's gaze. "I know some of you are in my advanced math classes, but not all. Even so, I want you to know I'm here if you need any extra help getting ready for your exams." He smirked when he saw a few eyes roll.

"Even if you don't become mathematicians, and I realize a lot of you aren't interested right now, it's not just about learning math. It's about learning to solve complex problems quickly. Beyond that, it's about learning to do something you don't like and to do it well. Mike Tyson used to say discipline is doing what you hate to do, but doing it like you love it. And he was right. Good discipline will get you far in life." He held up a hand. "Don't ask me who that was, please. I already know I'm old, and he's one of my favorites." Scattered laughter filled the room.

"Who's Mike Tyson, Mr. A?" One of the class's chronic jokesters called out, but Abraham let it slide.

"But beyond exams, there's something else I want you to know. I've had students in the past who didn't want to graduate because they thought I wouldn't be willing to help them anymore. I want you to know that is categorically untrue. All of you are more than my students. I've grown to love you as my kids. So, simply because you're graduating this spring doesn't mean we can't keep in touch. I want you to know that you'll always find my door open should you want to talk."

He was interrupted by a knock at the door. His mind flashed to Javier, to the videos, and he half-expected to see a cop standing outside. Instead, it was another student. Edward Garcia was an honors student, and he had dimples to die for. Abraham had helped his family a few times, and Edward's father Jorge always insisted on paying him back since he didn't like owing anyone money. More importantly for now, Edward usually acted as a hall monitor during homeroom, and the dean often asked him to run errands.

Not the cops, but still concerning.

"Sorry to interrupt your class, Mr. Alvarez," Edward started in a quiet voice. "The dean asked to see you. He sent me to keep an eye on everyone and said it should be quick."

Fuck. The dean always had his back, surely he didn't need to worry? And yet he was very worried.

C'mon, God, weren't you listening? I'll even go to mass with Maria if that's what you want.

"Thanks, Edward." He managed to keep his voice calm. He turned back to the class. "Everyone, mind what Edward says. I would like for you to work on finishing up any homework you have for today, and then I'll be back so we can keep talking. Feel free to write down any questions for when I get back." He nodded to Edward as he slipped out into the hall, but he didn't go straight to the dean's office. First, he headed for the teacher's lounge and the private bathroom inside.

"If You're real," he murmured while shakily pulling out his stash. "Let this meeting be nothing terrible." He took a quick bump to harden his nerves, cleaned up his hand and checked for any residue, splashed water on his sweaty face, and then headed to the second floor.

Abraham hated climbing the stairs at school. There were thirteen steep steps, a landing that wrapped around, and thirteen more. The school needed an elevator. Hell, he had donated to fund one, but the school was caught in red tape trying to get bids and align with all the regulations for modifying the building.

Floor two was home to the student lounge in Room 222, and Dean Gomez's office was attached. Abraham and the dean were good friends, having been working together the past six years. Surely he would have more warning if the meeting were about him? Especially with how much Abraham donated to the dean's charity, something about helping obese Latinx get healthy. He didn't really care about the mission, just enough to feign interest and give Gomez a reason to have his back. Dean Gomez even attended his fundraiser dinners, and he often brought his wife to Abraham's famous Christmas feasts.

By the time Abraham reached the office, he was short of breath. His mind flashed back to running from Jinx's, and he nervously straightened his shirt before knocking on the dean's door. He once more smoothed his nervousness with a public-pleasing mask as he entered when invited, and reached to shake the dean's hand.

Gomez pointed to the leather chair across from his own. "Have a seat, Abraham. How are you and the family doing?"

Abraham relaxed. This was familiar. Expected. Surely everything was fine? "You know how it is, this time of year. Maria is trying to navigate buying the gifts while I focus on getting my classes ready for finals. Teamwork and all that." He rubbed his palms together. "Speaking of holidays, you and Priscilla still coming to dinner? I know James is looking forward to seeing your boy."

"We wouldn't miss it for the world— your barbecue is exquisite." Dean Gomez grinned widely. "Aside from that, I really just want the holidays done with. It's all about gifts these days, not enough about family."

"I hear that. Seems to be the name of the game for anything even moderately tied to the church these days."

The dean let out a groan. "Don't get me started on religion. A bunch of fucking hypocrites and those damn pedophile priests. I wouldn't hesitate to vote for the death penalty if I knew they would be convicted. Hell, I'd put them down myself."

"I agree completely. I don't want them anywhere near my kids, but Maria insists. If any of the priests at her church touch my boys, though…There'd be nowhere for them to hide," Abraham growled. "It's part of the reason I don't have any bad feelings against John. Guy just wanted to protect his kid, even if it was all bullshit."

"I was surprised how calm you were in front of him. It really helped keep the process moving to find a resolution."

"Oh, speaking of priests and religion, that reminds me. Thanks for putting up with the place to watch Jesús's christening. That necklace you gave him was beautiful."

Dean Gomez smiled. "I'm glad you liked it. It's supposed to be a charm against evil spirits. It should help protect him and keep him safe."

"Even better." Abraham shifted slightly, feeling a little nervous again. "Not that I want to interrupt such pleasant conversation, but you sent Edward to take over my homeroom?"

Dean Gomez sighed, leaning back in his chair. "Sorry about that. You know I hate taking you away from your students, but my schedule is very full and I needed to talk to you. One of your students is having trouble with his math, and he was wanting some extra help."

Abraham looked confused. "He came to you instead of me?"

"He was worried about the other kids talking behind his back, but he was even more worried about if his parents found out he needed a tutor. I know you understand how that feels."

Abraham nodded. "I understand all too well. My dad was an asshole. Never cared about any of us except when we messed up. I guess there's a lot of pressure, then?"

"It's Ethan Bísólá, the Nigerian boy."

Abraham let out a low whistle. "Ethan? Really?" He stroked his chin. "He did struggle on the last couple of tests, but I thought it might be nerves. He's such a quiet kid, but he normally does really well. Now I feel bad; I should have asked him. I'm not surprised he's got family pressure."

"That's why you're one of the best, Abraham. You care about your kids. I know you don't need to be here; you do it because you want to. This school is damn lucky you do."

"Thank you, dean. That means a lot to me. I love those kids as much as my own boys. Their parents have entrusted them to me, and I want to see them excel. I don't want them to lose themselves in all these shitty standardized lessons and tests."

"They're our future, and they've been set up to fail. The world keeps trying to make things too easy for them, and it's going to backfire if they aren't ready for it when they hit the real world."

"I do what I can to get them ready."

"And they appreciate it. We all do, really. You know, I still have an opening for principal if you want it. I can't hold it forever, but we just haven't found a fit."

"I'm flattered, really. But it isn't for me. I'm happy teaching at this level, and I'd miss being in class with the kids. I wouldn't be able to give them the same attention."

Dean Gomez folded his arms. "I completely understand. Stop by the office and talk to Mike about setting up a time to study with Ethan. He'll act as a go-between for now to help Ethan keep his cover. He needs to get an 85 on the final, so you'll likely be meeting with him more than once. I know you *want* him to pass, but I also need to remind you we have analytics to consider. Between our funding and our reputation, we can't afford for a kid of his status to fail."

"Have I ever let you down?"

"Never. Thanks, Abraham." The pair stood, but then the dean held up a hand. "Before you go, want a quick shot? A toast for success and finals prep."

"I certainly won't turn you down."

Gomez moved behind his desk to fetch a bottle of Fireball and two shot glasses, pouring generously. "To health, happiness, and continuing stipends." They laughed before downing the drinks and then hugging like old friends.

On his way back to class, Abraham took another detour to the teacher's restroom. He grinned at his reflection, knowing that everything was going to be fine. It always was. He celebrated with a quick line, thanked the God he barely believed in, and left. He stopped by Mike's desk to get Ethan's schedule and pick a time for them to meet.

Abraham Alvarez returned to his class feeling invincible.

Chapter 4

With final exams approaching, the school schedule had gotten a shake up. Every Wednesday and Friday were designated study days so that students could hunker down in the libraries, meet with tutors or mentor figures, or get help from their teachers.

Abraham had selected nine on Wednesday to meet with Ethan. The libraries in the school had small study rooms that could be booked for an hour at a time, or taken first-come first-serve. He often booked room six in the first floor library to meet with his students. It had hookups to project problems onto the wall, and it was farther back and out of the way to help keep their privacy.

The school libraries were all fairly large, with high ceilings, rolling ladders, and shelves upon shelves of books. Six larger tables were in the middle, with several smaller cubby desks and a few comfy chairs scattered throughout. The study rooms lined the left and back wall, and the right wall had the circulation desk, the computer lab, restrooms, and an office equipment area where the kids could make copies or print files from their thumb drives.

All of the wood in the library was a deep, polished red mahogany. The black leather cushioning the study chairs was starting to fade and crack in places, but it just added to the lived-in, cozy feel.

Abraham arrived at the room prior to his reservation, but since it was empty, he went in. He worked to get his laptop and the projector on speaking terms and pulled out his books and study aids. A part of him was nervous. Ethan was incredibly attractive, everything the fictional Joseph was supposed to be— tall for his age, muscular, into basketball. Dark-skinned with delicious chocolate eyes. But Abraham had sworn to be more careful, and he couldn't risk acting up at school. Besides, Ethan was untouchable. He wasn't just some immigrant or scholarship kid. His parents had money, status. And a second accusation at work would be a lot harder to escape than the first.

He had a few minutes before their meeting, so he ducked out to the restrooms. Rather than having the big gendered and stalled bathrooms like the rest of the school, the library had four individual bathrooms with their own lockable doors. Abraham locked the door behind him and gripped the sink to stare at his reflection.

"Ok, God. Here we are. Today's gotta go well, right? I know You made me with these thoughts, so You gotta stop them. You made Ethan beautiful, so You gotta keep him from tempting me, right? I'm gonna be a better guy, and You're going to make it happen. And if those thoughts don't go away, it's gotta be You, right? 'Cause You wouldn't just leave me to drown if it was actually bad." He nodded, satisfied, and reached into his pocket. A small bump to steady his nerves, and then he could go meet with Ethan. Everything would be fine, and yet he still felt nervous. Instead of a small bump, he decided to do a line instead. Then he washed off his face, straightened his clothes, and headed back for the study room.

Ethan had arrived while he was gone. He was sitting in the study room, AirPods in and laptop up while he waited. What Abraham wouldn't give to slip in behind him and take a whiff of those chocolate cherry curls. Ethan always smelled like vanilla and coconuts, the scent wafting over Abraham as he entered. Abraham wiped his palms on his pants before walking up and tapping Ethan lightly on the shoulder in an attempt not to startle him.

Ethan didn't jump, but he turned those beautiful dark eyes right to Abraham. He quickly turned off his AirPods and took them out. "Mr. Alvarez. Thank you again for meeting with me." He was always so polite. So formal.

"Call me Mr. A, Ethan. I'm happy to help. But why all the secrecy? Surely your parents wouldn't be against additional prep for exams?" Abraham moved around to his own seat.

"Unfortunately, they would. Don't get me wrong, Mr. A, they're great parents. They just expect a lot, and they can be pretty strict about it. They have such high expectations for me, and needing a tutor would be accepting defeat. They want me to have straight A's while playing sports, and they're already talking about a job when I'm old enough. Since I started having a hard time with math, they've been all over me. Now coach is saying if I don't pull up my grades, I might get blocked from extra-curriculars next semester." His eyes were starting to water, so he reached up and wiped at them. "It's just so fucking much. I don't know how much longer I can take it. I don't even get to have a winter break, my parents are signing us all up for volunteer work. I'm so tired, Mr. A. And it's only going to get worse once I'm in high school."

While he was talking, Abraham reached into his laptop bag and pulled out some travel tissues. He slid the pack across to Ethan, who took them gratefully.

"Sorry, Mr. A. Got a little carried away."

"No, Ethan, it's ok. I'm here to listen. Sometimes you need to get these things off of your chest. Otherwise they'll start to fester, and they can lead you to dark places."

"I feel so bad complaining. I know they care. They love me. They take care of anything I need. But I don't know if I can handle all the pressure."

"Of course you can. You're a strong, handsome, intelligent young man. You can handle whatever the world decides to throw at you. You just need some practice with coping techniques— keeping that pressure from getting to your head, messing you up."

"H-handsome?" Ethan was dabbing at his eyes. Abraham mentally cursed. He needed to deflect that. It didn't help that Ethan's puppy-dog eyes were on him again.

"I'm sure you have quite the fan club among the other students."

"I don't know about that, Mr. A. Most of them only seem to like me because my parents are rich. I thought I had some great friends until they started getting mad when I wouldn't pay for things. But I'm not my parents, they don't give me all that money."

"It can be hard when you're wealthy," Abraham agreed. "You have to use a bit more discernment when making friends. But that doesn't mean every one of your peers is just after your parents' money."

Ethan nodded, sniffling as he took another tissue. "Sorry to dump everything on you like this. I know you said it's ok, but...I must sound like a whiny little kid."

"We all struggle with things, Ethan. And it's especially hard for young men to find support."

"We're not really getting any work done, though."

"Sure we are. Not everything needs to be about math. Your emotions can affect things, too, such as concentration and focus. Getting things off your chest can be just as helpful as working over practice problems." While Ethan dried his eyes, Abraham pulled out his wallet. "Tell you what. Why don't you go grab yourself something from the vending machines? Anything you want. And then we can take a look at some trig."

Ethan nodded. "Do you want me to grab you anything?"

"Just a Diet Coke."

As Ethan stood and moved for the door, Abraham couldn't help a wandering gaze. Those toned muscles; that ass. Once the boy was out of the room, he let out a breath. That had gotten close. He hadn't meant to call Ethan handsome, but he managed to distract him. Poor kid seemed to have no idea what a catch he was growing up to be. Abraham would love to show him. Perhaps coming from someone who was also wealthy would help him understand it was genuine. Oh, the things he could do to that boy to help him feel loved and cherished.

Abraham logged into his math software, pulling up some practice problems and setting them up on the wall. He was here to tutor Ethan, nothing more. Not unless he got some kind of sign it was ok.

We still have a deal, right God?

He glanced up from the computer when Ethan returned with his Diet Coke, as well as an apple juice and a packet of trail mix.

"Hope you don't mind, Mr. A. I know the trail mix is a bit more expensive, but it's the only vegan option."

"I don't mind at all, Ethan. I didn't know you were vegan?"

"The whole family. Mom got dad into it, and the rest was history."

"It's great the whole family can come together over food. My wife is vegan, but I never took to it. We agree to disagree, and she lets our kids get a bit of both so they can decide for themselves when they're older." Frankly, he didn't want her pushing diets on their kids. But it was what it was. James, luckily, had a healthy appetite for meat. He was even getting interested in his dad's barbecue. Another skill passed through the sons in his family. He was already teaching James how to appraise a slaughter, to ensure his meat was handled well. Anytime Abraham ordered a pig or a cow, he had the butcher send him video to be sure everything was done right. Though, he had to admit, it wasn't just about the meat— watching the life fade from the eyes of his meal called to something primal in him.

"I get curious about some foods, but I'll probably wait until I'm out of the house to try."

"That's the best time to branch out and try new things," Abraham confirmed. "Find what fits you without having to worry about your parents' rules. They do what they think is best until you're old enough to decide for yourself." He laughed. "Take me for example. I have noticed I have a weakness for nuts." He gestured to Ethan's trail mix as though still talking about food. "All right, settle in. We should talk a little about math while we're here," he added in a teasing tone.

Once Ethan had settled in, Abraham had him run through a few practice problems to get a feel for how comfortable the boy was with the current material and then the material from the past few tests. He helped clarify ideas and processes, but Ethan did fairly well. He was attentive, eyes on Abraham when they weren't on the projector screen. At one point when Abraham was typing into the computer, he caught Ethan's gaze wandering. Along him. And then the boy looked up and met his gaze. Ethan quickly looked away, his cheeks warming.

"Everything alright, Ethan?" he prompted.

"Uh...Yeah. I just..."

Abraham leaned back in his seat and folded his arms. "Ethan, I'm your teacher," he cautioned.

"I know. I'm sorry. I just...You've always been a great teacher. And nice, and helpful, and...Do you really think I'm handsome?"

"Is there not a single mirror in your home?" Ethan snorted into a laugh, and Abraham grinned. "In all seriousness Ethan, yes. You're a very handsome young man. And you're rather intelligent. I'm beginning to think you don't need my help, you just let all that pressure get to you."

Ethan hesitated, and Abraham raised an eyebrow.

"I...well..."

"Go on, Ethan. It's just us in here."

"I...I'm not into girls, Mr. A."

Oh.

"And I'm not really finding anyone my age that I *am* into, you know?"

Oh, thank you, Lord.

"How am I supposed to figure anything out if I don't have anyone to learn with, right?" Abraham watched Ethan steadily. The boy squirmed in his seat slightly. "I heard from Levi that you were checking him out, and I...I don't necessarily think that's true but it made me wonder if it was and if you might be open to the idea but I know you have a wife and—" Abraham raised a hand, and Ethan stopped.

"Teachers getting together with students is really frowned upon." Ethan started to melt in his chair. "So it would have to be a very closely guarded secret. Our secret." Ethan sat up a bit straighter, nervousness growing into a grin. "You can practice whatever you want. It doesn't even have to go anywhere. I know flirting can be awkward at your age, and it's nice to have someone as a sounding board. But it can only be when we're alone, ok?" Start soft. Start small. Surely this was permission. His sign. Everything was going to be all right. "I wasn't lying, Ethan. You're handsome and intelligent. You're also sweet and kind. And, since we're being honest, you have an amazing ass."

"Would you like to see more of it, Mr. A?"

"I would. But not here. Since Friday is another study day, why don't we study at my home, instead?"

"Won't your family be there?"

"No. It will be just you and me. We can talk, we can study... Whatever you want. But it's our secret. Your parents need to think you're at school. Think you can do that?"

"Yes, sir."

"All right. Then here's the plan. Treat Friday like a normal school day. Study with some of your friends. Hang out in the library. I have some other tutoring sessions in the morning, and then in the afternoon I'll take you to my place. Deal?"

"Deal."

Chapter 5

Abraham had a bargain to keep. He had promised to start praying, start being a better husband. So when Thursday morning rolled around, he got up early. First he made breakfast for himself and the kids. But then he dug into the fridge and pulled out a bunch of his wife's fruits and some açai. He stared at them a moment before grabbing his phone and searching for smoothie recipes.

By the time Maria came downstairs, wrapped in her plush robe, Abraham had breakfast ready for everyone. He had even managed to wash and put away the shot glass from his morning indulgence. Maria stared at the table and then looked over at him.

"You…You're up early," she commented lightly, though Abraham didn't miss the hesitation.

"Mornin', baby," he greeted, moving over to kiss her on the cheek. She reached a hand to it, stunned. When was the last time he had kissed her, shown affection? "I was hoping to get some extra time with you and the kids before you head to your mom's tomorrow."

"Aren't you still planning to join us?"

"Yeah, but it won't be until Saturday. I've got some students scheduled for tutoring, and I've heard it's gonna ice. I don't wanna be driving in the dark if it's slick." He moved for the table, snatching a piece of bacon. "I was also going to see if you wanted me to have a driver take you out. I want you and the kids to be safe and relax."

"I...No, it's ok. I like the drive." Maria was following his every movement. First the unexpected hug on Sunday, now this? "Are you..."

Abraham glanced up at her. He caught the confusion, the hesitation, and something angry flared in the back of his mind. But he stamped it down. "Feeling okay?" He finished her question with a teasing tone. "I'm fine." He paused, glancing down that the table. "I just...I've been doing a lot of thinking, baby. With Jesús getting older and stronger, I haven't been as on edge. And I..." He sighed, standing and moving over to her. He wrapped his arms around her and pulled her close. "I know I've not been the best. I get angry and stressed out. We fight a lot, and a lot of that's on me. So I'm trying to be better. For you. For the kids. For myself. I know it's not...me. But I'm gonna try."

Maria slowly wrapped her arms around him. "I...I want to believe you. I do. But the past few months— no, years —I've felt like I was living with a stranger..."

"I'm sorry. I know it's not gonna be an overnight thing. But I'll prove it to you. Starting with breakfast today and tomorrow, and then the weekend at your mom's." He stepped away, touching a hand to her cheek before letting her go. "You should drink your smoothie before it gets all watery. I'll go get the kids."

***

It was like a switch had flipped for her husband. Maria watched in mounting surprise as he took care of the kids that morning so she could relax and enjoy her breakfast. Once the kids were fed and dressed, he invited her into his shower. Then it was off to the school with a smile on his face. He had even said a prayer over breakfast!

> *I don't know what's gotten into him.*

Sure it's not aliens?

> *Oh, haha.*

In seriousness, chica, maybe he's telling the truth. Or maybe he had a stroke. Do you want to call off tonight and see how the rest of today plays out?

> *No...no, let's still meet. He's usually out late on Thursdays to hang with the guys, and I already have a babysitter for the kids. I would love for this to be genuine, but I have no reason to believe it. I don't want to get my hopes up.*

Ok. I'll see you at the gym.

Maria smiled to herself as she put the phone down. She wanted to believe. She did. But she couldn't. Abraham had a lot to answer for. He had a lot to prove before she let herself fall for him again.

Still, she wanted this to be real.

***

The next morning was the same. Abraham got up early, started breakfast for everyone, and even put on a pot of Maria's mushroom coffee. He let Maria sleep in, getting the boys ready and downstairs to eat. He knew she had training with Carlos in the evening on Thursdays, and that usually left her worn out the next morning. Frankly, he knew she had more than just training with Carlos, but he was trying not to pick fights right now. Besides, she had a long drive to her mom's.

Maria's mother, Mary, had lived in Providence, Rhode Island her entire life. She grew up there, went to college, got married, moved in with her husband, built a family with him, and then buried him there. Maria had lost her father to colon cancer, and now that same disease was threatening Mary. She was going through radiation, but she was also ignoring most of her doctor's advice— she refused to give up her cigarettes and whiskey. Abraham could respect that.

Maria was a bit of a black sheep. Unlike the rest of her family, she was vegan and had a personal trainer. She knew cancer ran in her family, and she took it seriously. But she still deeply loved her mother. She possessed fond memories of spending time at her family's home, which included a treehouse her father built for her and her siblings in the backyard.

By the time Maria had showered and made it downstairs, all three of her boys were dressed for the day. Abraham had thrown on a comfy sweater, one of the only things she had convinced him to buy in a proper size. He looked every bit the teacher with his fuzzy wool socks and slacks. He had been tempted to throw on some cologne, but that always got Maria to start asking questions. Heaven forbid he wanted to smell nice. As she entered the kitchen, Maria wrinkled her nose. The scent of bacon was heavy in the air. She had given up on getting Abraham to stop eating meat, but maybe with his newfound spark…

"It smells like you cooked an entire pig in here." She tried to keep her tone light.

"This is nothing compared to what I'll make for Christmas," he boasted, cutting into the eggs to make small pieces that Jesús could grab up with his fingers. Maria sighed. Too early to broach that idea, then. She moved to the fridge and pulled out some extra fruits and granola. "Did I not make you enough? I'm sorry."

"No, no, you did. But it's Friday. The boys get fruit, too."

"Ah."

"Mommy, do I have to?" James whined. "You don't make daddy eat fruit."

"It's not like I'm taking away your eggs and bacon, James," Maria scolded lightly. "I just want to ensure you have balance. Mommy loves you, and wants you to be healthy. Mommy loves daddy, too, but he's an adult. I don't control what he eats, and he doesn't control what I eat."

"Listen to your mother, James."

Maria stared at Abraham. "Are you sure you haven't been abducted by aliens?" she blurted. Abraham laughed. James sighed and pouted, but he didn't push away the little dairy-free parfait she had thrown together. For Jesús, she cut up some bite-size fruits and set them alongside his eggs. Unlike James, the little one gobbled them up happily alongside what his father gave him. He would still get a bottle, but they were introducing different solids.

Abraham was checking the weather on his phone. He glanced up to look out the window. "Are you sure you don't want a car? Even a limo?"

"No, thank you. I love the drive there. It makes me feel so good to leave the city sometimes and revert back to my childhood. Such simpler times, but I do miss them. There's just something magical about New England that makes me want to go back and visit." Maria closed her eyes and smiled to herself.

Abraham shook his head. "It's nice, but too quiet for me. I remember going out to dad's vacation home. The lake, the barbecue…Still, I wouldn't say I liked it. I just wanted to get back to the city and hang with my friends." He took a bite of pork, and while his mouth was still full, added, "Besides, too many Jews in New England."

"What an awful thing to say. Don't you have students that are Jewish?"

Abraham snorted, wiping a napkin to clear some of the grease building on his chin. "Oh, sure, but I don't hold it against the kids. Besides, their families donate plenty of money to our programs so long as we flatter them."

Maria shook her head. James was looking between them hesitantly. "I'll always be a New England girl. But more than anything, I need to go see my mom. I can't let her be alone, not now. Not after I couldn't be there for Dad." Her eyes started to water, and she grabbed a napkin to dab at them.

"I promise I'll be there." Abraham met her gaze across the table. "Everything will be fine. And if you want her to come stay with us so she's not alone, that's fine with me, too. We have lots of extra space."

Maria sniffled but nodded. "Thanks. I'll try and talk to her about it today. I know she loves that house, but I'm so worried about her."

"What time are you planning to head out?"

Maria snorted. "What, trying to get rid of us?" she teased.

"No, I just wondered if you needed help loading up the car before I go in to school. I wanna start helping you a lot more, and I'm sorry because I don't think I've been doing that for a little while now."

"Well, at least you noticed, and I respect that. Thank you."

"You don't have to thank me. It's my honor to support my lovely wife and children."

"That's sweet, but I still wanna know what those aliens did to my hubby. If you haven't been abducted, what did you do wrong?"

"Do we have to go to Grandma's?" James interrupted, stabbing at his eggs. "I want to help Daddy pick out the pigs for Christmas."

Maria opened her mouth, but Abraham leaned over and touched a hand to James's hand. "Now, now. Your grandma is sick, remember? We should spend time with her while we can. Adults don't live forever, but we can keep them alive in our hearts with memories. You can help Daddy buy the pigs next year."

James sighed dramatically, as kids often did. "Everything dies. Why make a big deal out of it?"

"Where have you been learning that?" Maria asked with concern.

"Online," he answered nonchalantly, shoving a forkful of eggs in his mouth. The light caught the ring on his hand, a smaller version of his dad's. He wasn't allowed to wear it everywhere, but at home, he insisted. As the lights danced through the ruby and diamond, it looked alive. Magical.

"Everything dies, but that makes living life all the more important," Abraham cut in, not nearly as concerned as Maria. After all, James had started watching slaughters with him. He always made the kid a nice juicy steak to demonstrate what could be done with good meat. "We need to enjoy the time we have together while we can. And you and I have a lot more time ahead of us than your grandma does."

James reluctantly agreed, and Maria didn't voice her concerns about what else the kid was finding on the internet. She did make a mental note to ask Esmeralda about it later so the young woman could show her how to set up better parental controls.

After breakfast, Abraham helped Maria get all the luggage loaded into the truck. Next they helped the kids get on their hats, coats, and gloves, and Abraham hefted Jesús into his arms and carried him out to the car. Once the youngest was all buckled in, he bent to pick up James.

"Boy, I'm gonna have to stop feeding you so much if I want to keep picking you up," he teased as he set James into the car seat. He kissed James' forehead. "Be good for Mommy and Grandma. I'll see you tomorrow." Both kids secured and settled, he shut the door and moved to Maria. "After such a big breakfast, hopefully they'll both pass out and you can have a nice, quiet drive."

"I don't mind if they don't. I really do enjoy being with them, especially since we're headed to Mom's."

"Do you need any cash?"

"No, I should be fine. I've got the bank card in my wallet and the credit cards on tap-to-pay."

Abraham pulled out his wallet and counted out ten crisp one hundreds. "Take it, just in case. If the power goes out or something, I want you all taken care of."

Maria hesitantly took the cash. Abraham was feeling oddly generous today, but she tried to push down her suspicions. "Alright. I'll give it back to you once we're together." She tucked the cash into her purse. "We should be heading out. I'll see you tomorrow."

"You definitely will. Early." He touched her chin, drawing her gaze to meet his. "Drive safe, mi vida. You know you have my three most precious treasures in that truck." Maria blushed. "Oh, by the way. I sent over some things you all might enjoy for the weekend. Fresh fruits, produce, and some vegan delicacies from that market you like there, Nourish. There are more options than I once remembered, so they must be doing good."

"That's very sweet of you. Mom loves that place, but she hates spending money. I'm sure she'll appreciate it. You know you didn't have to..."

"Hush. I love being able to spoil my family. It's my pleasure as a man to take care of you. I promised I would when we got married."

Maria smiled. A small voice in the back of her mind reminded her that his words had meant little in the past. But she wanted to believe. She reached up and kissed Abraham, and he pulled her into a warm hug before whispering in her ear, "Baby, sometimes I haven't been the greatest of husbands or even friends, yet you've always stood by me no matter what. I promised God that I would be better to you and the kids and to help you more and be less selfish, and I mean it. I know that I'm not the easiest person to deal with, and you're a saint for putting up with me, but I don't want you to be a martyr for anyone but God."

Maria sighed into his hold. "I want to believe you. And I know it won't happen overnight. I haven't been the greatest wife, either. I miss being your girl. I know I'm a mother now, but I'm still a woman. I want to feel like one. You can't pay for that, Abraham." She pulled back to meet his gaze. "So let's keep doing this. Talking. Laughing. Not just at Mom's."

Abraham kissed her forehead. "I'll do my best. But don't forget the big dinner is coming up. So we might need to wait to work out some things, 'cause we're gonna have a lot on our plates." He stepped away to open her door. "I'll see you tomorrow. Let me know if the food doesn't show up by four. I paid and tipped, so they shouldn't ask for anything. And I gave them a little extra to help carry everything inside. Just make sure they take off their shoes— I know what your mom's like."

"Thanks, Abraham. I love you."

"I love you too, baby." As Maria moved to get in the truck, Abraham grabbed her hand and gently helped her up the step. "I love you all very much. You're my entire life. I'll check in with you between students."

"All right. We'll check in, too. Right boys?" She turned to check on the pair, but both were out like a light. Maria chuckled as she closed the truck door and set up her music. Abraham moved to open the garage, steam forming where the cold and warm air collided. As Maria began to pull away, Abraham lifted a hand to wave. The morning sun glinted off his ring, bringing the diamond and ruby to life and making them appear magical. He waved until he couldn't see the truck any longer and then closed the garage.

Chapter 6

Abraham spent the first part of the day in the teacher's lounge, humming as he sorted through emails and updated his calendar. He had spoken with Mike to book out study room 6 for the second half of the school day.

Once his admin was caught up, he spent some time going over homework. But he found he couldn't really focus. His mind kept flashing between having Ethan in his arms and holding Maria. His soul couldn't seem to decide which he was looking forward to more: that afternoon or the weekend. Finally, he stood and moved to the restroom. He needed a line to bring his mind into gear.

He wound up doing two, then cursing softly when he got a nosebleed. Damn, that stuff was strong. The kind of blow that could stop a strong man's heart. As he sat on the toilet with a tissue stuffed up his nose, his mind ran off without him. If he died in the teacher's lounge restroom, how long would it take anyone to notice?

"What the fuck is wrong with me?" he muttered crossly. "Why am I doing this to myself?" He checked his nose and went back to sulking.

Getting high used to be exciting, but now he couldn't get away with being sober. This shit was expensive. And why was he drinking so much? He had a gorgeous wife, two great kids, and plenty other conquests to his name. So why was he pushing his luck when he still hadn't heard from Jose?

"But you deserve to have a little bit of fun," a voice whispered. He glanced around, startled, and then realized it was his own thoughts. *"You work so hard...You do so much for your family, your friends, your students— even the community. Maria has never had to work a day in her life. So what if you want to let off a little steam? You know your limits."*

Abraham nodded along. He did work hard. He took care of his family. He kept a roof over their heads, food in their bellies. And he poured into his students. Why shouldn't he accept the gifts of the universe? Obviously God loved him. Look at his house, his wife, Ethan... The universe served him. Everything always turned out to his benefit.

"After all, You didn't take away the urges. You had him come on to me," Abraham announced to the air.

Verifying that his nose had stopped bleeding, he washed his face in the sink, dried off with a paper towel, and headed back out into the lounge.

***

No matter how many ways she turned the conversation around in her mind, Maria couldn't decide if she trusted Abraham. They had so much they needed to go over, and yet he had already tried to deflect conversation by talking about the holidays. She needed to know he was serious. Committed. She pulled up her phone and tried to FaceTime him, but he declined. Soon, her phone pinged with a message instead.

> *I'm at the school, Hun. You know I can't use video here.*

> *Show me your desk.*

Another message came in; a photo of a cluttered desk in the teacher's lounge, with a digital clock in the corner showing the date and time. She quickly checked it against her dash.

> *See? I'm gonna be here for a while. How's the drive?*

> *Smooth sailing so far. Only a little traffic. The boys have been sleeping for most of it. I should be at mom's for lunch.*

> *Sounds good. Let me know when you get there.*

Maria sighed and put her phone down. It was Friday, where else would he be? Even if it was a study day, he stayed on campus in case the students needed him. Why was she feeling so suspicious? Something had settled in her heart, something dark. Softly, so as not to wake the boys, she started reciting Hail Mary, followed by Our Father.

***

Abraham let out a breath as he plopped his phone back on his desk. It was good he had been in the teacher's lounge to get a quick photo. He would need to snatch a few photos of the library and the study room with different problems on the wall before he left with Ethan. At least the school's privacy policy gave him an easy out on video calls. He could keep her complacent and have his fun. Everything was going to turn out well, just like it always did. Sure, he hadn't heard from Jose, but he hadn't heard from Dean Gomez, Javier, or anyone else, either. He could call Jose during his drive tomorrow just to be sure, but he had a feeling everything was water under the bridge. After all, God was on his side now, too.

Abraham headed down the to library, pulling out his phone to snap a few photos. He took some pictures of the cracked and fading leather on the seats and some of the worn-looking books in the shelves while he was there. Maybe he could look into funding some repairs. The school was far too prestigious to have such disrepair in the library of all places. Then he headed to study room 6 and started hooking up his laptop to the projector. He scattered some papers on the desk, laid out a couple of pencils and worksheets, then put some problems on the wall and showed partial progress.

He had the workspace cleaned up again just in time for his first student. He sneaked a few more pictures as they worked, though he didn't risk taking photos of his students or their personal items aside from a backpack or two. Whenever Maria pinged to check in, he would send a couple of snapshots and a few quick messages. He told his students when they arrived that his wife was traveling and he would be checking his messages, so they didn't think anything about it.

A little before noon, Maria had let him know they were at her mother's. By two, she let him know the food had arrived earlier than expected and had nothing but good things to say about the delivery. Everything was going smoothly. Abraham took a break to get out of the library and stretch his legs. He greeted a couple of students on his way to the side door, then stepped out into the brisk December chill.

If anything ever convinced him to lose weight, it would be finally getting fed up about being hot and sweaty all the time. Even in the middle of winter, if he wasn't outside or in his own home, he was too damn hot.

Abraham paused when he heard a low noise, looking up to see a drone with an even number of red and green lights. He frowned, wondering if it could pick up sound. He cupped his hand to his mouth. "This is a no fly, no record zone. If you're a student, the suspension isn't worth it!" he warned. The drone hovered a moment longer, and he was just about to dial campus security for advice when it slowly rose up and into the clouds. Kids and their toys. They never weighed the risks. He glanced down at his phone and realized he had a missed call. From Maria. Oh boy. Ten minutes ago. Why hadn't he noticed his phone go off? He quickly dialed back.

As soon as she answered, he knew she was upset. "Hi."

"Hi baby, I'm so sorry, I apparently hit DND mode in my pocket. I was just checking to see if you had messaged and saw a missed call. What's wrong? Your mom OK?"

Maria sighed. "I just don't like it when you don't respond," she confessed. "It makes me think of all the other times...

Times you said you were in one place and I found out you lied. You say you're trying to be better, and I'm getting my hopes up against my better judgment. You gotta mean it this time, Abraham. I can't go through the lies again. I deserve better than that. So do the kids."

"I understand, Maria. I'm sorry. I love you and our family more than anything. I've made a commitment to God to be better, and I'm doing everything I can to keep it. Do you need more photos? More proof? What can I do, babe?"

"I don't know. I don't know, Abraham. I've just had a bad feeling in the pit of my stomach all day, and then you didn't answer and…You've hurt me, A. So many times."

"I know. I've been a mess. We've been a mess. But I'm going to do everything I can to make it up to you and the kids."

"We want you in our lives. You don't need to make anything up, just be there for us. Maybe scale back on how often you go out with the other guys and spend more time with us. The kids won't stay this young." She hesitated before adding, "I want my husband back. The one I saw a glimpse of this morning and the person I fell in love with years ago. Can you be that man again?"

Abraham hesitated. "I'll see what I can do, baby. But I do need some downtime, too. We can look at the schedule and see what works."

"Ok. I should let you get back to work."

Abraham checked his phone. "My next session is in fifteen minutes. Do you want me to stay on a bit longer?"

"No, that's ok. I know you're not supposed to be on your phone for personal calls that much. You don't have to send more photos, either. Maybe we can FaceTime tonight, though?"

"Of course. I need to call about the pigs so I don't miss the cut off, but I'll see if you're free after that."

Maria bit back a sigh. Those poor pigs. But she didn't want to argue, not now. "Ok. I'll talk to you later."

"Ok, baby. Love you." Abraham let out a breath as he clicked off the call, then grinned. That couldn't have gone better. Maria really was on board to let him fulfill his deal with God. The world was his. And soon, Ethan would be, too. Abraham was the luckiest man alive.

Since he had a few minutes to spare, he headed to one of the library restrooms to spoil himself with a full line.

Chapter 7

Abraham met Ethan in study room 6 at precisely 2:30 that afternoon. Ethan had arrived a few minutes early, so the scent of vanilla and coconuts wafted over Abraham as he walked in.

"Hey, Ethan. Sorry to keep you waiting."

The boy looked up and smiled brightly. "No worries, Mr. A, I haven't been here long." He gestured to his worksheets scattered on the table. "I wasn't sure if we were going to stay here for a while or not, so I got set up."

"We'll work here for a bit," Abraham confirmed, moving over to where he had left his computer hooked in. "What time are your parents expecting you home?"

"I don't usually go home right away on Fridays. I stay at the school until the library closes, then I go to the gym for a run or a workout. Sometimes I'll go to the public library and get in more studying. I...like to stay out of the house, when I can get away with it."

Abraham nodded. "Understandable, with all the pressure you've been feeling. Nothing wrong with needing a little space." He pulled up one of the practice exams. "Do your parents track your phone at all? We might need to leave it here so it looks like you're sticking to your routine."

"Not that I know. At least not my browser history." Ethan flushed slightly, embarrassed. "Otherwise they would know a lot more about me," he confessed. Abraham smirked.

"I know the feeling. I have a few secrets of my own on my little device. Adults look at embarrassing things, too."

Ethan's eyes widened. "Wait, you mean I still need to keep what I'm watching secret?"

"Not always. Just make sure you trust who you're sharing with. Some people have different beliefs about good and bad behavior and want to control everyone else, or they might be looking for an excuse to get you in trouble."

Abraham had several secrets on his own phone. He had set up biometrics so that only a facial scan and thumbprint would give access to the little device. And Jose had taught him how to wipe the memory, just in case. A few buttons, drop it in some water 'on accident', and voila— his secrets would always be safe.

"Here, let me see what kind of phone you have." Ethan readily handed over his cell. "See here in settings? You can change your lock screen code to a biometric unlock instead. Makes it harder for anyone to go snooping, but remember your parents can just ask you to open it, so you'll still want to keep some things hidden." Ethan was nodding as Abraham navigated through his menus. "As for browser history, using privacy mode can help. It won't store anything. And you can regularly clear your cache and stuff."

"Geez, Mr. A, you really do have some embarrassing things to hide, huh?" Ethan teased. Abraham grinned at him.

"Have you forgotten our other plans?"

"No, but I had hoped I might be special."

Abraham set down the phone. "Ethan. Of course you are. But that doesn't mean I haven't sought gratification in other places before." He slid Ethan back his phone. "I can show you a few sites, too. Other places to learn than a fat old man." He grinned, and Ethan grinned back.

"You just enjoy good food, Mr. A."

"That I do. So let's get some work done so we can treat ourselves later."

"Yes, sir!"

***

Despite their eagerness to finish the school day, Abraham and Ethan took their time going over practice problems and things that might be covered on the exams. Abraham and the other teachers had subject summaries, but even they didn't get to see the problems ahead of time— the exams were from a third party to avoid "inflated" results. Ethan seemed to have a fairly solid grasp on the concepts, at least, so Abraham started having him take practice exams to work on his focus and anxiety in a timed situation.

Since it was the Friday before exams week, the school would be open late. But Abraham didn't want to sit in the study room forever; too many other far more delicious scenarios were playing through his mind. He kept the study session to ninety minutes. A nice, long session for their alibis, with more to come off the record. Nice and safe. Calculated. He was entirely in control of the situation.

"You normally walk to the gym, right Ethan? Go ahead and leave the school heading that way, but stop around the corner. I'll come pick you up."

Once he left, Abraham started packing up his computer. His mind was lost in the different things he wanted to introduce Ethan to. So much so, that he was actually startled when Jenna opened the door.

"Oh, sorry, Mr. A! I thought the room was free."

"No worries, Jenna. I was just packing up. How is exam prep going?"

"I'm feeling pretty good, but do you think I could ask you some questions?"

Abraham checked the clock. "Unfortunately I have to pack to meet up with my mother-in-law this weekend. Why don't you send me your questions in an email?"

"Perfect. Thanks!"

"No problem," he assured her as he slipped out of the room.

A few moments earlier, and she would have seen Ethan in the room. They really needed a better protocol for private study sessions. Because they needed to protect the students' identities, of course...though there could be some added benefits in other scenarios. Not needing to take students home, for instance. Ah well. He had a plan. Everything would be fine.

Abraham whistled a merry tune as he exited the side door to the teacher's parking lot and climbed into his car. He gave the security camera a small wave as he always did, playing nice with the guards who kept them safe.

***

Ethan was a quiet passenger. The type to just stare out the window and watch the world pass by. Abraham didn't mind too much; he was planning on ways to spoil Ethan once they arrived at his house. So it surprised him when Ethan commented, "Someone is really enjoying their new drone this year."

He glanced over at the kid and then past him through the window, noting the small shape disappearing into the clouds. "Gift of the year, apparently. Must be some new model, I don't think I'd noticed one quite like it before."

"Do you ever wonder if someone is spying on you?"

Abraham snorted. "From that high up? Nah. Besides, I'm not that interesting to watch."

"You don't think so? Aren't you, like, a local celebrity?"

Now Abraham laughed. "Nah. I host a few fundraisers, but that's about it. I try to keep out of the spotlight. Too many people think they're entitled to your life if you're famous, ya know? Had a cousin try and break into streaming at one point, and even people in chat would get weirdly personal."

"...You know what streaming is, Mr. A?"

"Oh, haha."

Ethan grinned at him and went back to staring out the window. "What do you even do with all that money?"

"Take care of my family, first and foremost. And help out friends."

"Do you give any away?"

"Only to people I know. Don't believe every sob story on the street, Ethan. Most panhandlers make bank betting on people's emotions. They'll get together and compare what streets get better results. They'll help each other with their signs for the most impact. Then they go waste it all on booze and drugs. Imagine if they turned all that analytical experience into an actual job?" He shook his head. "If you really want to give handouts, get yourself some gift cards so you know where the money is going. Hell, the cops even busted a street violinist for using recorded music and pretending to play."

"They can't all be bad."

"But it's a gamble. And the house always wins."

"You don't like risks?"

Abraham glanced at him. "If I didn't take the occasional risk, we wouldn't be here," he pointed out with a grin. He reached up to hit his garage door opener. "But I pick my risks carefully."

"So were you really checking out Levi?"

"I don't check out students unless they want it." Or if he knew he wouldn't get caught. Or could get away with it.

"What about kids that aren't your students?"

Abraham gave him a side glance as he put the car in park and unbuckled. "Let's get inside. We can talk over some food." Where had all this come from? Ethan wanted to flirt and have fun, didn't he? Why the twenty questions about Abraham's business? He checked his phone to make sure the security system was off, including the cameras, before opening the door.

"This place is huge!" Ethan exclaimed, stepping just beside the door to slide off his shoes. Abraham smirked. He moved over to Ethan, stepping right in front of him and moving to unzip the boy's coat. He moved slowly, not breaking eye contact, and Ethan shivered in delight. Then Abraham slid the coat away and promptly turned, carrying it to the closet.

"Make yourself comfortable," he teased as he moved to the kitchen.

The kitchen was always well-stocked with organic fruits and vegetables for Maria and Esmeralda, so he had plenty to choose from. And since he had been making Maria's smoothies the past couple of mornings, he had been practicing cleaning and preparing them. Now he was going to use those newfound skills to spoil Ethan. Maria always soaked any new stock in alkaline water with baking soda, so he just needed to rinse them under some filtered water. He took out a silver strainer and a selection of strawberries, blueberries, bananas, mangoes, peaches, and oranges. He opened his pantry, grabbed the blender, and cut the fruits before putting everything inside with some chocolate almond milk. He glanced to see if Ethan was nearby, spotting him in the living room, before slipping in some little extras to make their day special. Then he tossed in some ice and mixed it all together.

While the blender ran, Abraham leaned against his counter and stared out his large, panoramic windows to the park. He could hear birds chirping and dogs barking.

You continue to bless me, Lord. Now help me bless Ethan.

He moved towards the pantry and took out two table settings before decorating the kitchen island. He even pulled out the fancy embroidered napkins. Since the smoothies were done, he poured them in goblets and then served Ethan a selection of Maria's vegan goodies and got himself a plate of leftover brisket. He also pressed a button on the wall to close the blinds.

"Is this whole place yours, Mr. A?" Ethan wandered into the room, but before Abraham could answer, he spied the plates. "Those look delicious!"

"I'm glad you think so. Help yourself."

Ethan pulled out one of the stools and slid up to the counter, making a show of picking up a fruit and popping it in his mouth. Abraham grinned at him from the sink, washing out the blender. Ethan eyed the brisket.

"Do you want to try some? I won't tell."

"Why don't you feed it to me?"

Abraham set the blender back in the dish drainer. He moved around the island and took his own stool before stabbing his fork into the brisket. He started with a small piece; he didn't want to get the kid stuck on the toilet instead of in his bed, after all. Ethan closed his eyes and opened his mouth. Rather than slide the food in, Abraham kissed him first. Ethan hummed in surprise but didn't pull away. Abraham lifted a hand to his jaw, sliding a thumb along that dark, delicious flesh before pulling away.

"Couldn't resist," he teased as he offered the forkful of brisket for real. Ethan grinned as he ate it.

"Anyone else might think you're happy to see me, Mr. A," he practically purred.

"Oh, Ethan. You have no idea. But we're wearing entirely too much clothing for you to see for certain."

Ethan's eyes dropped to his crotch and then slid back up to his gaze. "Then maybe we should rectify that."

"Now, now. No need to rush. We have some time together. So let's enjoy it." Abraham slid the smoothie towards Ethan. "Let me spoil you good and proper."

"I rather like the sound of that." Ethan took the smoothie and drank.

"Do you want to try other meats?"

"I don't want to do too much at once. My stomach isn't used to it, you know?"

Abraham nodded. He paused when he felt his phone buzz with a message. "Go ahead and work on your food. I need to make a quick call."

"I'll be quiet," Ethan promised.

Abraham stepped out to the room, checked his messages, and then hit the call button instead of typing out a reply.

"Hey, baby. I just got home, so I thought I'd call you instead." He noticed Ethan slide from the counter and wander around the kitchen, looking at things.

"Hey. I just wanted to check in with you. How was school?" Maria's voice pulled him back to the phone.

"It was pretty good. I got to catch up on some admin and grading before I had all those tutor sessions."

"What does the rest of your day look like? I know you said you aren't leaving until tomorrow."

"I need to order the pigs for Christmas. I thought about trying to get in some Christmas shopping before the weather gets too bad. And I haven't heard from Jose in a while, so I thought I might check up on him."

"Didn't you see him Thursday?"

"No, he didn't join us this week. Part of why I was planning to check in."

"Maybe you should do that instead of shopping today."

"Oh?"

"Sorry. I've just got a bad feeling. At first I was worried you decided to brave the ice after all, but now I'm worried about your cousin."

"I appreciate that, baby. Don't worry, I'll make sure he's ok. How are you and the boys?"

"We're doing good." She paused as uproarious laughter filled the background. "Mom's got James enthralled with charades," she added with a soft laugh of her own. "Though I think Jesús might be enjoying it the most."

"That sounds like a blast. You don't need to worry about me; I'll stay home and just make some calls. Go enjoy your time with them."

"All right. Please let me know everything's okay?"

"Will do, babe." He glanced up as Ethan entered the room bearing a strand of grapes. The lad arched a playful eyebrow and held them up for Abraham. Abraham slid his teeth over one and bit off the stem. He slid the grape into his cheek. "I'm going to get myself some actual food, hun. I'll talk to you later." Once Maria hung up, he chewed and swallowed. Then he followed Ethan back into the kitchen. "I don't think you need my help to flirt," he pointed out with a smirk. "You're doing pretty good on that front. You aren't nearly as shy as I was expecting."

Ethan grinned at him. "I'm not shy at all, Mr. A." He hesitated. "Well, ok. I was a bit shy about approaching you because I thought you might get mad. And I used to be shy in your class because I had a crush on you."

Abraham stepped up to Ethan, wrapping his arms around him and pulling him close. "I was worried I might go mad tutoring you, unable to touch you," he confessed. Ethan grinned up at him.

"Touch me all you want, Mr. A," he invited. "But I've got a question first."

Abraham frowned. "Oh?"

Ethan slid away to the counter, pulling out his phone and digging into his files. He set the phone on the counter, and Abraham saw a familiar scene playing out over video. "Is that you?"

Chapter 8

Abraham watched himself push through the crowd, heard Javier calling after him. Dammit, so Jose hadn't found all of them. At least not yet. He reached towards the phone, but Ethan snatched it and danced away, grinning playfully.

"I can't confirm or deny if I can't get a good look at it." Abraham kept his voice calm. The kid was already in his grasp. Right?

"I suppose." Ethan slid the phone in his pocket. Abraham rolled his eyes and moved to the living room.

"Forget it for now, then." He turned on some music, jazz crooning from his vintage record player. He faced Ethan and held out his hand. "Come dance with me." He kept his gaze locked with Ethan's, though he knew exactly what pocket the phone was in. As Ethan approached him, he took the kid's hand and twined fingers with him before pulling him close. He hummed as Ethan reached up to kiss his neck and then nuzzle against him. He slid a hand down to tease Ethan's cock, feeling the muscle harden beneath his hand. Even as he toyed with Ethan, his mind was on the video. The phone. If Ethan had figured out it was him, who else knew?

He slid his hand around Ethan's waist and into his jeans, sliding along his buttocks. The molly should be kicking in.

Ethan would be nice and relaxed. They could have their fun, and then he could get his hands on that phone. He felt Ethan's hand start to explore as well, cautious at first and then more bold, just like the lad had been acting towards him.

"How far are you wanting to go, Ethan?" he whispered, finally taking in a deep whiff of the lad's hair. "I want to fuck that tight ass of yours so badly, but only if you're up for it." Otherwise, he would build him up to it, of course.

"That's pretty quick, Mr. A, but I'm pretty tempted. I've never felt so…loose on a first date." Ethan grinned up at Abraham. "It's not like I'm a virgin or anything. Kids my age aren't that innocent, you know." He leaned his cheek against Abraham's chest. "I feel crazy about you."

"I'm feeling pretty crazy myself. I don't even feel this attracted to my wife."

"That's horrible to be in a marriage like that, Mr. A."

"I'm glad I have you to help distract me from that part of my miserable life. If there's one thing I've learned from my father, a man needs distractions to keep himself from going insane."

Ethan glanced up suspiciously. "Is that what I am to you? A distraction?"

"You're much more than that, Ethan."

They continued slow dancing, Abraham toying with Ethan's body and slowly relaxing him.

"I'm not sure that meat agreed with me, Mr. A. I'm not feeling so good. Can we sit down for a minute?" Ethan's words were starting to sound a bit sluggish.

"Sure. Do you want some water?" Abraham moved over to the couch, pulling Ethan down with him.

"I don' want you to leave...Don't stop touching me..."

Abraham grinned as he obliged. This was going perfectly. "I won't. But I need to answer a text really quick, ok?" He pulled out his phone and opened his messenger, sending more than one text. Then he set the phone aside. "Want to show me that video again?"

"No...I want to keep having fun...Fuck Javier." Ethan slid his hand down to retrieve the phone since it was digging through his pocket. He half-heartedly tossed it next to Abraham's.

"Who's Javier?" Abraham prompted, sliding his hand down to Ethan's cock to continue toying with him.

"Guy at Jinx's...I know it was you, Mr. A, I was jus' playin'... we set up the whole sting..."

Abraham kept himself calm. "Why are you here, Ethan?"

"Javier said we could get you to stop...Get you to help his program to get more people help so they stop...going after kids...But I had you in class so long...s'it really bad?"

"I told you before, E. People have different beliefs, want to get other people in trouble. That's why you have to be careful. That's why Javier tries to be so sneaky to learn about people." He paused. "Does Javier know where you are right now?"

"Noooo...He knows we were gonna study today...But I didn't tell him. I...I wanted to find out for myself."

"And?"

"And I don' want you to stop touching me."

"I hadn't realized I did," Abraham said in way of apology. He guided Ethan to slide off his shirt, whistling in approval at the toned build. Yup, this kid was an athlete. Abs for days. "So, what now?"

"What if you jus' give him the money. He doesn't gotta know if we keep seeing each other, right?"

"You tricked me, Ethan. Can I trust you?"

"I didn' wanna." His eyes drooped before turning a pleading gaze up at Abraham.

"Didn't you tell me you had friends who got mad at you for not paying for things?"

"Ya...But look at this houze. Yer loaded."

Abraham fell silent, enjoying the work of his hands. Ethan was starting to make some delicious noises in response. So. This was a lie. Ethan was working with Javier. And if he agreed to the kid's plan? How long would it last until they were blackmailing him again? How many other kids would they send his way, begging for help, drawing him in, just to stab him in the back? "Think more of the smoothie would help? Or some water? We can walk there together."

Ethan made a humming noise, so Abraham stood and helped him up. He slid behind Ethan and wrapped his arms around his waist, pressing his own hardened self against the lad's jeans and smirking when Ethan giggled. He continued playing with Ethan's body as they walked, showering him in kisses. So what if it was a trap? Why shouldn't he have his fun? He had plenty of ways to deal with Ethan and Javier.

He had been careful. Was being careful. There weren't any texts to tie him to Ethan, and plenty of witnesses had seen them at school. There was video of him leaving alone. Ethan had a routine away from home. They had time to figure out what they were doing. He let Ethan lean on the counter while he rinsed out the smoothie glass and filled it with fresh water. He supported the lad and tipped the glass against his lips, watching as a little water dripped past and highlight his jawline and neck.

How dare he. How dare such a delicious thing offer himself up as bait and try to ensnare Abraham. How dare those delicious dark eyes continue to draw him in, even as the thought of the boy trying to ransom his affection gnawed at Abraham's insides.

He set the glass aside and drew Ethan closer, licking the water from his jaw before pulling him into a kiss. He licked Ethan's lips before sliding his tongue between them. Ethan groggily reciprocated, reaching up to wrap his arms around Abraham's neck.

Ethan really was delicious. It was such a shame. He slid a hand up to cradle Ethan's head. Such a shame the corruption of the world, the greed, had already taken a hold of the boy's soul. His other hand slid up to Ethan's neck. He deepened the kiss, and then in one solid movement, snapped the boy's neck.

Chapter 9

The bone-sickening crunch vibrated through Abraham's hands. He slid his grip down and held Ethan close.

"Shame, shame," he murmured to himself, tucking Ethan's head against his neck and rocking him softly. "But you're free now. No more pressure. No more Javier. All mine." He reverently lowered Ethan to the floor. "You're safe now. Safe from this awful world. Safe with me." Once he was sure the boy was comfortable, he moved to make himself an espresso. Maria had bought him a fancy machine for Christmas last year, but he rarely used it. Now was a good time to treat himself.

While the machine was working, he put away the leftover fruits and rinsed the extra dishes. "This wasn't how I expected things to go, you know," he told Ethan calmly. "I was rather looking forward to our little tryst. But you had to go and show you were just another cog in the fucking machine." He shook his head, putting the dishes away. "It's alright. I forgive you. We can still have this evening together, we just won't get to do everything I wanted. But it will work out in the end."

He leaned against the island, looking down at the cooling corpse. Then he looked up. "You see what You made me do? You couldn't be bothered to save him, so I had to kill him to free him?" He tsked. This hadn't been the plan. Ethan was meant to be a conquest, not part of the collection. "The Lord will provide...I suppose you were meant to be my sacrifice..." This hadn't been the plan, but he could work with it. He could. There were just extra complications. Abraham sighed as he pulled out his phone. He needed to make a few phone calls while he came up with a plan. Perhaps he should take Ethan upstairs and get them both into something more comfortable.

He sipped his espresso and called Jose.

"Twice in one week? You spoil me."

"Hey, Jose. We missed you last night."

"Ah, mijo, such is the life. Everyone is sick. You know how it is."

"How's the missus feeling?"

"Better, slowly. I felt like I was in the plague for a little bit. The kids are taking longer, I think they keep getting each other sick again."

"That's rough, cuz. You guys need anything?"

"Just promise you're still doing pork feasts for your besties, eh?"

"You know it. I'm ordering the stock tonight."

"Man, I'm already feeling better."

"Maybe you can cheer me up, too?"

He heard Jose snicker over the phone. "About your little pest problem? Ah, bro, you got nothin' to worry about. Most of the ones that did hit the web were crappy quality. And I hunted down a few others. The man himself seems to be quiet for now, but don't go fallin' for anymore sob stories, eh?"

Abraham glanced down at Ethan's corpse. "Nah, mijo. I'll stick to helping the folks I know. I'm done with scammers."

"I'mma hold you to that. Start chargin' double if I gotta to dissuade you." Something happened in the background, and Jose muffled the phone for a moment to talk to someone. "Sorry, man. I gotta bounce. Need to get some food for the patients."

"Alright, bro. Tell the fam I hope they start feeling better." After saying his goodbyes, Abraham paused to look at Ethan again. "I'm sorry, lovely. You must be cold down there. Why don't we get you more comfortable?" He bent down and, with some effort, hauled Ethan up into his arms. He had expected the kid to be at least a little stiff by now, but perhaps the minutes just seemed to stretch since they were together.

Huffing slightly, he hauled the lad up the thirteen stairs to the second floor and into his and Maria's bedroom. He got the body settled on the duvet, then propped up some pillows to help him lounge. As he moved for the closet, he made another phone call. He closed the door so Ethan couldn't eavesdrop or see what he was up to in the walk-in space.

He had just hung up when Maria tried to FaceTime.

Abraham cursed, quickly setting aside everything he had in his arms and pulling up her call. "Hey, babe. Sorry it took a minute, I'm arms deep in the closet."

"You're in the closet? Why?"

Abraham felt a flash of irritation. "I haven't packed yet, hun."

"You don't need to, remember? I brought your suitcase."

Abraham stopped, staring at the screen for a minute. Then he bust out laughing. "Oh, babe, you're the best. I hate packing. I didn't realize…"

"You loaded the car," she reminded him, laughing as well.

"When I tell you it's been a long day…" He left the closet, careful to keep Ethan out of the frame. Luckily he had promised to be quiet. Abraham moved for the hall to head downstairs. "Did you need something? I thought you were gonna join in on the games?"

"Did you reach your cousin?"

"Yeah, a little bit ago. He's taking care of the family since they've all caught something." He started rummaging through a few drawers. "I'm just about to order the food. Are Carlos and Esmeralda still coming?"

"Yeah. I left a list of what to order. Are you sure you don't want me to call?"

"I've got it, babe. You know these feasts are my passion." He pulled out the list and the brochure for the vegan caterer Maria had chosen, setting them aside. He checked the time. "I should get those calls done. Don't want to keep anyone late this time of year."

"Alright. I can let you go…"

"What's up?"

"Are you sure you're ok? You seem…stressed."

"I'm fine. I had a lot of sessions."

"Who did you tutor today?"

Abraham kept his expression pleasant, but the woman was grating on his nerves. "One of the Jewish kids, Jacob Schwartz. Kid normally gets a free pass since his family donates a ton of cash, but we've gotta justify the grade. Those fucking Jews take advantage of everything and everyone around them. I remember my grandfather talking about how they thought they controlled the world…"

"What the fuck are you on about? No. No, it doesn't matter. Who else?"

Abraham listed off a few names, then paused as if he couldn't remember. "Oh, and Ethan Bísólá."

"Ethan Bísólá? Isn't he, like, your star student or something?"

"My thoughts, too. Turns out the kid's starting to feel the pressure and just needed some extra help preparing… Babe, I'm sorry, can I let you go? My stomach is killing me, I think I'm going to be on the toilet for a bit."

"Are you surprised? You eat like crap, drink too much, and never take care of yourself. Look at how much weight you've gained, and you think that's healthy? How long have I been telling you to go to the doctor and get yourself checked from head to toe."

Abraham grimaced. He needed to get her off the damn phone. "I know, you're right. I'm thankful you care so much."

"If you're serious about being there for us, that means getting your health in order to."

"Ok. I'll see what I can do after the holidays. Getting in anywhere right now would be hell."

Maria sighed. "Fine. I'll let you go. How about I call you again when James is getting ready for bed? I'm sure he'd like to say goodnight."

Abraham smiled. He kept the twitch from his eye. How many times was she going to say she would leave him alone and then not? "Sounds like a plan, Ma. I'll talk to you then. Love you."

"…Love you. Bye for now."

As she hung up, Abraham let out a breath. He was just going to keep getting interrupted. It was fine. It would be fine. Just annoying. Was winning her trust back and keeping his promise worth this hassle? So far his only reward was freeing Ethan, and it didn't feel like much of a reward. He could still have some fun, at least.

Since he was downstairs, he made Maria's order and then pulled up his contact entry for The Happy Pig. The staff there always took good care of him, especially since he had bailed them out of so many fines and court fees. Fucking activists trying to take a butcher down for 'animal cruelty.' Pathetic.

"Hey, Jess. It's time for the Alvarez Feast!"

"I thought I recognized your dulcet tones, Abraham! Cutting it close this year, are we? I was beginning to worry you found someone else…"

"Nonsense. I'd never let anyone else take care of my meat. You know how loyal my family is."

"And we're always glad to serve you. How's the family?"

"Good, good, how about yours?

"Fantastic! The little one will be two soon, so he's getting into everything, but we're blessed."

"We are, too. I'm glad everything is good. Hey, love catching up, but can I put my order in? I have so much going on I almost forgot, and I'm headed out of town tomorrow."

"Of course. What are we doing this year?"

"I think we're going pretty big."

He heard Jessie moving a few things around on her desk. "Alright, hit me."

"Do you have those sucklings like last year? The sixty-pounders? They were so sweet and tender."

"I've got six around that size."

"That's perfect. And then I'll take two whole adults."

"You *are* going big this year. Expecting an army?"

"Well, you know I've got the big shindig at my place. Then I'm donating to the police, firemen, EMS…a few homeless shelters in town. And I've got some friends that I cook for. They love it, and I love making it."

"That's awful generous of you."

"I do what I can do. God blessed me, so I think I should do the same."

"Any specifics on the adults?"

"Let me have the breeding stock. Hell, you may as well give me the sucklings' sows."

"Breeding stock? You're not looking to put us out of business, are you?" He could hear her curiosity under the tease.

"Nah, I just like eating them. It makes me feel powerful, ending their line."

"If you say so. They're more expensive, though."

"Not a problem. Just let me know the total."

"Well the two adults are gonna run you 1,600 each since they're breeders. That's twice the price of our normal butchers. Then 250 each suckling. How do you want those prepared? Any special instructions?"

"You know how I am. I'm going to bring my own feed tomorrow morning, so please don't give them anymore from your stock. What pen are they in?"

"I'll have them all moved to pen six for you."

"Great. Then let me have three of those sucklings in tact. I'm going to roast them whole. The other three can be divided up like the adults. You know the drill: some tenderloins, pork chops, and ham. Sausage and bacon. The works. Just package things in groups instead of by pig so I can cook in batches."

"You got it. And I know you want the blood to keep them moist."

"It really helps with marinating."

"Still want the videos, or do you trust us?"

"Aw, c'mon, Jessie. You know I gotta watch my pigs. James is taking an interest in the family recipes, too, so I've been letting him watch."

"Taking after the man of the house, is he?"

"Such a daddy's boy. You know he'll be taking my place some day. Boy needs to know how to ensure his meat is handled. When can you deliver these?"

"Your dinner is on Christmas, right? How's Christmas Eve sound? That will give them time to cure and us to butcher."

"Eve is great. When do you plan to butcher? Should I bring more than one feeding?"

"When are you planning to come by?"

"Early tomorrow morning. I'll be driving through."

"One should be enough. We'll start butchering tomorrow."

"Alright. Give my regards to the crew, Jess."

"And say hi to the family, Abraham. We'll see you around."

Abraham whistled as he headed upstairs and lay out a line of coke on his bathroom counter. He rolled his eyes harder than some of his students when his phone pinged, whipping it out and glaring at Maria's message. He typed something back and then went to check on Ethan.

"Looks like you're still resting. Sorry I had so much to do. Now Maria—" his phone pinged again, and he whipped it out of his pocket. "—pain in my ass, such a nightmare," he muttered as he answered, ending the text with a smiley.

"What do you expect?" Ethan's voice shot through his mind. "Of course she doesn't trust you, fucking pedophile. You're a demon in human skin. A fat pig who wants to own the world but can barely keep his own damn pants on."

"How dare you." Abraham tossed his phone on the bed, but his voice was steady. "After all I've done for you? You had better clean up that attitude, or I'll—"

"You'll what? Kill me?" Ethan quipped. "I'm not afraid of you, fucking fatass. No one is. They just suck up to your ego for your money and then laugh behind your back. You know they all hate you. And you deserve it."

"Ethan, shut the fuck up. Let's just enjoy our time."

"What is there to enjoy? I'm dead, you asshole! And it's your fault! You are so fucked once my parents and Javier realize I'm missing."

Abraham growled, stalking to the side of the bed and roughly rolling Ethan over so he was facing the wall. "Now, think about what you've done, baby. I'll be right back. I've got a surprise, not that you deserve it."

He moved for the walk-in closet again. When he emerged, he was wearing makeup, high heels, a red dress, earrings, and a red wig. He had supplies to doll up Ethan, as well. Abraham sashayed around the bed and struck a pose. "Ta-da! And look, I've got some for you, too." He rolled Ethan onto his back and started applying the make up. As he was working on the lad's lipstick, Ethan's eyes opened. He looked wildly around, then at Abraham. He didn't say anything, but tears welled in his eyes.

"Well, well. You get to enjoy this after all," Abraham greeted in a sing-song voice. "See? Everything will be fine." He frowned when Ethan started to cry. "Oh, baby, there's no need to cry. Are you thirsty? Do you want some water? Is that why you aren't saying anything?" He reached for a glass by the bed, holding it to Ethan's lips. But as the water tilted in, the boy couldn't move to drink or swallow, and it all came spilling back out. Abraham sighed, setting the glass back.

"Don't worry, Ethan," he crooned, smoothing the boy's hair. "I won't let you suffer, baby. You can blame God when you see Him. It's all His fault, after all. He's the one who guided everything to this point. I won't forsake you to the life of a cripple." Abraham slid from the bed and moved to his safe for more supplies. "It's just going to be another missing kid. Another set of parents temporarily distraught," he hummed to himself. "Everyone learns to cope. They'll be fine. Eventually."

When he returned to Ethan, he had a clear plastic bag and duct tape. He sat on the side of the bed and kissed him goodbye. "I'm going to miss you, baby. The smell of your hair, the taste of your lips. It's such a shame. But don't worry— you won't be all gone. I'll keep your youthful energy, your spirit alive. And I'll never forget you. I never forget anyone." Abraham smiled, watching Ethan's eyes as he slid the bag ritualistically over the boy's head and carefully wrapped the duct tape around his neck. The smile remained as he watched the light fade from the boy's eyes.

Chapter 10

Abraham went into the bathroom to change out of his heels and dress. He thoroughly cleaned the makeup off his face. "Father, why have you forsaken me? I told You to just let us study, and now look what You've made me do! I'm not Your butcher. Why couldn't I just have what I wanted? What are You trying to prove? I already know this world is hell. But now You're letting little boys lose their souls? Why can't you let your fake-ass priests do this dirty work? They're already enjoying the fun part. I get it, God. You agree. Little boys are the best. So You want them all to yourself. But that's not fair— let us enjoy them, too! Or I'll never pray to You again!"

Abraham angrily stashed his clothing and make up. Then he stripped Ethan and washed off his face. He was still fuming, so once everything was safely secured, he returned to the bathroom and did a few more lines of coke. He scowled at the supply; he was running low. Hadn't he just restocked? No matter, it was too late in the day. He would have to ration until Monday, and then he could go restock.

He almost jumped out of his skin when his phone went off. He quickly checked his reflection to make sure all the makeup and cocaine were gone before answering.

"Hey, little man! You all ready for bed?"

***

Abraham had gotten into Ethan's phone and deleted the video. He also went through the boy's text messages and deleted anything from Javier related to the set up at Jinx or approaching Abraham at school. He deleted a few other things, wiped the browser's location history, and then dropped the phone in water and let it soak while he got dressed in something casual. Once he was ready, he pulled the phone out, dried it, and wiped the surface with alcohol. He held it to the light to make sure the thing was practically sparkling, then headed to his car. He wouldn't make Ethan leave yet, but the phone needed to go.

First, he drove to the gym Ethan said he liked to work out at, but it had been long enough he decided that wasn't the best place. Instead, he went to the public library. He wasn't about to touch foot in that place, but it was somewhere they would look for Ethan. His smile widened when he realized there was a river nearby. Even better. He parked the car and strolled along. No one paid him any mind, lost in their own realities. Once he was absolutely sure everyone was just as self-absorbed as he was, he tossed the phone in the river. Step one. Now he could go home and enjoy his company. Besides, they would need an early start in the morning.

***

It was barely Saturday when Abraham's alarm went off, but he forced himself out of bed. He had a lot to do, after all. He planned on leaving by 2:00 so he could avoid traffic, his neighbors, and anyone else walking their dogs in the early morning hours. He was looking forward to seeing his family, but he had some errands to run.

First, however, he wanted to treat himself for breakfast. Maria had picked up some of his favorite filet mignon. There was a little note attached to the wrapped package: *Miss you, baby. Make sure you eat while we're gone. There's also mashed potatoes and some broccoli (not that I really expect you to eat that). Enjoy.*

It was too dark and cold to cook outside, and really he didn't have enough time to fire the slow cooker. Instead, he decided to pan-sear the steaks. He liked his steaks crisp and brown on the outside but rare and bloody on the inside. He tossed the potatoes into the microwave and moved to pour himself a glass of his favorite blood-red wine. Once everything was ready, he had a feast fit for a king. As he cut into the steaks, the bloody juices seeped across his plate and into the potatoes.

It was too dark to see much through the panoramic windows aside from the security lights out back. The moon was hidden behind the wintry clouds. Abraham said a quick prayer over his meal and dug in. The potatoes started to stain red from the steaks, but even they didn't absorb all the excess. He used Italian bread to sop up the rest, making sure he ate every drop.

Normally he would leave the dishes in the sink for someone else, but he was turning over a new leaf. He washed them all and put them in the dishwasher. Then he headed upstairs to get Ethan. He couldn't wait to show the kid the scenery during their drive. He smiled as he looked to Maria's side of the bed, where the boy still lay.

"Hey, baby, are you still sleeping? We're driving to New England today. I wish you could enjoy the scenery, but

I'm going to have to keep you hidden away in the back. I'm going to get cleaned up first, and then I'll help you get ready." Once Ethan knew the plan, Abraham moved to shower and clean up. Since he knew he would need to carry Ethan downstairs, he took a line to prepare himself. At least going downstairs would be easier with gravity on his side. He would also need to take a few things downstairs first, so the boost would help. He had no plans to take Maria up on her offer to exercise. Stairs were hell enough.

First, he got his supplies ready. A tarp, his special knife, pliers, and a couple of towels went into the garage. He laid out the tarp neatly; only the best for Ethan. Once the bed was prepared, he went to retrieve his guest. He laid Ethan out properly before stripping him. Then it was back up the stairs to strip the bed and put on new sheets. He even sprayed fabric freshener on them so the place would smell nice. He surveyed his work a moment before fetching a few candles and decorating the room, then pulling out a special pair of goblets. He would wait to pull out the wine until he and Maria were home.

That done, he bundled up the sheets and Ethan's clothes. Another trip downstairs, and he was huffing from the marathon. Still, he was on a schedule. He went outside and tossed the fabrics into his slow cooker, setting it for a few hours. Now it was time to prepare Ethan.

He moved into the garage and knelt beside his sacrifice. "Don't worry, this won't hurt," he promised Ethan, picking up a small syringe. "This will make sure you don't feel a thing." He had to force the needle into the rigid skin, but he wasn't going to let Ethan endure this without a little morphine. "I'm sorry it had to be this way. Such a shame for me, but you're blessed. God has chosen you, little lamb." He took the knife and cut away the plastic bag he had used to free Ethan. Then, he started to pray.

"Father, forgive me, for I have sinned," he began as he picked up the pliers. "I lie. I cheat. I steal. I kill." He listed every one of his sins, taking a tooth for each. Removing the teeth made a bone-shattering crunch that reverberated through Abraham's eardrums, each seeming louder than the last. He was familiar with the noise, but for some reason it seemed worse this time.

At least there wasn't any blood. That was always a pain to deal with. But Ethan had been sleeping for so long that all the blood had pooled down his backside and started to congeal. "So sweet of you not to make a big mess for me to worry about," he hummed as he transferred the teeth to a baggie. Then he retrieved the knife. It had started out as a hunting knife, but he had made a few modifications and painted dark symbols along the blade and hilt.

"Father, let this sacrifice assist you in overlooking my sins. Let this new vibrant life be transferred to me, that I may truly start fresh in Your eyes," he resumed his prayer while methodically searing away Ethan's scalp. He moved with practiced care, not missing a single hair or patch of skin from the top of the boy's head. He placed the scalp in a separate bag from the teeth and set them aside. Next he grabbed another clear plastic bag and the duct tape, resealing Ethan's head before carefully wrapping him up in the tarp.

Since Maria had taken the truck, Abraham was left with their SUV. He opened the hatch and hefted the shrouded Ethan into the back. He pulled the hatch cover over the top, then closed the gate for now. Next he cleaned up his work area and headed inside. He cursed at having to take the stairs again, but took comfort in the fact that he was almost ready to leave. First he moved to the bathroom and started hot water in the sink, shoving first the pliers, and then the knife under the hot water. Once the residue had washed off, he set them to drip on a hand towel and grabbed out his stash. Everything was going perfectly, so he celebrated with a quick bump. He wanted a full line, but he was getting a bit too low to go all out.

After his small distraction, he finished drying the tools by hand and then collected the rest of his items and went into the walk-in closet. He had a large safe inside that only he could access. After a facial recognition scan, a thumbprint scan, and a password, he slid his supplies inside. He stored the knife in it's special case, then used a small key to open an opaque container. He gently added Ethan's scalp and teeth to the collection inside, relocked the case, hid the key, and secured the safe.

Now to prepare for the pigs. He huffed his way downstairs and back into the garage, moving to the storage system built along the back wall. One of the cabinets held his supply of pig feed, a special family blend. After counting out how many bags he should take, he opened the SUV's back hatch again. "Hey, Ethan. Sorry for the wait. I'm going to help keep you comfortable and safe, ok?" He moved back to the shelf and started hauling the feed bags, using them to cover the tarp. He unrolled the trunk cover so all the bags would fit.

All of that horrid exercise out of the way, he moved inside and straight to the kitchen. The preparation had made him hungry again, so he pulled out more of the brisket to heat up in the microwave. He gorged himself on more than one sandwich as he flicked through the news on the television. Wars, murders, crime. Everything was entirely too dreary for how he was feeling, so he kept changing the channel. "Fucking pigs. All they care about is the ratings," he grumbled with a full mouth. He finally landed on late-night game show reruns until he was done eating.

Abraham sighed as he hauled himself off of the couch. He wanted to sit there and watch more trash for the dopamine rush, but he had places to be. He took a moment to disinfect the kitchen, bedroom, and garage before warming up the SUV.

"Comfy back there?" he asked as he climbed into the driver's seat. He could just imagine the 'fuck you' in response, but he brushed off Ethan's new attitude. The boy would learn, and he only had to put up with him a little while longer. He hit the garage button and then started backing out. As he pulled past the sidewalk, he saw his neighbor, Carl, out with his new dog. Carl waved, and Abraham plastered a smile as he rolled down his window.

"Morning, Carl! Little early for a walk, isn't it?"

"Oh, you know how pups are. Once they start whining to pee, you either get up or have to clean the carpets," Carl joked, stifling a yawn. "What has you out so early?"

"I'm heading out to New England. Maria and the kids headed to her mother's yesterday, but I had to stay back for school," Abraham explained. "I figured a nice early start would help me avoid most of the traffic, but you know, I also just miss them."

"I can sympathize. Luckily the ice isn't too bad this morning."

"No surprise the forecast was exaggerated. You know they have to make everything dramatic while they're on air."

Carl laughed. "Man, if that ain't the truth of it. They can't just broadcast the happy stuff anymore— they gotta shove all that into a single evening broadcast and fill the rest with drama and violence. I barely watch the news anymore, it's all trash." He shivered. "Well, I won't make you waste any more hot air. Drive safe."

"Thanks, Carl. Don't let that dog give you frostbite, now."

Carl was laughing as Abraham rolled up the window and pulled away. He glanced in the rear-view to see if the man was watching him, but Carl had already turned back towards his own house. Abraham was a bit surprised the stench of death hadn't made it through the front window.

Carl could be nosy, like all wealthy people were, but he knew better than to stick his nose too far into Abraham's business. The latter's uncanny luck with the stock market had increased Carl's wealth exponentially; he didn't want to acknowledge anything peculiar about his golden goose, lest he lose his edge.

Abraham had filled up his tank after getting rid of Ethan's phone, so he didn't have to stop until The Happy Pig. Or at least, that was the plan. But it was very early in the morning, and he had barely slept. What sleep he had was filled with the things he had wanted to do to Ethan but didn't have time for. About an hour out of the city, he pulled over for a quick bump, then cursed vehemently when flashing lights filled his mirror. He quickly checked his reflection and straightened his shirt, but he didn't roll down the window until the officer was close.

"Everything all right, sir?"

"Yes?" Abraham gave the officer an innocently confused look. "Why do you ask?"

"Any reason you're on the side of the highway so early in the morning?"

"I lost my phone connection and GPS stalled out. I decided to pull over so I could safely download the map. Figured I could rest my eyes while I waited."

"That's fair. Where are you headed to this early?"

"My mother-in-law lives in New England. My family headed out yesterday, but I had to stay late since I'm a teacher. Figured a nice early start would give us more time to all be together. My mother-in-law has cancer, so every hour counts, ya know?"

"Sorry to hear that, man. Let's work on getting you back on the road. Can I see your license, registration, and insurance please?"

"I mean, yeah, but why? I'm not doing anything wrong."

"Yeah, but dispatch is really strict on following traffic stop protocols when it's this early in the morning. Lot of stolen vehicles getting moved around and the like. You know how it is." Though he didn't mention it, Abraham had a feeling he was also eyeballing the luxury SUV with a teacher sitting inside. As the officer took his papers and moved back to the patrol car, Abraham could just envision pulling out his magnum when the man returned.

He already had his sacrifice, however. A dangerous prey on its own without going after a cop. Those assholes always got more up in arms when one of their own was missing, though they tended to hand wave most missing kids and insist they were just runaways. He rolled his window down again when he saw the officer returning.

"Alright, you're all clear. Sorry to keep you. Sounds like you have a lot on your plate. You drive safe, Mr. Alvarez. Get to your family in one piece."

"Thanks, officer. You, too. And I hope your family has a good holiday season." As the officer moved to walk away, Abraham started to roll up his window. But the cop glanced in the back window and paused.

"Is that pig feed you got there?"

Abraham's heart hammered in his chest. Not a search, not now. "Yes, sir. You ever heard of The Happy Pig?" The officer walked back to the window.

"Who hasn't? They've got some great stock."

"Right? I order them every year for Christmas. My family has ordered from them even longer. My cousin has a feed store, and we've got a running deal with the shop to use his blend. Healthier, ya know? Figured I would save the delivery fee this time around since I'm passing through."

"What shop does your cousin run? My wife's got backyard chickens, but I hate those chain shops. Corporate bullshit, though you didn't hear that from me."

Abraham laughed, the sound coming easier as he relaxed. "You good if I pull out a business card?" With the officer's nod, Abraham reached for his center console and pulled out a business card wallet, rifling through to find the feed shop. "Here ya go, man. Tell him I sent ya, he'll make you a deal for the first purchase." He wrote his name on the back of the card before handing it over.

"Thanks, man. I appreciate it. I'll let you get going."

Abraham nodded as he rolled up his window. He made sure to turn on his blinker and check for traffic before carefully pulling back out onto the road. His face split into a wide grin as the officer faded behind him. Everything was going perfectly. Everything would be fine. Just like it always was.

Chapter 11

Abraham allowed himself to enjoy the drive to The Happy Pig. It was still fairly early in the morning, and the crew didn't usually show up until six. He had several hours to work with.

While he had been told before in casual conversation that the outside cameras were busted and too expensive to fix, Abraham didn't press his luck by going to the parking lot. Instead, he pulled off the road and looped behind the barn. He knew the slaughterhouse layout quite well, so he parked close to where he could access pen 6. He opened the hatch and started unloading, but he stacked everything by the pen and went to get more. Finally, he brought in Ethan. The pigs squealed incessantly at him, begging for food, anything they could shovel into their snouts. He ripped open the first bag of feed and poured it in, then he unbound Ethan's burial shroud and tossed him in on top. The rest of the feed covered the body as the pigs dug in.

They devoured everything Abraham gave them, not hesitating in the slightest when grain and seed and slop gave way to flesh and bone. Abraham pulled out his phone, adding a few more photos to his library as the pigs annihilated all evidence of the dead boy. He watched in glee as they ripped through his flesh, chomped and chewed on his bones. Even when they were done, they screamed at Abraham for more.

Abraham shoved the empty feed bags to the side for the crew to clean up, grabbing the tarp from beneath them. He left a couple of extra bags of feed in case the slaughterhouse decided to give them a final meal. He also pulled out a wad of cash and weighed it down on the extra bags with a rock as a tip.

Abraham whistled as he strolled back to his SUV, running through the few Christmas songs he knew. The security lights from the slaughterhouse caught his ring, the artificial light making the stones seem alive. Magical. Everything was going his way. God was on his side.

***

As Abraham was pulling into Mary's driveway, the team at The Happy Pig slaughter house was starting to arrive. Abraham's gift was a welcome surprise, as the crew eagerly split it among themselves and then set some aside for the front-end workers. They pulled the feed bags, empty and full, into their storage room for now so they could walk through the aisles unimpeded. One after another, they started emptying the slaughter pens.

Each squealing pig was lined up in a row. The stench of death lay heavy in the air. Some pigs kicked up a fuss as they got closer, but others tried to pull ahead of the herders, expecting a meal.

One by one, the pigs were led into the chute. One worker held a rod along their spine, stunning them with electricity, before another quickly hauled them out, shackled them to a hoist, and lifted them up to slit their throat with a sharp knife. A metal bucket collected the blood.

Once it stopped dripping, the dead pig was hauled into a metal tank and dropped into a scalding solution to remove hairs. The pig would be hauled out after a set time, and any remaining hairs manually removed.

Most pigs would then have their heads removed, followed by their intestines and organs. Then they are washed, weighed, and placed in a cooler to chill. After rigor mortis begins to set in, they will be pulled back out for processing. Their bodies would be cut in half and then pieces.

The buttocks would be salted and pressed into ham. The ribcage meat salted and smoked for bacon. Some meat would be ground up for sausages. Bits of fat would be cut into small pieces, some fried for cracklings while others were heated and reduced into a simmering grease to make lard.

Blood and death and the cries of pigs saturated the air. The workers barely even heard the squeals anymore, or smelled the blood. This was every day for them. Killing, bleeding, scalding, eviscerating, butchering. Again and again, in a well-practiced routine of death.

***

Maria had woken early at her mother's house and started some coffee. She knew she wouldn't fall asleep again. She had woken so many times during the night. That sinking feeling just wouldn't leave the pit of her stomach. She settled into her mother's patio furniture, bundled against the winter chill to watch the dawn. She nursed her coffee as a light snow fell through the neighborhood. It was so peaceful. Why couldn't the rest of her life be this calm?

Why couldn't Abraham be sitting across from her, enjoying the serenity? Why did he have to despise the things that brought her peace? She closed her eyes and sighed, taking a sip. There were so many things they needed to discuss.

Father Peter's suggestion of counseling slid through her mind, but that would likely have to wait until they started discussing New Year's resolutions. She also considered the gossip from her aerobics classmate, Ruth. Something about Abraham getting in trouble with the father of one of his students. Of course Abraham hadn't told her anything about the incident. Ruth didn't really know any details aside from the fact that the father, John something, had come to the school and shouted at the dean before shouting at Abraham. And then the whole thing had been swept under the rug.

Maria took another sip of her coffee. Was she really willing to give this man another chance with her heart? She wanted this to work out. She wanted to be his princess again, to have a stable household for their boys. And yet. Every hateful comment, every time he cooked meat in their kitchen, every time he brushed her peace aside, she gained another emotional scar.

"Penny for your thoughts?"

Maria jumped as her mother slid into the other chair, her own cup of coffee in hand and a cigarette in her mouth.

"Let's start with the wish you would quit that," Maria noted flatly. Mary snorted.

"Let a dying woman have her pleasures."

"Even when getting rid of those 'pleasures' might help her not die?" Maria prompted. Mary sighed, but she extinguished the cigarette and dropped it in an ash tray.

"There. Better?" she groused.

"Yes." Maria sipped her coffee. "You know I love you, Mom. I'm not trying to be a nag. But I want you to be around as long as possible."

Mary sighed. "I know. But maybe I should start being a nag in turn, eh?" Maria arched an eyebrow, and Mary took the invitation. "You and those boys deserve better. And you know it."

Maria didn't answer for a moment, watching the snowfall. "I'm...I don't know, Momma. Every time I start to feel the same way, something happens. And then there's the pre-nup..."

"Who cares about the money? You know I have plenty to leave you."

Maria continued as though her mother hadn't interrupted. "And finding somewhere to live, and getting the boys settled. At least when we're together, I can help balance his influence on the boys. If we have to split custody..." She trailed off. "I don't know if I can do that to them. It's so chaotic for kids going between households."

"Is it any better being stuck in a warzone of a house?"

Maria didn't answer.

"I know the terms in the pre-nup wouldn't let you all move in with me. But what if I moved in somewhere with you in that big city?"

Maria glanced at her. "You hate cities."

"I'm already planning to move in with you," Mary pointed out flatly. "We just wouldn't have that pig of a man around. I might enjoy the city more if I don't have to deal with him any more than necessary for the boys."

Maria considered, staring into her now-empty mug. "You would have to make some pretty big changes, you know. If I get away from him, I'm not letting any more meat in my house."

Mary huffed a dramatic sigh. "I suppose it's a good thing you've got me eating all that rabbit food on occasion," she teased.

"And I don't want any alcohol around the boys."

"I'll only pull it out when they're at school."

"I might need to get a job." Mary scoffed, and Maria raised her eyebrow once more.

"Girl, your father didn't leave me with nothing. Just because I don't like spending money doesn't mean I don't have it. And if you don't have that lug to pay for things, I'll just have to take over."

"And what would Mark and John have to say about you spending all that money on their sister?"

"I'd just tell them I'm spending it on me. I've got plenty set aside for them to inherit. Besides, they're not the ones bringing their kids to visit grandmum while they can."

Maria sighed, finally setting her cup over on the table. "I'll think about it. But it's not a change I'm willing to make in the middle of holiday chaos."

"I'll be there for you, whatever you choose."

Maria reached over to touch her mom's arm, smiling gratefully. They both looked over when they heard the crunch of tires on snow, and a dark SUV pulled onto the street. "Is that...?"

"How early did he get up this morning?" Mary asked in disbelief. Abraham wasn't the type to sacrifice his personal comfort for others, let alone her daughter, and yet there he was pulling into her driveway just past sunrise. Maria's boots crunched as she stood and moved to greet him. Mary's disbelief only grew as the man hopped out with a smile on his face and pulled her girl into a hug. Now she understood Maria's confusion and jokes about aliens.

The entire weekend, he acted like a new man. He sent Mary and Maria out to a spa Saturday morning while he watched the boys, then he took them out to eat and see a show. Sunday, he took them out shopping and paid for all of their purchases. He helped Maria get the boys ready and put them to bed. And yet, despite all the evidence he was presenting, Mary understood her daughter's reluctance to trust him. After all, she had been the one to console her daughter with every wound. Every affair. Every fight. Men like Abraham didn't change. Right?

Mary had never considered herself to be an overly cynical person. But Abraham had long ago lost the status of 'decent person' in her mind. He had seemed like quite the gentleman when he was courting Maria, even when he married her, but then the secrets had slowly started coming to the surface. And they knew there were more. But she had promised to support her daughter come what may. Time would tell if the man had actually changed or was just trying to cover up something more abhorrent than his usual trysts.

One thing was certain. If she was going to support her daughter, whether through healing her relationship or helping her rebuild after ending it, then she needed to start taking her health more seriously.

***

Even though Abraham had arrived separately, he decided to stay with his family and then drive everyone home. He hired a service to deliver his car back to their house. After dinner Sunday evening, he helped Maria load everyone into the truck. Maria had been tempted to stay later, but Abraham had already sent his car away. He would need to be home at a reasonable hour since he would have to be at the school in the morning. He kept the car running and waited with the boys while Maria said goodbye to her mother. The pair shared a long hug before Maria pulled herself away and hopped into the passenger seat.

"And?" Abraham prompted as he reversed and pulled out of the driveway.

"After Christmas. She's planning to come to dinner, then return home and start putting her affairs in order to move. Thank you again for offering, dear. After this weekend, I'm even more convinced it will be good for her."

Abraham nodded. "Anything for you. I know Mary and I can clash from time to time, but I'll do my best to get along with her. It will be easier, I think, now that I'm committed to being a better man. Some of her criticisms have been pretty valid."

Some? Maria bit her tongue. "I agreed to give you this chance, and she supports my decision. The rest is up to you. Though I daresay you've made a good start this weekend."

"I'm glad to hear it, baby."

Maria lapsed into silence, enjoying the scenery, the ride, and whoever she was texting, so Abraham eventually turned on some music. James was playing on his tablet, while Jesús was lulled to sleep by the movement.

About halfway back, after the sun started to sink, Abraham saw dark skin and cherry-chocolate hair in the headlights. He cursed, swerving, but when he looked in the rear Ethan was gone.

"What the hell was that??"

"Something in the road. Caught me off guard."

Maria sighed as she settled back into her seat, but she didn't lose herself in the phone again. She ran her hand down her face, trying to calm the adrenaline spike. "Did you get all the orders in Friday?" she asked in an effort to distract herself.

"I did. Tomorrow we need to rearrange some things in the cold storage so we can fit everything." The giant refrigerated space in their basement was great for when they were planning large meals. Neither of them liked to freeze their food if they could get away with it. "I'll start the barbecue as soon as the pigs are delivered. I've got a lot to make this year. I figure a few right away, take the next day to get things ready for our dinner, then start cooking the rest on the twenty-sixth."

Maria nodded along numbly. Most of her dishes would be ready-to-serve, though she had a few that would go in the oven before dinner. Abraham didn't make his pork in the oven, so they never had to fight for the space. "What time should I tell Carlos and Esmeralda to arrive?"

They spent the rest of the drive discussing logistics for the party. Abraham planned to expand the guest list a little if Jose and his family were feeling better so they didn't have to stress about Christmas dinner after having been sick. The fresh snowfall made them run a little late, so it was close to eleven by the time they reached home. Abraham pulled into the garage, not even blinking when he saw Ethan lying in his burial shroud on the floor. Maria didn't react, so he knew he was just seeing things. That was on him for letting his stash run low; rationing was making him see things. Everything was fine.

"Why does it smell like disinfectant in here?" Maria asked, wrinkling her nose as she slid out of the car.

"What?"

"It smells like cleaner in here. We weren't scheduled to have a housekeeper come through."

"Oh, that was me," Abraham explained as he carried the first suitcases in. "I spilled some of the feed while I was loading up."

"You...cleaned?"

"Yes?" He stamped down a flash of anger. No suspicion; not now. "What, you want mice in here?" He shrugged a shoulder. "I tried to get some cleaning done inside, too. Wanted to surprise you."

"I...see. Thank you."

"Mommy, please, I just wanna go to bed," James interrupted in a whine. Maria stifled a laugh to avoid encouraging his whining.

"Go ahead and get them to bed. I'll finish unloading."

Maria nodded, turning to James. "Alright, buddy. It's pretty late, huh? Come on."

"Please don't make me take a bath..."

"Not tonight. We'll make up for it tomorrow."

Abraham could hear James groaning as he followed Maria inside. Maria paused long enough to turn off the alarm before herding James upstairs, Jesús in her arms.

***

While Maria finished up with the boys, Abraham started a shower. He moved into the room and lit the candles he had set around, though he doubted they would do more than enjoy some wine and company before falling asleep. He had school in the morning and felt exhausted.

Still, the look on Maria's face when she entered the room to fresh sheets, candles, a goblet of wine, and a warming shower was priceless. The candlelight accented her flesh and reminded Abraham all over again just how beautiful his wife was. A part of him wanted to ensure time never touched her. But he didn't want to raise his boys alone, so for now he enjoyed her as she was.

After their shower, they propped up on their pillows and Abraham turned on the news and landed on Channel 6, barely listening. Maria curled against Abraham, eyes sliding closed, while Abraham imagined she was Ethan. Just as she started to doze away, anchorwoman Sofia Guzman said the words "Amber Alert." Maria's eyes snapped open as a picture of a dark-skinned boy with reddish brown hair popped onto the screen. "...Ethan Bísólá was last seen at his school on Friday," Guzman explained as an infograph of Ethan's age, height, and weight popped up alongside the picture. "If you have any information on his whereabouts, please call the number on the screen."

Abraham had gone very still. As Maria turned to look at him, his eyes were glued to the screen. "Oh, my God," he breathed as the news moved on, seeming to come out of his trance. He met her gaze. "That's the kid from my class."

Chapter 12

Abraham and Maria barely slept, for different reasons. Finally around five, Abraham gave up and slid out of bed into his Versace slippers.

"Are we going to talk about Ethan missing, or are we just going to ignore that?" Maria asked softly from her side of the bed. She was facing away from Abraham, staring at the family photos on the wall.

"I'm not ignoring anything," he snapped, but then he sighed and sat back down. "What is there to say? We don't really know anything aside from what was on the news. They'll start an investigation, and I'll do what I can to help."

Maria was silent for a moment. Her mind was everywhere. Ruth's rumor about Abraham and a student. All of the kids constantly going missing. The competency of police. "I want to help, too."

"Of course. But we don't know how to help yet." He sighed, running a hand through his receding hair. "I'm sure everything will be fine. Do you want a coffee? Maybe a shower while the kids are still asleep?"

"A shower sounds fantastic. Fuck coffee...Until after."

The pair laughed together as they moved for the rain shower. Since Abraham had a little extra time that morning, they spent the shower intimately reacquainting themselves. They only stopped when Maria's phone reacted to the baby monitor, letting them know Jesús was awake and crying. Maria moved to take care of the boys while Abraham got ready for school.

He threw on a red wool sweater and Christmas-patterned socks. He wasn't sure how many of the kids would know about Ethan being declared missing, but he hoped to keep their minds off of things and keep them entertained before taking their first exams.

"You look ready for the holidays," Maria commented as she joined him downstairs. "If only you had white hair and a beard, you could be Santa Claus."

"That's not nice, Mommy," James murmured groggily as he moved to sit at the table.

"It's ok, buddy. Momma's only joking," Abraham assured him with a chortle.

The morning was surprisingly normal. No, better than normal. Despite the news of Abraham's missing student, he and Maria enjoyed their time over breakfast. They flirted like they had in college. Abraham's mood only dimmed when he was putting on his coat, scarf, and gloves to head to school. He took a moment to kiss both his sons on their foreheads and then Maria on her cheek. "Love you all. I'll see you after school." It was as much to reassure himself as to promise them.

As he drove to school, Abraham made a quick call to his dealer and arranged to meet with him later that day. There was no way he would get through the next few days sober, let alone if he started going into withdrawal.

***

As students started filing into his homeroom, Abraham noted that they were in relatively high spirits. Discussions in the air involved things like confidence for exams and the upcoming holidays. Only a few whispers reached his ears about Ethan. He let everyone find their seats before rapping his knuckles on his desk.

"All right, everyone, settle in. This is your last chance to ask any questions or finish up exam prep. Tests start after homeroom today, and I can't help you during the actual thing."

A few laughs chittered through the air. A few of the kids were still pulling out their books.

"Let's use our time—" he had started to say 'wisely' when there was a knock on the door. He frowned and moved to the hall, where Edward was waiting again.

"Hey, Mr. Alvarez. The dean has asked everyone to gather in the assembly hall. And he asked me to have you go to his office first. Said it was urgent."

Abraham nodded gravely. He turned to the class, every eye on him. Those who had been discussing Ethan had paled. "Everyone, it seems there is a last-minute assembly being called. Please gather your things and follow Edward to the hall. I'll talk to the dean about starting the exams a little late so we can discuss anything you wanted to ask." He saw relief pass across more than one face. Even if Dean Gomez couldn't accommodate the request, he was once again in his students' good graces for even trying.

Every step to Gomez's office felt heavy. Abraham couldn't help being apprehensive. If an assembly was being called, this likely had to do with Ethan going missing. Still. He had covered his tracks perfectly. Everything would be fine.

By the time he reached Room 222, he was sweating. The dean's door was closed, so he knocked.

"Come on in, Abraham. Close the door behind you."

"Dean Gomez. Don't you need to be at the assembly?"

"It's alright. I have Rachel handling the announcement, and a few of the teachers and the guidance counselor are there."

"The guidance counselor?" Abraham moved into the room, sitting across from Gomez at his desk. "That's pretty serious. What's happened?"

"We have a pretty big problem. Have you seen the news?"

"No, we got back from New England late last night."

Gomez sighed, leaning back in his chair. "Abraham, Ethan never made it home on Friday."

Abraham didn't say anything. He didn't move. He stared at Gomez, doing his best to look stunned.

"The police have already started an investigation, and his parents have asked us to have all of his teachers cooperate. Abraham, this isn't like that incident with Levi. This is a different animal entirely. The boy's parents work for the embassy, for fuck's sake. That means the FBI are watching the investigation. His parents are worried sick. He's their only kid, you know."

"I understand completely. I'll help however the police request. Would you like me to reach out to his parents?"

"Absolutely not. Don't talk to anyone about this outside of the official investigation."

"And if they reach out to me?"

"Then that's up to you. But if there is anything you want to tell me now, in private, please do so. What I don't know can and will come back to bite you and any of his other teachers."

"Nothing. We met at 2:30 and had a 90 minute study session. I'll answer any questions they have, but he said he was headed to the gym next."

Gomez nodded. "Alright. I am obligated to let them know about the study sessions now. And they're going to ask if you've had any issues with students in the past. I have to tell the truth."

"You don't need to lie about anything. I promise."

Dean Gomez sighed. "Glad to hear it. Hopefully he'll be found, and all of this will blow over before Christmas."

"You know, when I was his age, I ran away at least five times before I got it in my head I really did have it better at home."

Gomez shook his head. "Time will tell. For now I've given the police a list of Ethan's teachers and the rosters for his classes." He glanced at the door before leaning in slightly. "I'm told they're exploring a possible private relationship, but you didn't hear it from me."

"Really?" Abraham leaned in, too. "I wouldn't have thought he would run off with a girl."

"Who said it's a girl?"

"*Oh.*"

Gomez shook his head, resting his elbows on his desk. "For now we have to wait and let law enforcement do their job. Hopefully the weather stays pretty clear. Please don't tell anyone what we've discussed."

"I won't say a word."

"Especially to your students."

"Of course not." Abraham paused. "Although it's only a matter of time before they see something on social media or whatever."

"That's why I'm getting ahead of the curve with the assembly. We're keeping it to the basics, just what's already in the news. We need to try and keep a lid on this as much as possible. A lot of jobs are at stake, including ours."

"That's ridiculous. We didn't do anything wrong."

"It's a missing student, Abraham, last seen on our property. A foreign student with influential parents. I don't see this going away without somebody paying a steep price."

"It won't be either of us. Especially if we cooperate fully."

"Let's hope not." Gomez sighed, pinching the bridge of his nose. "I need something to calm down. Join me for a shot?" At Abraham's agreement, he pulled out the whiskey and poured them both a double. "To a quick investigation and a calm holiday." After they drank, Gomez stood and came around the desk to hug Abraham. They patted each other's backs before pulling away.

Abraham did stop on the way out, broaching the idea of delaying the exams by at least an hour. Gomez agreed before heading towards the assembly hall, while Abraham took a detour to the teacher's restroom. He was running low, but he was going to need all the help he could get to make it through the rest of the day acting like everything was fine. Because it would be. Just like it always was.

Right?

***

"Ask him."

Despite the whispered tones, Abraham heard the urge clearly. "Ask me what?" He glanced up from the papers on his desk, and Tyrell hesitantly raised a hand. He nodded.

"Is Ethan really missing?"

Abraham glanced around the classroom, noting the looks of concern. He sighed, sitting back in his chair. "Do you think they called that assembly for fun?" he asked softly. Tyrell shook his head, looking abashed. "I know it's hard to believe. A lot of you are Ethan's classmates, his friends. But it's important that we don't jump to conclusions. Watch for any messages from him, but let the police do their jobs. I'm sure he'll turn up quickly."

Jenna raised her hand next. "But he's going to miss exams!"

"Don't worry. The dean isn't heartless, despite how tough he wants to appear to students." There were a few scattered smiles. "He'll get to take his tests once we're sure he's all right. But you all start your tests today. I know it's hard, but you need to focus on your grades for now."

He spent the rest of homeroom answering questions about the tests and helping his students relax. Exam days weren't full days at the school. The kids would have homeroom, then a three hour exam slot, and then they got to go home at lunch— though it would be a little after lunch, today. Monday's tests would be math, so Abraham fielded several questions and practice problems. Tuesday would be Sciences, and then Literature and Language Arts on

Wednesday. Social Studies would be Thursday, and then everyone would be free for winter break.

When the bell rang, the students were split into groups according to grade level. They were gathered in the assembly hall, with teachers on the stage, in the aisles, and in the back of the room to monitor. Once all the students were seated in the right section, the front row students were handed a stack of exams with instructions to take one, place it face down on their desk, and pass the stack along. The teachers along the aisles watched closely to make sure the papers kept moving and didn't accidentally cross the aisles to another grade.

Abraham stood on the stage, watching the other teachers. Once each section had signaled, he tapped on the mic. "Alright, everyone. You have three hours. Please read the instructions throughout the tests very carefully before starting the problem. If your pencil stops working, raise your hand and we'll get you another. When you have finished, flip your test face down. Once you pull out your reading material, you may not turn the test back over. Your time starts...now."

By the time the assembly hall had cleared and most of the teachers had left for the day, Abraham sat in his car in the parking lot with his eyes closed. He was exhausted even though nothing had happened. A few of the teachers on the stage had whispered to each other about Ethan, but no one said anything to him about it. He had three hours to stew over everything. To relive every moment. To pray that everything would blow over, and to blame God for the situation He had created.

Abraham jumped when his phone rang. He didn't recognize the number, but he answered anyway. Soon he was on his way to the nearest police station to meet with a Detective Jimenez. He called Maria on his way and let her know where he was going and why so she didn't get suspicious when he was late coming home. Once he arrived, he parked in visitor parking and entered the precinct, approaching the watch commander at the front desk. Her badge read "P.O. Hope."

"Excuse me, Officer Hope? I'm Abraham Alvarez. I have an appointment with Detective Jimenez."

Officer Hope smiled up at him. "Yes, Mr. Alvarez, welcome. Detective Jimenez let us know to expect you." She stood and shook his hand. "If you'll follow me to room six?"

"My favorite number." He nodded as she slid from behind the desk.

"Maybe it's your lucky day."

"I've been lucky my entire life."

Officer Hope gave him a public-facing smile before turning to lead him down the hall on the left. Abraham's eyes slid down her form, and he hid a smile as he imagined all the things he could do with such a body in his bed. He thanked her as she let him into the room, and then he was left to wait.

Chapter 13

Luckily the detective arrived only a few minutes later, so he didn't have to stew further. Abraham started to stand, but the Detective assured him he didn't need to before shaking his hand awkwardly across the table and sitting.

"Good afternoon, Mr. Alvarez, and thank you for coming with such short notice. I'm Detective Jimenez, and I'm taking the lead on Ethan Bísólá's disappearance. I'll be asking you some questions, but I would like to record your answers. Do I have your permission to do so?"

"Yes, of course."

Detective Jimenez took out a small portable audio recorder, placed it on the table before Abraham, and turned it on. "Good afternoon, Mr. Alvarez. My name is Detective Jimenez, and I'm handling the investigation into the disappearance of Ethan Bísólá. First, do I have your permission to take audio and video of this conversation?"

"You do."

"Do you understand that you are not being detained, nor are you a suspect at this time?"

"Yes, I do."

"Do you understand that you have a right to an attorney, and to remain silent, and that any information obtained may be used against you in a court of law?"

"Yes, I completely understand."

"Are you under the influence of any drugs which would impair your ability to understand my questions?"

"No, I am not."

"Are you on any prescription medication which you failed to take today?"

"No, I'm not on any medication."

"Do you still want to talk to us?"

"Yes, I do."

"Do you understand you have a right to an attorney?"

"Yes, I don't want one. Lawyers are all crooks, just like most cops. No offense."

"None taken." Detective Jimenez took down a few notes in a little flip pad. Abraham's gaze wandered to the one-way mirror along one wall, surprised to see such things weren't just made up for television dramas. His attention snapped back to the detective when he cleared his throat. "Mr. Alvarez, do you know why you are here?"

"I'm one of Ethan's teachers. And I was informed you are aware we had two private tutoring sessions."

"Who told you that?"

"I spoke with the Dean. He was letting us know that the police had a list of Ethan's teachers and activities so we wouldn't be anxious if you called."

"When did you speak with him?"

"This morning, at school."

"And why would speaking with police make teachers anxious?"

"Who wouldn't be worried about getting a call from a cop without knowing why?"

The detective inclined his head to concede the point. "When was the last time you saw Ethan?"

"Friday at school. Around four."

"Around?"

"We had a tutoring session at 2:30 and aimed for 90 minutes, but we might have gone a few minutes over. I'm not certain."

"Did you meet before then?"

"Yes, Wednesday morning."

"Did anyone see you two together?"

"Only one person. Ethan had requested the other students not learn he had asked for tutoring, so I worked with our receptionist Mike to schedule things and help keep other students away from the room while we worked."

"So you were in a private room?"

"The library has private study rooms, yes. We met in room 6 both times."

"Why did Ethan not want anyone to know he was tutoring?"

"He was embarrassed." Abraham paused, and Detective Jimenez lifted his gaze from his notes to watch him. "And he was worried his parents would find out," Abraham continued.

"And that would be bad?"

"To him. We want to help our kids succeed and feel comfortable, so we let him have the privacy. We know when things shouldn't be kept from parents, but a stressed out kid is usually pretty average."

"Usually?"

"Well, he's missing now, isn't he?"

"And no one came into the room while you were studying? Even on accident?"

"No...Well, hang on. It wasn't while we were studying, but after Ethan had left one of my other students came in while I was packing up my laptop. Jenna Bowman."

"Why did she enter if you were still there?"

"She had the next reservation. You know how kids can be staring at their phones, she probably just went for the doorknob without thinking."

"Did she see Ethan?"

"I don't know. Probably not if she was absorbed in her phone."

"You said her name was Bowman?" At Abraham's nod, Jimenez asked him to spell it. "Alright. Next Question: Do you know a man named John Finn?"

"Yes. His boys go to the school, and his middle kid was in my class last year until he moved classes."

"And why did he switch?"

"Levi alleged that I was checking him out."

"And were you?"

"No."

"Why would he say such a thing?"

Abraham shrugged. "Why do kids say anything? They want to push boundaries, they want to get a reaction, they want to see what happens...Maybe he really thought he saw something and was scared. Kids have a lot on their plate and they can read into things that aren't there."

"Did you disclose the allegations to your wife?"

"No, why would I?" Abraham sighed, leaning in his chair. "She's a worrier, detective. She gets anxiety spikes and freaks out about things. I didn't want to set her into a panic attack. You know what those kinds of allegations can do to a man if the right wind hits the sails, regardless of the truth."

"Did you ever meet with John and the dean about this incident?"

"There was no incident, but yes, we met. John yelled at us and threatened my job. I sat and listened and let him vent—that's part of my job, taking bullshit from parents."

Jimenez frowned at him. "Mr. Alvarez, do you think this is a joke?"

"No. There's nothing funny about this."

"There's a missing kid out there. His parents want answers, and I'm going to find them."

"You're the one who brought up my wife and John, Detective." He folded his arms. "I want to help with this investigation. Whatever Levi thinks happened has nothing to do with Ethan. So let's focus on him, hm?" He paused, considering. "Is there currently a reward being offered?"

Jimenez paused. "Yes. From his parents, though I'm told the embassy is considering adding to it."

"I would like to add to it as well."

"Of course, but you must know this won't influence our investigation."

"I'm aware. But I'm more worried about my student than about you and your investigation. So I'd like to add a million dollars for Ethan's safe return, and five hundred for tips that have solid leads."

"That's...very generous of you." Abraham arched an eyebrow, so Jimenez added, "And an awful lot of money for a school teacher."

"I don't teach because I need the money. If you look into my background, you'll find my father and his father before him were quite wealthy. Real estate, stock market, those sorts of things. I teach because I want to invest in the next generation."

Jimenez nodded, taking a few notes. He asked Abraham a few more questions about the school, his meetings with Ethan, and if he had seen him leave the school premises. He quickly wrote down what Abraham told him about the outside cameras. After a while longer, he set down his notepad.

"Thank you again for your time, Mr. Alvarez. You're free to go for today, but do please let us know if you hear or see something or remember anything. No matter how trivial it might seem." He reached into his breast pocket and pulled out a business card. "This is my direct office line."

"Of course, Detective. Thank you. I'll pray that Ethan is found, alive and unharmed, quickly."

"Thank you. I'll be in touch if I have any questions. There will likely be a search party organized soon. For now, go home and try to enjoy the rest of your day."

"I will. Hopefully this clears up in time for a peaceful holiday."

Chapter 14

Rather than head straight home, Abraham drove through the city for a little while. He kept an eye on his mirrors to be sure no one from the precinct was tailing him before heading to his dealer's house.

Julio had his quarter pound ready to go when he arrived.

"You're a godsend, man. How much do I owe you?"

"Each ounce is 2-K, so a total of 8. You sure you want this much? Didn't I just fill you up?"

"It's been a long few weeks. Sure I can't get a bulk discount or something?"

"Sorry, bro. I could easily get twice that for each ounce, especially if I cut it. I'm already cutting you some slack. You need to be careful with this stuff, man. It's a really strong batch."

"That's what you said about the last batch, but here we are." Abraham took out ten thousand dollars wrapped, counted two thousand, and gave the rest to Julio, who counted out each crisp one hundred dollar bill to verify.

"The only reason I'll sell you that uncut is because I know you can handle it. Don't even try to smoke it, though, because you've come a long way since then. That shit will land you straight back to hell."

"I know. I'd never do that shit again. I'm paranoid already from doing lines. Thanks for hooking me up. I won't see you before Christmas, God willing."

"Remember me if you'll have any of that barbecue leftover. You make the best roasted pig I've ever had."

"I got a list of people I give to yearly, and you're on it. I'll give you enough to feed you and your entire family."

"Thanks so much, Abraham. You're among the nicest and wildest people I've ever met."

They laughed, shook hands, and hugged like men sometimes do.

***

By the time Abraham made it home, the NYC teacher's union had set up a social media page to draw attention to Ethan's disappearance and garner more public interest. He reached out to his union rep and learned that some teachers and their families would be starting their own search parties that evening. They planned to stay out for as long as the temperature allowed. Abraham got the details and then called Jose.

"Abraham? What's wrong? You never call me during the school week, bro."

"Hey, Jose. Sorry to bug you, but one of my kids— er, students has turned up missing. Do you think the missus could spare you while we get some of the guys together? I'll pay 'em, though let's be honest, they should be willing to do this regardless..."

"I don't know if I can come out tonight, but how many guys are ya wanting?"

"Whoever can make it. We've got a lot of ground to cover, starting at the school and spreading out. The teacher's union has a search party meeting, too."

"All right, I'll put out the call. Give me the deets."

Abraham spent a few minutes planning out a meeting spot and route with Jose before letting him go to head inside. He caught Maria up on the case and the search efforts. Once he had a quick meal (and a secret double line in the bathroom), he changed into fresh, warm clothes that would keep him comfortable out in the cold and went to meet up with Jose's guys.

The union let him know the police had set up a helpline, and they had extra posters with the information at the school. Abraham picked up a few stacks and passed them around his own crew. It was freezing and the sun was fading, but still the rescuers came in droves, bundled up in parkas and face masks, boots and insulated gloves. Some had little hand warmers to put in pockets, and everyone brought a strong desire to find Ethan and bring him home.

Abraham had run to the store before meeting up at the school, and he brought high-powered flashlights for the search parties. He gave the union workers Maria's number in case they needed anything she could order, and then he set off with his crew.

Each group split into smaller groups of four and spread out through the streets, checking alleys and questioning any passers-by. A few journalists stopped by through the night, but they didn't help with search efforts.

The men combed through the streets as darkness descended, and they kept going even as the first flakes fell. Once the snow whipped up into more of a fury, however, the search had to be called off for safety reasons. They had made it quite far, but no sign of Ethan had been found.

Abraham was on top of the world. No one suspected a thing. Here he was, the beloved teacher leading the charge to find his wayward student. It was the perfect crime. Everything was going to be fine. It always was.

***

The next several days were more of the same. Homeroom in the morning, exams, a short break, and then search efforts resumed pending the weather. They had been told to go home early a couple of nights to keep the would-be rescuers safe, but then everyone would hit the streets again as soon as they were cleared.

Maria helped Abraham coordinate most days, but on Thursday, she let him know that she had an appointment. He assumed she was meeting Carlos, but that was only half true. She was also meeting with Detective Jimenez. She left the boys with Esmeralda and went to the precinct. The front desk was staffed by Officer Harris today, who greeted her politely and led her to the detective's office. He knocked twice, and when a voice answered, tucked his head inside.

"Mrs. Alvarez is here."

"Thank you, Officer. Please let her in and then close the door." Jimenez stood as Maria entered, extending his hand to shake hers. "Good afternoon, Mrs. Alvarez. Thank you for agreeing to meet. I'm the detective in charge of Ethan Bísólá's disappearance. Please, have a seat."

Maria shook his hand as she stepped up to his desk before lowering into a chair. Jimenez's office was clean and well-organized, with pictures of his wife and children on display. She felt a slight pang of jealousy; Abraham didn't have her picture on his desk in the teacher's lounge.

"It's a pleasure to meet you. I just wish it was under better circumstances."

"Indeed. It's a difficult time for everyone, especially Ethan's family."

"I can't even imagine what they're going through. A parent's worst nightmare."

Detective Jimenez sighed, sitting back and taking a sip of his coffee. He asked Maria if she would like anything to drink, but she declined for now. He set the mug down and folded his hands.

"Mrs. Alvarez—"

"Please, call me Maria."

"Maria," he started again, nodding in acknowledgment. "I want you to know you aren't required to speak with us. Anything between a husband and wife may be privileged and confidential unless one or both of you voluntarily divulge that information. Do you understand?"

"I do."

"And are you willing to let me record this conversation for easy review?"

"I am."

Jimenez nodded. He pulled out his recorder and turned it on before repeating the questions for the record. He also went through her rights, including to an attorney, which she declined much like her husband had.

"Have you met Ethan Bísólá?"

"No, not in person. Abraham has mentioned him before when he talks about work. Said he was one of his best students but seemed to be struggling lately and stressed."

"How long has he been a student under your husband?"

"I don't know. But Go-- er, Dean Gomez keeps roster records at the school. You could check those."

"Did you know that your husband was tutoring Ethan outside of class?"

"Yes, to help him prepare for exams."

"Do you know how often they met?"

"I know about two sessions. I'm not sure if that was all."

"Do you know where they studied?"

"Most likely in the school library. Abraham likes to use Room 6 because it has the better projection hookups for his laptop. It's also his favorite number."

"Do you know when they last met?"

"Friday, last week."

"And what time?"

"I'm not certain. He had more than one student that day, but he didn't tell me who he was meeting when. I asked him to send me photos of where he was from time to time so I could be sure he was still at school."

Jimenez paused in his notes, looking up at her. "Why did you ask him to do that?"

Maria was quiet for a moment. Then she sighed. "Our marriage is not in a healthy place," she confessed. "It's one of the steps I requested while I rebuild my trust."

"Do you have reason not to trust him?"

Maria scoffed. "It's more surprising when I *can* trust him."

"Why do you say that?"

"The man can be very secretive. Deceptive. Manipulative. He's cheated on me before, several times. And I still don't really know where all of his money comes from."

Jimenez frowned slightly, but he shifted the conversation. "Where were you while Abraham was tutoring at school?"

"The kids and I drove to my mom's in Rhode Island."

"And you spoke to Abraham during that time?"

"Yes, we kept in touch throughout the day."

"Did his demeanor seem different?"

"No, he seemed normal. But he's always strange."

"Did he come to meet you and your family on Friday?"

"No, he got to my mom's on Saturday morning. I don't remember the exact time, but it was early. Shortly after sunrise. I was surprised; he would have been up rather early to make it by then. It's a good four hours, though it was probably closer to three and a half for him with no traffic."

Jimenez nodded, checking something on his desk and then scribbling a note on that paper. "This may seem random after the last few questions, but are you aware of an incident with a student in Abraham's class last year, where the boy's father came to the school?"

Maria thought of Ruth's rumor, but she shook her head. "No. Can you tell me?"

Jimenez shook his head. "Not today, sorry. How's your marriage, Mrs...Maria?"

"What does that have to do with the investigation?"

"Hopefully nothing."

"No relationship is perfect, Detective, and that's true even if your husband's rich. My husband is a liar, a cheater, and an asshole, but he's not a child predator nor a kidnapper."

"That's good to hear. I hope you're right."

"Thank you, Detective. Good luck on your investigation."

Chapter 15

Once she was back in the car, Maria set her phone in its cradle and FaceTimed Abraham. She was met by a face covered in cloth.

"Hey, baby." He was a bit muffled but understandable.

"Hello, A. Are you out searching in this weather?"

"Yeah. Jose is here." He turned the camera a bit, and she saw his cousin wave. "We're making good distance, but nothing's come up. They always say the first 72 hours are the most important, so we're trying our damnedest to find any kind of clues today."

"I hope you find something. I did want to let you know I met with that detective today. Jimenez."

She couldn't read his expression behind the scarf. "Oh, he asked to meet with you, too, eh? How'd it go?"

"Fine. He asked a bunch of questions about you and Ethan and a few about us."

"What did you tell him?"

"Don't sound so nervous. I told him about your tutoring and how we were talking through the day. And I let him know you can be a damned dirty liar at times, and an asshole to boot." She glanced at the screen and thought his face paled.

"Aw, what did you have to tell him that for?"

"Did I lie?" Abraham sighed, but she continued. "Besides. I told him you were trying to be better, and that as much of a jerk as you could be, you weren't a kidnapper and he was barking up the wrong tree."

"Thank you, Ma."

"We're in this together, Abraham. And if you really mean it with this whole new leaf thing, then 'til death do us part."

"With you by my side, everything will be fine. We just have to let justice take its course."

Maria sighed, but nodded. "Oh, speaking of time and courses and all. Mom got the order today that she's not supposed to be driving anymore. Am I good to call a car for her for Christmas?"

Abraham shivered as he considered. "It's a bit last minute. We could ask my mom to swing by and pick her up on the way. Why don't you try her first?"

"Are you sure? It's an hour out of her way."

"It should be fine, so long as she has the time to spare. If not, go ahead and call around for a car. Spend whatever you need. And let your ma know we can help with her moving expenses after the New Year if she needs it."

"That's very sweet of you, baby. But you know you aren't going to bribe her to like you?"

Abraham laughed. "I know. She's got plenty of reasons to hate me."

Maria grimaced. "Sorry, not sorry? Sometimes I need to talk to my momma."

"I know baby. And I'll do anything for you, including pay a bunch of your money to move your mom around even though she doesn't like me. I'll never make you feel alone again."

Maria was quiet for a moment, but she sighed. "You're right. You won't. I've got my momma, and I've got God. Even if you fail me again, I'll be ok. But will you, Abraham? Have you really repented? Atoned? Or is this another act?"

He didn't answer, stunned.

"What, now you got nothing to say?"

"No, not really. I'm just listening to you, mi vida."

"Nothing to add? No questions or promises?"

"No, not right now."

"Ok. You just think on what I said. I'll let you go so you can help with the search. I can only imagine how that boy's parents feel, especially so close to Christmas. No parent should have to deal with this. I hope you find whatever monster is behind this."

"What makes you so sure something happened to him?"

"Good kids like that don't just disappear."

"Don't you remember when you were a teen? I know I do. I'd disappear for days, especially if I was getting laid."

Maria scoffed. "You're still like that," she pointed out flatly before sighing. "It's been too long, baby. Especially with all the fuss. I don't know if he was kidnapped or sex trafficked or what, but something sinister has happened. You've seen him in person, and now I've seen the photos. He's a good-looking, athletic young man. Some sickos are really into that. I'm telling you, someone took him. Maybe they were jealous they couldn't have him."

Abraham felt a spike of jealousy as Maria commented on Ethan's body. "Yeah. I know. But I can't give up. Not yet." He shook his head, then glanced at the clock on his phone. "Baby, if I text you an address, can you order some hot chocolate? Maybe something hot to eat, like pizza? Or heavy calories for stamina…Donuts?"

"Will do. I'll let you go so you can text me and get back to looking. Bye for now, babe."

* * *

The search parties ballooned in size over the weekend, only to be hampered by a record sixteen inches of snow. Two days of clear skies and sunshine meant the delay wasn't long, and no school meant the search parties stayed large. When Tuesday rolled around, the temperatures had turned unseasonably warm. People wearing parkas, hats, and gloves a few days earlier had T-shirts and shorts on. What should have been a cheerful time of year was somber for Ethan's parents and everyone in the search party. Some of the volunteers selfishly wanted to return home to complete their last-minute shopping, but instead, they stayed and continued to search as they promised. Their commitment to continue searching for Ethan wasn't purely altruistic. Word had spread of the growing rewards being offered for information and his safe return.

Volunteers and law enforcement weren't the only people out. Blissfully unaware members of the public offered automatic well wishes before returning to their daily routine. More newscasters were poking about, dressed to the nines and faces painted with concern as the viewership numbers rolled in.

By now, the streets were plastered with missing posters; there were flyers on every pole, every board, every available surface for miles and miles. And yet nothing turned up, no one came forward...

Until a homeless man presented the police with a drenched phone. He said it had washed up under the bridge where he stayed, and something told him the police needed it more than he needed to pawn it. Information from Ethan's parents and the phone company confirmed it belonged to the missing young man, but they were worried about the state of it. Still, it was their first solid lead. Detective Jimenez put in a request for Clyde Richardson, an authoritative forensics analyst in the FBI.

Unfortunately for the detective, Clyde was on holiday until after the New Year. The police advised the search parties to disband for now as they brought in K9 units, but the investigation would likely be on hold until Clyde could get his hands on that phone.

Chapter 16

Christmas Eve had crept up on the Alvarezes. They had been so caught up in the investigation and the search parties that they hadn't realized the day was coming closer. Now they had one day to get the house ready for company, and the pigs and vegan dishes would be arriving. Even though it wasn't a standard workday for Esmeralda, Maria offered to pay her time-and-a-half to come help get the house ready. It still wasn't enough to pay the woman what she was actually worth, but she stayed on for the boys and because Maria would often buy her things or pass on designer clothes and purses she no longer liked.

While the weather had been unseasonably warm, suddenly it was almost freezing. It was a brisk six degrees outside when Abraham and Maria brewed their coffee. Six minutes past six, Abraham's phone went off.

"That's Happy Pig. They'll be here in about a half an hour," he announced.

"Ok. My order should arrive closer to noon. Will you be able to watch the kids for a bit? I have a couple appointments."

"Oh? Where are you headed?"

"The gym and then the sauna. Afterwards I have an appointment at the salon."

"How long do you think you'll be? I've got some things to take care of this evening."

"Just a few hours. I know you always have plans Christmas Eve." She kept the bitterness out of her voice. She did.

"Are you training with Carlos today? Is he still coming tomorrow?"

"Yeah. He doesn't have any family around, so he'll be here."

"Good. I like having him around. He's a pretty great guy, takes good care of himself. Not gonna lie, I envy him a bit."

"You could take good care of yourself too, you know. But you don't want to work out with me. How many times have I offered?"

"A lot."

"And have you ever come?"

"Never...But, baby, be reasonable. Can you imagine me in the gym? A sweaty fat guy surrounded by all those chiseled bodybuilders? You really think I want to put myself through that?"

"We don't have to go when it's busy. We don't have to go at all. We could buy some equipment and have Carlos come here. That is, if you really wanted to try and stay fit for your family."

Abraham sighed. "I know you're right, and yet I'm hesitating. Besides, I've always felt like I was gonna die young. Shouldn't I enjoy what life has to offer? Good food, good times. What's so wrong with that?"

"Do you ever stop and listen to yourself? It's the day before Christmas, and you're talking about dying young. How is that fair to me, to the kids? How do you think that makes us feel?"

Before he could answer, Jesús's baby monitor alerted Maria that he was awake. She gave Abraham a look before moving upstairs to change him and get a bottle ready. Since Abraham was waiting for a delivery, she got the boys up and ready for breakfast. When Maria came down with the boys, she put James on the couch and Jesús in his playpen so she'd have time to make them breakfast.

James demanded she make breakfast like Daddy, but Maria patiently reminded him it was her turn and that he had liked the breakfast she made at Grandma's. His stubborn streak tried to rear up, but she calmly tamped it back down. Finally he let out a defeated sigh.

"Okay, Mommy. I'm sorry I'm being mean. You just love me and want me to be healthy."

"That's right, James. Thank you. Now watch your cartoons with your brother and see if you can tell Mommy what the stories were about later."

While Maria prepared açai bowls for James and herself, Abraham attended to the delivery of meat, which took up more space than he anticipated. He had Manuel and David load the first few boxes into the large cold storage downstairs, but he picked out a few things for them to set out in the snow. Since he planned to start cooking them within the next hour, he could take advantage of the frigid air.

The pigs took up several boxes, with one separate box for the each of the three whole roast sucklings. The rest were packed according to cut and clearly labeled. Each box was heavily insulated, and Jessie knew Abraham would send them back once they were empty.

Once the boxes were unloaded, Manuel gave Abraham his invoice, stamped 'paid in full'. There was no note about the tip; Abraham always tipped them in cash so they didn't have to report it in their taxes. It was meant for them, not some government stooge.

Abraham signed the invoice to confirm delivery, and Manuel pulled off the carbon copy, stapling Abraham's credit card receipt on top before handing it over.

"You have a good day, Mr. Alvarez. And Merry Christmas!"

Abraham reached into his wallet, pulling out a couple hundreds for each of them. "Thanks for everything, guys. Take this, please."

"That's mighty kind of you."

"You guys are working on Christmas Eve. I'm sure you'd rather be home. It's the least I could do. Do you guys wanna take home some food?"

"No, thank you. We appreciate that for sure. Have a great holiday, you and your family."

Abraham walked them to the front door, where they removed the cotton covering for their shoes. "You guys can leave them at the door. We'll have them thrown out."

Maria poked her head from the kitchen when she heard them readying to leave. "Have a great holiday, you two!"

"Thank you, Maria. Enjoy your dinner tomorrow! It's always a pleasure. Take care, Abraham."

"Drive carefully. It's supposed to snow more later," Abraham cautioned.

"Man, this weather is crazy."

"It really is."

Abraham waved as they pulled away and then closed the door. When he turned around, Maria was staring at the invoice. He must have set it on the entryway table while letting them out.

"What in God's name did you order, Abraham?" she demanded. "Over two thousand dollars?!"

"Baby, you know I love cooking for everyone. It's the only time of year I order this much, and it's not like we can't afford it. Besides, I get to write some of it off since I donate a bunch of the food."

Maria shook her head. "I'll never understand you. Thousands of dollars to slaughter those poor pigs. How is spending that much on pork rational? You could just as easily give out something healthy! We have two growing boys to care for, and my ailing mother. Hell, you haven't been to a doctor since before I was pregnant with James, and you're gonna blow all this money on pork?!"

Abraham bit back a sigh. He really didn't want to get into this right now. Best to let her hear what she wanted to hear. "I'm sorry, baby. We can take a look at the budget closer to next Christmas and figure out how much to spend together."

Maria sighed, setting down the paper. "Alright. Fine. I need to be heading out. Please make sure the boys aren't sitting in front of screens all day." She moved to the coat closet and pulled out her Moncler down jacket before moving to the living room to kiss the boys goodbye. "Esmeralda will be here in about an hour to help around the house," she added to Abraham as she headed for the garage.

"Have fun at the gym. Drive careful." He watched her leave, already positive that she wouldn't just be seeing Carlos at the gym.

As soon as she was in the car, her phone pinged. The message was accompanied by a photo of Carlos stretched out on a bed in the motel, naked and hard.

Have you left yet? I'm waiting for you xoxo

Just now. I'll be there in ten. Don't put the chain on the door. Just be good and ready.

That an order?

Damn right it is. I want you stroking that hard cock

when I get there. Otherwise I'll turn around and walk right back out that door.

So demanding. I like it. I'll be waiting as you wish.

Like other illicit guests, Maria hid her car around the back of the Motel 6. Carlos had left a key at the front desk under her nickname, so she claimed it and headed straight to the third floor as promised, Room 333. She didn't bother knocking, striding in and stripping to join him.

Chapter 17

Abraham had given up on waiting to hear from Maria. Esmeralda had gotten the house clean, and he had gotten a good start on cooking. Once the slow cooker was done and he had packaged the cooked meat, he left the boy's in the care of their nanny. He didn't return home until the sun was rising on Christmas Day.

The house was silent as he crept his way upstairs and into the closet, digging around a bit and then grinning as he retrieved his prize. He peeked through the door to be sure Maria was still asleep before moving to the bathroom. After a quick shower, he emerged from the bathroom dressed like Santa Claus. As he stepped out, Maria suddenly woke up screaming. The grin slipped as he hurried to the bed.

"Easy, babe, it's just me. What's wrong? I was just trying to surprise you and the kids…" He carefully wrapped his arms around her and pulled her close. Maria shook her head, leaning into his hold. She tried to say something, but she was shaking too much. "Nightmare, then?" he prompted, and she nodded as she started to cry. "Easy, baby, easy. It's ok. I'm here. Let me grab you some tissues." He leaned to the side to snatch the box off of her nightstand. He continued holding her until she started to calm.

"Oh, my God. Oh, my God, Abraham. I saw Ethan. He was lying next to me in bed, dressed up in some obnoxious sequined thing and a wig. Someone had put make-up on him, but his head was wrapped in a plastic bag. Abraham, he was dead. Oh, my God..." She sobbed, blowing her nose into the tissue. "Someone's killed him. Oh, God, Abraham, he's dead. It was so real. It has to be real. I need...I need to..."

"Maria, it was just a dream. You don't need to do anything except let yourself wake up," Abraham reasoned, keeping his tone gentle. "What could you even do? The police aren't going to accept a dream as evidence. It was just a nightmare, baby. I know it's hard, but you need to block it out. It's Christmas."

Maria took a deep, calming breath. As much as she wanted to argue, she knew he was right. What could the police do with some stressed-out woman's dream? And yet she couldn't shake another question— why had her vision of Ethan been on her own bed? Instead, she asked, "How can we enjoy Christmas when his family is grieving alone?"

Abraham sighed, scooting away and taking off the Santa hat, wig, and fake beard. "I doubt they're alone. Besides, we're doing everything in our power to help find whoever is responsible for Ethan's disappearance. There's nothing else we can do except pray."

Maria sighed, running her hand through her hair. "You're right. I know you're right. And yet it still doesn't feel like enough." She stood from the bed. "I should take a shower. Introduce the boys to Santa." She started towards the bathroom.

"I thought you went to the salon yesterday?"

Maria frowned, looking back at Abraham. "So?"

"You never shower after a salon day. Something about fresh hair and ruining your nails. Or did you forget you said you had an appointment yesterday?"

Maria held up her hands, showing off the new polish. "Oh, look, new nails," she said flatly. "Yeah, showering the day after can cut into how long they last. But it's Christmas, and I'm tired and stressed out." Her eyes narrowed, and she placed a hand on her hips. "What is this, anyway, an inquisition? Because that's real rich coming from you."

"I'm just saying, you were gone an awful long time yesterday. Longer than you said. I had to pay Esmeralda overtime so the kids wouldn't be alone."

"How does it feel, A?" she quipped. "Constantly questioning? Not able to trust where someone is, what they were doing? Unfortunately for you, you aren't catching me in some big lie. I lost track of time. It happens. I ran into some of the girls from my aerobics class and we went for coffee. I even have the receipt, though you always tell me to throw them away. Believe it or not, A, not everybody lies about where they're gonna be." All she did was omit some things.

"You've been riding my case this whole time I've been trying to be a better husband, but I don't get to be the least bit suspicious?" Abraham spat back.

"You keep saying you want to be better, and then you go and do something that grates on my nerves. You say something hateful, you eat something disgusting, you spend two thousand dollars on pork, you disappear all night on Christmas Eve...And you're gonna get mad at me, Daddy? Uh-uh. The spider webs of lies are woven together tighter until one day they catch a sneaky fly. Who is that sneaky fly going to be, A? You think it's gonna be me or you that's gonna get caught in that spider web? 'Cause believe it or not, I already know some of the things you think you're hiding. I know you had a student taken out of your class because their dad got pissed. I know you're still doing drugs even though you swear you're sober. I know you're drinking more even though you try and wash the shot glasses before I get downstairs."

Abraham rolled his eyes. "Oh for the love... You can spout whatever nonsense you want, but it's as solid as that nightmare. No proof, just suspicion. Kids get switched between classes all the time, it's the easy solution to calm a parent down. Nothing happened."

"Proof? You want proof? You suck at washing dishes, A. I know you're drinking more because the glasses aren't clean. And I know you pulled out the fancy dishware while I was in New England. Gonna tell me who you had over? God, I knew I should have trusted my gut feelings. I was so worried I almost turned around and came back without telling you. Wanna tell me what I was gonna find, A? Cause you certainly made sure the cameras were off."

For one horrifying moment, Abraham imagined Maria walking in the door with Ethan dead in their bed. But he stamped down the concern. He had done nothing wrong. God ordained that sacrifice, but Maria wouldn't understand. She never would. "Do you hear yourself? I hate cleaning, Maria. Why the fuck would I mess with all that fancy nonsense if I didn't have to? How much of this is you deflecting from the fact that I'm catching you in something for once?"

"You haven't caught me in anything."

"Keep telling yourself that." Abraham shook his head, standing and moving to a mirror to put the wig and beard back on. "It's fucking Christmas. Get off your high horse and let's try to at least pretend to have a good day for the boys."

"Fine. Whatever." Maria rolled her eyes, resuming her trek to the bathroom. She paused in the doorway. "Did my order come in?"

"Yeah, yeah, it's split between the fridge and the cold storage. You sure did have me order a bunch of that rabbit food. Awful lot for three people."

"Three vegans will need three full meals. Besides, not all meat eaters avoid healthy food like you do."

"Good for them. I'll stick with real meat instead of that fake-ass cardboard."

"Oh, here we go again. Fake this, cardboard that. And yet you look one meal away from a heart-attack."

"Oh, sure, more insults on Christmas. At least we don't have any guests over yet."

"You're the one making an ass out of yourself. One minute you're lamenting how much you envy our health, and the next you're insulting everything we do to be that healthy. Look in a damn mirror and actually see yourself for once. You've got one foot in the grave, and I am getting damn tired of trying to pull you out." She shut the bathroom door before he could say anything more.

***

Since Maria had claimed the shower and the boys were still in bed, Abraham decided to get a head start on cooking. He had taken off the Santa suit, no longer in the mood to play the jovial Christmas spirit. He had changed into jeans and an ugly Christmas sweater that had lights built in. He could at least pretend to be festive for the boys. Besides, working with the meat would help calm him. As he dipped his basting brush in some of the stored blood and slid it over the pork in his slow cooker, he thought back to feeding the pigs. Only instead of Ethan's corpse, it was Maria he was throwing in the trough.

He had a strict schedule for his cooking today. The first batch would be more community pork, but the second batch he would need to start on the roast suckling for dinner. He had to take extra care with that one. The whole batch was a sacrifice, but the suckling would be for him and his boys. It had to be perfect so they could receive their blessing. By the time Abraham finished seasoning and basting the meat, Maria had brought the boys downstairs for breakfast. He headed inside, shedding his coat and moving to the kitchen to make a hot cup of coffee.

"Merry Christmas, Daddy!" James greeted happily. "Mommy made us açai bowls! Look, look! I've got bananas and blueberries and strawberries and honey!!"

"Sounds like you're enjoying it this morning. But can you really say it beats Daddy's eggs and bacon?" Abraham teased.

"Hmmm, that's a hard one, Daddy. Eggs are really yummy, especially when I put syrup on them! But Mommy's breakfasts are healthier, and I wanna be healthy, too. I'm tired of not being able to run with my friends at school…"

"You don't have to give up eggs and bacon to be healthy."

"I guess…" James took a bite of his breakfast, considering. "But we don't have to kill anything for fruit, right? Didn't you say we should make what life there is count? So why kill something—"

"That's enough, James." Abraham cut him off. "There's nothing wrong with taking our place in the food chain. Besides, the pigs Daddy orders are humanely killed."

Maria scoffed. "That's the stupidest thing I've ever heard come from your mouth. There's nothing humane about killing something that doesn't want to die."

"I'm not gonna have you disrespect me in front of my kids."

"You do a perfectly good job of making a fool of yourself without my help."

"I'm sorry I said anything about it, please don't fight," James pleaded, tears forming in his eyes.

Abraham sighed but shut his mouth, moving to make his own breakfast. He glanced at Jesús in his playpen and then reached to turn on the lights in his sweater. The toddler babbled excitedly before pointing.

"Da! Ligh!"

Maria and Abraham both spun towards him, surprised to be blessed with his first words on Christmas.

"He said 'Daddy is the light'!" Abraham cheered. "Did you hear that, baby?"

"No, he said 'Daddy, light' for the light on your shirt, you dumbass."

"Perfect, now call me names in front of the kids on Christmas."

"You deserve much more than that for the things I know about, and I'm sure there's a lot more that I don't know."

Abraham reined in his temper. He was being tested, that's all. A test because today was his big offering. But Maria was fast on her way to joining the Collection with her attitude lately. He shook his head and finished getting breakfast, determined to move past whatever the hell had gotten into her today. Besides, most of his day would be spent working on the barbecue, where he could finally relax.

"Look, boys, it's snowing!" Maria's voice pulled Abraham back to the present, and he looked outside with his family to see the large white flakes drifting through the sky.

2222: The Untold Stories

***

Abraham spun his ring in the light, watching the diamond and ruby facets dance. He loved how the stones seemed alive. Magical. Standing in the backyard, cooking the same feasts his ancestors had enjoyed, he felt complete. Calm. Whole. And now he got to make the centerpiece of tonight's meal.

Since Abraham's cooker was custom-made, it was large enough to hold all three sucklings at once. He pulled them from their boxes and slid them in, grinning. He could already imagine how flavorful and tender they would be. He took more of the blood from his order and started brushing it almost ritualistically over the three young pigs.

"God, thank you for the abundance of food you've provided us. Thank you for the abundance of wealth that continues to bless my family. And thank you for accepting this sacrifice that I make on behalf of my family and myself, in Your name. Amen."

"What on Earth are you muttering about? What sacrifice?"

Abraham's head snapped up in surprise as he looked over at Maria. "You hate coming out when I'm cooking. Now what do you want?" She just couldn't let up today. Now she was interrupting his work.

"I brought you some hot chocolate because it's freezing out here, and I find you muttering weird shit about sacrifices to God. You haven't sacrificed a day in your life. What did you do?"

"The fuck you mean 'what did I do'? I'm talking about all the things we've done through the year, the fundraisers and shit. Plus all the help we've given looking for Ethan." Abraham straightened to take the mug. "And as much as you don't like it, I'm talking about the pigs. You know they used to give up the best stock for sacrifices, and it seemed appropriate for Christmas to dedicate all the meals I'm making to God."

Maria rolled her eyes. "Whatever helps you sleep at night," she snapped. Her phone pinged, and it was Abraham's turn to sigh in exasperation.

"Who the hell are you texting on Christmas?"

Maria gave him a look before pulling her phone out. "Carlos and Esmeralda started a group chat about dinner. They're going to be coming together."

"Together? What, are they dating or something?" That would throw a wrench in Maria's little tryst. Serves her right.

"I doubt it. She doesn't strike me as his type. But I could be wrong." Maria shrugged a shoulder.

"How would you know what his type is?"

"They just have some big differences in personality, that's all. He can be pretty impulsive. Remember that time he canceled our training sessions for a week because he decided to go to Vegas on a whim?" Maria slid her phone back in her pocket. "But I suppose there have been stranger couples. Look at us." She turned and walked back inside before Abraham had a chance to respond. That was the second time in one day she had closed a door in his fat face, and she had to admit it felt good.

***

While Abraham stayed outside for hours dressing up those poor pigs, Maria arranged the ceremonial dining room. The room had a large, heavy African blackwood table that hadn't been moved in centuries. Supposedly it had been in Abraham's family even longer, with more than one actual king sitting at its head. Regardless of its true history, the large table could hold thirty people with room to spare.

Despite the table's age, it was polished and sturdy like new. Rather than cover up the beautiful structure, Maria opted for a long, thin runner with candles and Christmas decorations down the center. She then started setting each place. They weren't expecting thirty people this year, but she liked to have the full table decorated. Besides, they would be ready if any surprises knocked at their door.

Next came the dishes. There was a large cupboard of heirloom table settings they used for their fundraiser dinners, but in the closed cabinet beneath was another antique set that only got brought out for Christmas. Maria would never admit it, but she hated using these dishes. They gave her the creeps, though she couldn't explain why.

Once all the table settings were in place, she took small place cards Esmeralda had written out and started arranging them. She couldn't help a soft smile when she came to Carlos's name, so of course Abraham walked inside and saw her through the doorway.

"What's so funny?"

"Nothing. Am I not allowed to smile on Christmas?"

"You don't smile like that with me."

"Because you've given me so many reasons to smile," she noted flatly. "What time is it? I could use a drink."

"You and me, both. What sounds good?"

"Vodka and 7-Up?"

"You got it, babe." He went into the kitchen and opened up the set of cabinets they had refitted into a hidden minibar. He pulled out a Beluga Noble vodka to mix their drinks. He entertained the thought of slipping something extra into her drink to rid himself of her, but he knew now wasn't the time. They had a dinner to host, a masquerade to show themselves as the perfect family. He finished preparing the drinks and joined her in the main dining hall. "Our drinks, madame."

"Thanks, A." She took the glass and moved to drink from it, but he caught her hand.

"A toast?"

"...Sure."

"A toast to us. Despite our arguments, God really has blessed us. We have two handsome young boys, all the money we could ever want and more. We have everything we need and can buy anything our hearts desire."

"You're wrong."

"What's that supposed to mean?"

"Sure, we can have everything money can buy. But money can't buy the things that matter. The things we actually need. We used to be friends, A. We used to love each other. Have passion. Need I go on?"

Abraham just shook his head.

"I've made up my mind, A. We're just not good together anymore, and perhaps we never were in the first place. I'll help with your little show for the holidays, and then I'm done."

"Fine."

"That's all you have to say?"

"Of course not, but can you really say you wanna have this talk right now? We have too many things happening, and this is the most important meal of the year for my family. So let's get through the holidays as you said."

"Fine, but I expect you to talk then since you already know my feelings, and they're not likely to change. So, have a plan, A, or you'll force me to initiate mine, and we'll be free of each other. Merry Christmas."

"Merry Christmas," Abraham replied flatly, clinking their glasses together before downing his drink in one gulp.

Chapter 18

As Abraham opened the slow cooker, the delectable aromas that had been slowly filling the air now wafted across his face full force. He breathed in the scent, grinning widely as he pulled off a subtle piece to taste test. As he savored the bite, his mind remembered kissing Ethan. Dancing with him. Watching the light fade from his eyes. Abraham seemed to fill up with a renewed energy as he straightened, the confidence of a man who knew he could get away with murder. He closed the cooker and looked out across his backyard to truly enjoy the stunning views.

He thought back to the family Christmases in this home under his grandfather and eventually his father. Of men out on the patio around the cooker, enjoying their cigars, while the women flitted around the kitchen to create the rest of the spread and gossip about anyone who hadn't come. He was six when he first got to join the men and his father let him taste a cigar; they had laughed when he got sick.

The amount of family who came together for the feasts had faded in recent years. Everyone had started new traditions with their families, though there was talk of getting together once every five years or so for a large feast like their parents often hosted.

As he was lost in memories and potential future plans, the sound of the doorbell carried through their home. He glanced at the window to the kitchen, realizing his phone was still plugged in to charge, and saw Maria setting down his phone and moving to answer. He snorted, unconcerned. She could try all she wanted, she wouldn't be able to get into his phone. Dumb bitch probably didn't even know how the biometric logins worked. Still, he moved inside so he could help Maria greet their guests.

As they opened the solid antique oak door, they were greeted by Carlos, Esmeralda, Mary, and Abraham's mother Margaret. Carlos was holding two vases full of flowers for the table; Abraham couldn't help noticing they were Maria's favorite colors. He looked behind them to see Dean Gomez and his wife, Priscilla, were coming up the walkway with their son Jacob. Abraham gave them all a wide, well-practiced smile.

"Merry Christmas, everyone! Please, come in. It looks like we're going to get more snow." He stepped aside and started taking everyone's coats. "Please slip off your shoes by the little bench there so we can keep the place dry. You're welcome to use any of the slippers if you like." He greeted Dean Gomez with a hug and shook Priscilla's hand, hiding his jealous glare when Maria hugged Carlos in greeting. He moved to hug his mother, though Mary walked past him to Maria.

"Make yourself at home, everyone, please," Maria invited their guests. "I have some hors d'oeuvres in the living area. We have a few more people coming, so please enjoy."

Priscilla took Jacob to the playroom so he could hang out with James while the adults milled about the living room. Small talk filled the room as they chatted, ate, and drank a precursor of wine. Abraham occasionally moved outside to check on the meat, but otherwise he spoke with Gomez about random things or checked in with his mother.

Jose and his family weren't long in arriving. Their two children took off to play with James and Jacob, while Jose and his wife Amy warmed up in the living room. Margaret and Mary had taken over watching the kids, so Priscilla came out to meet Abraham's cousin.

Once everyone was merry and warm, Maria led them into the dining room. A fresh-cut California Baby Redwood stood in the corner of the room, trimmed with red ribbons and beautiful lights. Maria helped everyone find their place cards before moving to the kitchen to start carrying in the food. Abraham went outside to retrieve the sucklings. He took a little time to wrap the extra two in foil and carry them into the cold storage before returning upstairs to set the main roast suckling on the table with the rest of the food.

He took his place at the head of the table. Jesús sat in a high chair on his left, then James, Maria, Jose, Amy, their two children, and Esmeralda. On his right was his mother, then Mary, Gomez, Priscilla, Jacob, and lastly Carlos. Both Esmeralda and Carlos looked a little pale when the suckling was set on the table with a red apple in its mouth, but the sight of the pig made Abraham's chest swell with pride. He reached for his wine glass, holding it up and tapping the side with his knife.

"Please, everyone, a moment of your time. You are welcome to remain seated, but please join hands and bow your heads." He waited for everyone to settle in. "On this Christmas, we commemorate those who are no longer here but remain in our hearts. For my father and his siblings, their parents before them, and beyond. For Maria's father. In their names, we pray. Father, forgive us, as we are natural sinners. We are imperfect people, trying to survive in a corrupt world."

Maria slid her eyes down the table to catch Carlos's gaze. She wished she had broken protocol and sat the man near her so she could tease him while everyone else was occupied with Abraham's prayer.

"Additionally, Lord, we pray for Ethan Bísólá. We pray for his safe return, and if that cannot be had, for justice. We have left a seat open for him and his family. May they find peace and solace in Your love and protection, Your kindness. We pray that his family will find comfort in You, that they may move forward despite this tragedy and honor their son's life through the years to come. Glory be to the Father, the Son, and the Holy Spirit, as it was in the beginning, is now, and forever shall be, world without end, Amen."

Abraham remained standing, reaching for his Miyabi knife and carving the roast pig. He served his sons first, cutting little pieces for Jesús, then his mother, before moving down the table. Mary surprised him by declining, choosing instead to eat vegan like her daughter. While he was serving the Gomezes, Carlos excused himself to step outside. The smell of the meat and the site of the pig being carved were making him ill. Esmeralda moved to check on him, Maria's eyes following them both. Abraham glanced at her and then back down at his task. The pair returned after some fresh air, though the heavy scent of meat turned their stomachs.

The carnivores around the table, however, were in paradise. Jose was the only other person at the table who knew the recipe, though he insisted Abraham made it best. Margaret had never been told, explaining to Priscilla that it was a family recipe passed through the men of the family. The young ones at the table devoured the meat as if they couldn't get enough of the rich flavor and tender texture.

Abraham had already scheduled the first delivery of meat he made for the community to be delivered the next day. He had so much to cook that the deliveries would be picked up over the next several days. Anyone who received pork from the Alvarezes always praised the flavor, but none could find a way to replicate it. The secret was closely guarded.

Aside from Abraham's prayer, no one thought of Ethan Bísólá or his grieving parents, losing themselves in delicious delicacies and warm conversation.

***

After dinner, while the kids played and the adults milled about in the living room, Abraham invited his cousin and the dean into his den. He offered the men an after-dinner drink, pulling out a rare cognac. The Henri IV Dudognon Heritage was his most prized possession, and his father had taught him to be sparing. However, this year was a special occasion, and he poured generously. He also pulled out his cigars and offered them around.

"I'm glad you and your family were able to make it, Gomez, what with all the lunacy this year."

"Abraham, nothing could keep us away."

"And I can't thank ya enough for finding room for us, cuz. We didn't have time to plan anything."

"We always have room for you, Jose."

Gomez lifted his glass. "To health, happiness, and peace. Merry Christmas." The three touched glasses, drank, and smoked the best cigars Abraham's money could buy.

Eventually, their conversation turned to the search for Ethan. Gomez knew Abraham had been running a search party, but he was pleasantly surprised to hear Jose had been so involved. He took a deep breath of his cigar. "Well, whatever happened, shit's about to hit the fan in the case. About damn time."

"How so?" Abraham asked.

"Now, I probably shouldn't say anything. But you say you trust your cousin with your life. So this stays between us." He leaned forward in the thick leather chair he had taken. "Ethan's phone washed up from one of the rivers. Some bum brought it in." He glanced at Abraham. "That reward of yours probably changed his life."

Abraham scoffed, but before he could lament the five hundred being spent on booze and shit, Jose asked Gomez how he had learned about the phone.

"I have some friends in the department. The information isn't going to be released publicly until they can fly in some hoity-toity forensics guy from the FBI to take a look." He took a long drag on the cigar. "God-willing, they'll find something despite the water damage. They need to catch this damn murderer before he goes after someone else's kids. You know getting away with shit just makes them bolder."

"You think he's really dead, then?" Jose asked sadly.

"It's been too long. If he had just found a piece of ass, he'd be back by now. Besides, this is Ethan we're talking about. I know you never met him, but Abraham and I could tell you he isn't that kind of kid. He wouldn't just disappear like that."

Abraham sighed, swirling his cognac to watch the liquid dance. "I won't say a word. You know I won't," he assured Gomez. "I can't help but be a bit fascinated with what happens behind the scenes. Are they just keeping the phone at the precinct for now?"

Gomez shrugged a shoulder. "As far as I know. Why is it so interesting to you?"

"Maria got me started on this true crime shit everyone is obsessed with," he confessed with a laugh. "I find it morbidly fascinating. Putting together the puzzles of evidence, getting into the mind of a serial killer…"

"Who said anything about a serial killer?" Jose laughed.

"No one, no one. Just explaining my latest fascination. God, you don't think it is a serial killer, do you?"

"I don't know, Dexter, you have anything to tell us?" Jose quipped. Now Gomez and Abraham joined in his laughter.

"If I ever did have something to hide, you two would recognize the signs. Those missing posters would have more priests than kids."

"Hear, fucking hear." Gomez raised his glass before downing the rest of his drink. "On that note, gentlemen, perhaps we should return upstairs. I daresay the little ones should be wearing out."

"Let me get a moment of your time in the hall. Jose, you don't mind waiting in here a moment for me, do you?"

"Nah, cuz, go ahead."

Abraham walked out with Gomez. "I know things are uncertain right now. I'd like you to have this." He reached into his pocket and pulled out an envelope.

"Abraham, I thought we said gifts are only for kids?"

"I know how hard you work through the year, man. You don't get paid nearly enough, and now you have the Ethan case weighing on you. I want you to know you're appreciated." Abraham handed over the envelope. Gomez sobered as he felt the cash inside. The envelope was thick, and he knew Abraham rarely dealt in small bills.

"I can't take that. Surely that's too much."

"Yes, you can, and you will. There's lots more where that came from. I got you covered. Whatever you and your family need. Besides, it's cash. Keep it out of your bank and don't worry about the taxes."

The two men embraced as the dean wiped away tears, quietly putting the money away in his tailored jacket pocket. "I can't thank you enough, Abraham."

"You don't need to. We'll be upstairs with you soon."

Gomez nodded, and Abraham returned to Jose. He waited until the dean's footsteps receded.

"Feeling generous, were you?" Jose commented, his tone a fair bit too light.

"Not like he's some random bum on the street. We always take care of our true friends."

Jose lifted a glass. "I suppose I can't argue that. I just get worried about how much you flash all that cash around, mijo."

"You keep me honest."

"I keep you anonymous."

Abraham laughed. Jose also benefited from the family wealth, though each male line carried its own riches. They didn't openly compare, but Abraham knew he had more stored away than Jose. The man had learned much caution because his father, Abraham's uncle, never had. Unlike Abraham's father, his uncle had practically hemorrhaged money. Abraham's grandfather had stepped in before it went too far, and now Abraham hired his cousin for anything and everything to help him rebuild. Jose wanted to earn the wealth, and the rest of the family respected that approach. No one liked handouts. Keeping that money in the family was an additional perk to helping his favorite cousin, and Jose had plenty of skills to offer.

"Speaking of feeling generous," Abraham noted, reaching into his pocket and pulling out his stash. "Care to partake in some of the best blow money can buy?"

"Merry Christmas, indeed." Jose rubbed his hands together as he joined Abraham at the counter of his bar. "I thought I told you to cut back?"

"You think I listen to everything I'm told?"

The pair laughed as Abraham laid out a line for each of them. They partook, shared a hug, made sure they were cleaned up, and headed upstairs.

When the pair emerged from the stairwell, Abraham froze. Carlos was walking around with Jesús in his arms, the tot fast asleep as the man rocked him. Maria was nearby with a soft smile as she watched them. They looked like a perfect little family, and Abraham felt a spike of jealous rage. Jose's kids went running past the pair, laughing, and Abraham broke out of his stupor.

"Yo, why is Carlos holding my son?"

Carlos glanced up at Abraham and smiled. Was he imagining the smugness beneath?

"Sorry, Mr. A, no harm meant. Maria was helping the Gomezes get their coats and the little man was getting fussy. I was the closest."

Jose clapped Abraham on the shoulder as he walked past in a nonverbal signal to chill out, but Abraham was already riled up.

"I don't care if you were the only one in the whole damn room, I don't want you holding my boy," he spat, moving over and taking Jesús. Despite his rage, he was careful with the little boy. His boys were precious.

"Hold up, Mr. A. I already said I was sorry, but you're out of line here, bud."

"Abraham, would you relax?" Maria joined in, glaring at him from the entry hall. Gomez stood awkwardly by the door while Priscilla helped Jacob with his shoes. "He was trying to help me. Where were you? Why weren't you there to help me? Hell, why aren't you ever there when I need help? Be mad at yourself for not being the man you're supposed to be. You can't even be that man on Christmas! It's too much for you, apparently. Thankfully, you're not the only man in the world."

"That's the closest you're going to get to telling him the truth, you little slut?" Margaret blurted, standing from the couch. She turned to Abraham. "That wife of yours disappeared upstairs with mister babysitter. They only came down because Jesús started fussing."

No one moved. Amy looked to Jose, who held up a subtle hand and motioned her towards the entry. Mary was standing now, too, but she bit her tongue for the moment. Abraham was glaring at Maria.

"Thank you for coming, everyone, but I'm afraid the party

is over," he ground out as politely as he could manage. "I won't make you sit and listen to how this plays out. In fact, I think we should both take the evening to settle down."

Maria scowled at him, but she turned and started helping their guests claim their coats. "Merry Christmas, everyone. Don't worry, I plan on having a happy, free New Year. Please do drive safe."

"And Carlos?" Maria and the trainer turned to look at Abraham. "You're fucking fired."

Chapter 19

Six Months Earlier

John Finn was a man of routine. No matter the season, he rose at precisely 4:44 am to go for a run. After, he would return home for a quick shower and make himself a vegan breakfast. At 47 years old, he took his health seriously. He had been in Brazilian Jiu-Jitsu for the last twenty years, his current classes meeting on Tuesdays and Thursdays; on days he didn't have class, he went to the gym.

Every morning he would check on the stocks and his accounts, do some trading, and check in with the non-profits and startups he had invested in. He would check his emails to see if anyone needed his consulting, and then he would put the electronics away and choose a book from his shelves to read. He didn't read at home; instead, he would choose a local café for the day. He had a rotation of several, though he only frequented the ones that offered vegan menu items and tried their best to offset their carbon footprints. He never went to a chain; he wanted his money to go to local owners.

If school was out, his boys would often meet him for coffee and a treat. He had three with his ex-wife— Liam, 18; Levi, 14; and Luke, 13. Though he and their mother had divorced when Luke was young, they remained amicable and co-parented well together. Susan maintained custody for living arrangements so the boys could have a stable household, but John spent time with them throughout the week and several weekends. He also paid more than the court-ordered child support because he wanted to ensure his boys were taken care off. He had trusts set up for each, with the option to attend college or trade school to receive the money. Liam had chosen college, and was currently applying and touring. Luke and Levi had begged to go to a new summer camp, so John had paid their admission. But that meant he was looking at a week of coffee alone.

Or so he thought.

The morning had started like any other. It was gorgeous outside, and he had truly enjoyed his run. Stocks were going well, and none of his clients needed advice. He had the day to himself, so he reached for one of his favorite books and made his way outside. It was hot enough he decided biking would make him too sweaty, so he readied a water bottle and walked. The beauty of summer surrounded him, and he marveled at God's work even within the stones and concrete of the city. More than one sun flare across the glass or through a streetlight banner or flag took the shape of a cross, and John quickly snapped photos of the little blessings.

John arrived at the café at the same time as a Colombian woman with a complexion that reminded him of calla lilies. She smiled as he held the door for her, chestnut eyes grateful. John could barely take his eyes off of her; she was gorgeous. He estimated her around 5'6 against his 6'2. Despite her appearance, John didn't let himself stare. He didn't want to make her uncomfortable; he knew he could appear rather intimidating, both from simply being a strange man and his athletic build. Despite his concern, she turned to face him and started a conversation.

"Chivalry isn't truly dead, I see. Thanks for getting the door. I'm Selena." She held out her hand.

"John. It's nice to meet you, Selena." Her name slid from his tongue like honey. It felt magical to say. "I do try to be polite when I can. The world is dark enough, and it costs nothing to spread a little kindness."

Her smile brightened further, but she turned to order her coffee. "An iced latte with oat milk and an extra shot of espresso please, also…" she paused looking up at the menu. "Sorry, I haven't been here before. Do you have anything vegan to eat?"

"They have some amazing pastries, but I would recommend the apple cobbler," John piped up. He smiled when she turned to blink at him. "I come here specifically because they have vegan offerings. And Hannah makes the best cobbler." He nodded to one of the baristas currently preparing more food for the display.

"You flatter me, John. But it is pretty good," Hannah agreed with a laugh.

John smiled, then turned to the cashier. "Sara, add in my usual please, with two of the cobblers. My treat," he explained to Selena.

"Then the least I can do is ask you to join me at a table," she joked. John paid for their order and let Sara know they would be at a patio table. He held the door open for Selena again and led her to his favorite, just under the cherry blossom tree. He pulled out her chair.

"First the door, then the coffee, now the chair...what next, Prince Charming?" Selena teased. John blushed, but she held up a hand. "No, don't tell me. I rather like surprises."

As John sat across from her, Hannah brought out their order. As she walked back inside, she turned and flashed John an encouraging thumbs-up and a wink. He cleared his throat. "Do you mind if I say grace?"

"Please."

As John bowed his head to give grace over their meal, Selena watched him. A part of her wondered if the man was putting on a show since he had just met her, and yet another part of her knew he wasn't. Something in his eyes radiated kindness. She could practically feel the light from his soul; or was that the July sun? Selena usually trusted her intuition, but she hesitated trusting men. Too many times, she had been wrong in her estimations. Her wounded soul, her wounded heart, could not escape their suspicion.

Still, as John lifted his gaze, she met it and smiled. "Protestant or Catholic?" she asked curiously.

"Protestant is closest, but I don't really have a category for my faith," he explained. "I know that God has blessed me, and I follow His Word, not the words of men." He took a sip of his coffee. "Granted, I'm still interested to hear what people have to say. I just don't follow them blindly," he amended. "There are some fantastic scholars out there who help bring clarity to verses, especially when you look at the historical contexts and Jewish traditions."

"Have you taken any classes in Jewish studies?"

"I have, actually."

They spent the next hour discussing history and tradition and how it related to the Old Testament and the newer covenants before sliding into topics related to their pasts. They were so engrossed in the conversation that they didn't glance at their phones even once. From Biblical history to academic pursuits, to their reasons for going vegan and their favorite exercise, the conversation flowed as naturally as water from a spring. They had so much to share with each other, and they quickly felt like lifelong friends.

"I've always wanted to try jiu-jitsu," Selena confessed. "But I've always felt intimidated when I look into the classes."

"You should come to my school. We have some great beginner classes, and the advanced students are always happy to help out. We actually remember what it was like when we first started, so we try to make it easy."

From there they talked about past experiences, and John started laughing. "No, I'm sorry. I just remembered something from back in middle school," he explained. "I was athletic even then, partially out of spite. So I could do more than most kids my age. We had a PE test once where we had to do push-ups with our fists, but it wouldn't count unless we lowered our chest to our fist and then fully extended. Well, I did 90. Even though my buddy confirmed it, the teacher wouldn't believe us, so I did another 90 just for him. The look on his face as I kept going!"

Selena joined him in the laugh. "I have to ask, how can you be athletic out of spite?" John hesitated. "You don't have to tell me. I'm sorry."

"No, it's all right. That's a pretty natural follow-up. It's just not exactly a happy story. My father…" John grimaced. "Well. He didn't really deserve the title. He was a very irresponsible man, and that included his health. He completely ignored the signs of alcoholism in our family, and he fell victim. As a result, his health suffered, as did his mood."

"I'm sorry."

"He always told me I was destined to be a failure like him. So I dedicated myself to proving him wrong. By the time I was thirteen, he was in jail, and I was a straight-A student on the baseball team. My grandad took me in. I still visited my father on occasion, but his sharp words were like water on a duck. I knew better. It took a few years of therapy to move past excelling out of spite and the resulting burnout, but I'm at peace with it now."

Selena smiled softly. "I'm glad. My childhood was special simply because my mother was a wonderful woman who loved me and my brother to pieces. I was pretty average growing up. I wasn't a straight-A, but I wasn't bottom of the barrel, either. I just wasn't really inspired until I hit college."

They talked a little longer about the sort of classes she had enjoyed and his own college experience before John's phone went off. He checked to be sure it wasn't a business email and noticed the time. "I hope you didn't have anywhere important to be today?"

Selena quickly checked the time. "No, thankfully," she answered with a laugh. "My, the time has flown. I was actually planning to do some shopping today. Would you like to join me?"

"I would love to." Despite his words, he hesitated. "I'm sorry if this is too forward. But you're beautiful, and I've been having a wonderful time just talking to you. Surely someone with your looks and personality is taken? Am I reading too much into things?"

Selena couldn't help a soft laugh. "No, I know what you mean. I could ask you the same thing. No secret girlfriend, or wife?"

"Just an ex," he assured her.

"Several exes, unfortunately," she answered, grimacing. "I simply haven't found the one that sticks. But I don't want to give up and consign myself to loneliness."

John stood, moving to get her chair so they could walk while they continued talking. "I can't say I've been actively looking," he confessed. "I have three amazing young men that I'm helping raise. And I decided to spend the past few years focusing on them and myself. But now the oldest is 18 and the youngest is in middle school, so they don't need me as much." He let Selena lead the way, since she had been planning to shop. She asked him about his sons, so he spent the next few minutes talking about Liam's college applications, Levi's growing interest in music and band, and Luke's obsession with superheroes. Despite the depth of their conversation, John didn't miss the homeless man a little further down the street. "I'll be just a minute." Selena blinked at him, but he sped up to reach the man.

"Good morning, friend," he greeted warmly. "What's your name?"

The man gave him a suspicious look. "Name's Felix, mate. Who're you?"

"Felix, my name is John." He held out his hand, and Felix stared at it.

"First you're talking to me, now you're shaking my hand?" he asked hesitantly. "What do you want?"

"To let you know you're seen," John assured him softly. Felix shook his hand firmly.

"Ah, man, I'm sorry. I'm sorry. No one ever stops to talk to me unless they want something. God bless you, John."

"No, Felix, I would rather He bless you." John reached for his wallet and pulled out some cash. "Why don't you go have a hot meal? There should be enough there for a hotel room, too. I know it doesn't fix everything, but we can start getting you on your feet." He also pulled out a business card. "Give my friend here a call, too, once you've taken care of yourself. Ok?"

Felix was crying now. "Sir, please. It's so much."

"And it's all yours," John assured him gently. "I have a mission from God to help those in need, and today He led me to you."

"I know...I'm not the cleanest...but...?" Before Felix could finish, John pulled him into a hug.

Chapter 20

Selena had waited for John a little further down the sidewalk, not wanting to interrupt or crowd. She smiled as John rejoined her.

"That was very kind of you."

"I appreciate the compliment, but I don't do that kind of thing for attention," John confessed. "I wasn't kidding: it's my mission." He hesitated a moment, but so far he hadn't needed to keep any secrets from her. He knew he could trust her. "I know I don't necessarily look the part, but my family has been blessed through the years with a lot of money. My grandfather instilled the importance of giving to others, especially if they're in a rough patch. You know that old saying about if you give a man a fish, he'll eat for a day, but if you teach him how to fish, you'll feed him for a lifetime?" At her nod, he continued. "Well, my granddad always liked to point out that it's easier to teach a man to fish if he has a full stomach."

"But what if they don't take your help? What if they just spend the money on other things?"

"Then that's a reflection on their hearts, not mine. I do what I can to help; whether they accept the help is their decision." He folded his arms as they walked. "I help in other ways, too, but I always stop for a conversation when I see someone on the street. I invest in a lot of local initiatives to help the homeless, as well as a few others."

"You help fund non-profits?" she asked hesitantly. John arched an eyebrow.

"I sense another question there," he prompted.

"I don't want it to seem like I'm digging," she confessed. "I...well, I've actually got an organization that I've been struggling to get off the ground."

John laughed. "You're kidding? Well, I guess Felix isn't the only one the Lord has led to me today."

Selena blushed. "I won't tell you that it's based in veganism and helping the homeless," she added with a growing smile. She slowed as they approached a store. "Although, this is my first stop for the day."

John grinned at her. "Oh, really?"

"Don't tell me you know the place?"

"I did tell you Levi is getting really into music. I didn't tell you it's because he takes after his old man." He laughed. "Yeah, we shop here a lot. C'mon, I'll introduce you to Jamal." He offered his hand, and she took it. "We'll come back to our other conversation," he promised as they walked inside.

John had met Jamal around the time his marriage had fallen apart. Since he let Susan have the house in the divorce and moved back into the brownstone he inherited from his grandfather, he had needed to find a new records shop. Jamal was very involved in his shop and loved to chat with the customers. He had given John some great advice, as well as some good music recommendations, and the pair had been friends since.

"John, you didn't tell me you had such a beautiful girlfriend!"

"Nice to see you, too, Jamal," John joked in return. "Selena, this is Jamal. Jamal, Selena. And she isn't my girlfriend. Well, at least not yet."

"We only just met a couple of hours ago," Selena confessed with a laugh.

"Nope. I don't believe it. You too look like you've been together forever, and I mean that in the best possible way."

"That's very kind of you, Jamal. I'm beginning to think the same thing," Selena confessed, smiling up at John.

"Just wait until you meet his boys. If you aren't sold on their dad yet, I'm sure they'll seal the deal," Jamal assured her. "Fine boys, all three of them." Jamal smiled as if talking about his own family rather than his friend's.

"Oh, they're ok," John teased, and they all laughed.

"Levi's my favorite," Jamal teased in a loud whisper. "Voice of an angel, that one. So talented. I'm sure I'll be selling his albums some day."

"If that's what he wants, I've no doubt," John agreed.

The three spoke and laughed like old friends while Selena browsed the racks, discussing everything from the type of music they liked— "Really, you're a boygenius fan, too?" —to other entertainment— "I can't believe you both like Dexter. Are you sure you aren't dating yet?" Eventually, however, John became all too aware of the fact it was time for lunch when his stomach growled. They bid farewell to Jamal and resumed their walk, eventually passing Memorial Chapel.

"That's where my grandad's funeral was held," John noted. "He was such a good role model for me, especially after my father went to jail. I miss him."

"It's beautiful that you have such great memories with him. Cherishing those helps keep his memory alive. Why don't you tell me more about him?"

John led her to a nearby vegan eatery while they talked about their families. He learned that Selena's father had left when she was six, and he told her about how his mother had passed away when he was young. While John told her about his grandfather Moses, she taught him about her mother Diana and her brother Santos. Once again they lost themselves in a good, healthy meal and good company.

"I have to confess, I wasn't always on a good path," John explained, flushing slightly. "After my grandad died, I...didn't really know what to do with myself. I made some poor choices. I had always sworn never to drink, but I did end up getting into drugs. Things spiraled, and I almost took my own life." He hesitated before adding, "Surprisingly, it was my dad that saved me. I was desperate, so I called him. He'd been sober for a couple years at that point, and we were working on reconciling. He talked me down, and got me in touch with his therapist."

"That's incredible, John. I'm glad your father was able to talk you down, and that you didn't give up on yourself."

"It's God that never gave up on me," he corrected with a soft smile. "He's very loyal, even when we're not. Kind and forgiving. It's only right that we at least try to be the same." He grimaced slightly. "Though I suppose that was a bit heavy for a first date," he confessed with a dry laugh. "I'm sorry. I don't mean to weigh down the conversation. It just feels so good to talk to you, to tell you these things. My ex-wife doesn't even know what I just told you."

Selena smiled. "I don't mind. I know what you mean, honestly. I just...I have a hard time being vulnerable with anyone. I've been burned too many times before."

"I'm not the kind to run and leave you hanging," John promised, and she smiled.

"I believe you. It's just going to take some time for me to fully accept it."

"I understand. There's no rush. I'm rather hoping this is the first of many dates to come."

"I think that's a pretty safe bet."

"Though we have yet to talk about that non-profit of yours," John reminded her, raising his eyebrows. Selena smiled.

"Hmmm...Maybe on the third date," she teased. Then she sobered. "I know I said my childhood was pretty average. My mother loved me to pieces. But I still struggled. Growing up without a father took it's toll, and we never really had a lot of money. After my mother died...Well. I lived without a soul." She grimaced. "Not really something you bring up on a first date, I know, but...I trust you. I didn't always have such confidence and respect for myself. I essentially looked for any connection to try and fill the never-ending void I had within myself. For years, I was in a state of depression and had no one to truly open up to or even a place to call home. Santos tried to be there for me, but I didn't make it easy for him."

She kept her eyes on her plate, avoiding eye contact for now. "I had a few relationships, but none of them were good or healthy and none of them lasted. Finally, Santos sat me down for a serious conversation. I didn't want to hear what he had to say, but he wouldn't let me run away again. I ended up breaking down, and the next day I decided something had to change. I saw a job posting for an English teacher in Thailand and decided to leave the country for a while. I think those kids taught me more about life than I taught them about English." She smiled with the memories. "I found my footing. Found my faith. And I came back to New York City with a renewed interest in helping people at home."

"That's amazing. Have you ever been tempted to go back to Thailand?"

She laughed. "I would love to visit, but I just can't afford to travel right now. Both from a business standpoint and a finances one. While I work on getting the business going,

I'm also working as a cashier just to keep things running. What do you do for a living anyway? Besides give all your money away?" She grinned to show she was teasing. John rubbed the back of his head sheepishly.

"Officially, I'm an investor," he confessed. "I also freelance as a consultant, but mostly I volunteer my expertise to the businesses and organizations I'm helping. Honestly, I don't need to work; I just know I would get bored without being actively involved. I wasn't kidding when I said my family was blessed. My grandfather inherited a lot of wealth, and he spent his life growing it while paying it forward. He taught me everything he knew, and I inherited all of his wealth and passive income; he wrote my father out of the will because of the turn he had taken in life. Now I help forward-thinking companies get off the ground and invest in non-profits whose mission coincide with my values. I do set down some requirements to continue investing, but I help the company meet them as well."

"What kind of requirements?"

"Sustainable business practices, for one. Green initiatives. And I won't support any company that causes harm— to the planet, animals, people, anything. I'm not willing to sell my soul to the devil or the world."

"That's fantastic. Hopefully you don't mind that I haven't come from anything glamorous..."

"I have money, but you've heard how glamorous my life has been," he pointed out gently. "Being wealthy doesn't mean your life is stress-free, though I admittedly didn't face some of the barriers other kids my age faced. I know a lot of people who have just as much money, but they're miserable souls. No morals, entitled kids, families full of greed. What good is their money? Million-dollar houses, billion-dollar neighborhoods, and nothing but misery and loneliness. Hearts full of darkness." He shook his head.

"Sorry. I get a bit riled up about it" he confessed. "I refuse to become like them. I give back as much as I can without compromising my integrity or faith. My kids are the real treasures, not my wealth. I'm doing everything I can to prepare them for the world and teach them to be responsible with what they will inherit. I'm grateful my financial situation allows me to remove certain barriers, but I won't let them take it for granted."

"From what Jamal was saying earlier, you're doing a fine job," Selena assured him. They paused their conversation to order dessert. "All right. You've convinced me. But only if you put on your business hat and act like an investor, not a date."

John laughed, but he agreed. "Allow me to interview you. Just so it's official."

Selena laughed. "Fine. Ask your questions."

"What is the name and mission of your organization?"

"Don't laugh."

"Madam, I am a professional."

"The full name is Plant Love and Nourish the Soul, but I call it by the acronym: Plants. It's meant to be a free delivery service of plant-based food to designated areas for people in need. Sort of like a food truck, but we're giving the meals out for free." She started getting more passionate as she spoke. "I want to start with one truck, wrapping it in a design that advertises the mission and provides positive messaging. As we take on more routes, we would bring on more trucks. I want to help make healthy food accessible to the community, but especially low-income areas and the homeless. I would love for our trucks to become positive icons in various communities, almost like when you see an ice-cream truck, you know?"

John kept his face straight. "Where will the meals come from?"

"I really want to get to the point where we have a place to make the food ourselves, but I figured we could start by partnering with local vendors. I also had the idea to sell some merch for fundraising. Most of it would have to go back into the organization, but any excess would be donated to other initiatives."

"It sounds like you've put a lot of thought into this. What are your challenges?"

"Funding. I've been trying to raise money to buy the first truck, but I'm not having a lot of luck. I've applied for grants, but most places want you to have a financial history before they'll donate. And it's hard to get a meeting with investors." She smiled in thanks as the waitress dropped off their dessert.

John nodded, folding his arms. "To say I'm interested would be an understatement. This is something that aligns perfectly with what I stand for. How do you feel about using electric vehicles?"

"It would be a dream! But I worry about sustainable mining practices to make the batteries. It's hard to tell whether gas and oil and emissions are worse from a single vehicle than an entire mining operation."

John nodded again. "I can understand the concern. I'll see if anyone's done the math. Obviously I can't really write up a contract in a restaurant. But if you're willing to put me on the board of directors and let me make some pretty big decisions, I'm in." He leaned forward and met her gaze. "I'll fund your first vehicle and help you find a place for food prep. I'll pay for any renovations to make the building sustainable. I've got some connections with a screen printer who sources hemp clothing, so I'll fund a uniform shirt for any workers and volunteers we bring in. But I want to do more than just fund this. I want to help you with the labor, as well. Is that ok?"

Selena's hand had gradually risen to cover her mouth the more support he listed. "Oh, my God, John, yes. I would love to have your help! This...is so much. No one has ever done this much! Are...Are you serious??"

"I wouldn't kid around about something like this," he assured her. "I'm not that cruel."

"No, no, of course you aren't...I'm sorry, I'm just...You're an angel. I've been trying so hard to get this going, and you've guaranteed I can!"

"I'll do more than help you get it started. From now on, we're partners." He held up a hand. "Regardless if we actually date or not. I'm not going to make others suffer over something petty like that. And I'm not doing this so that you'll sleep with me." He lowered his hand to continue.

"Even when it comes to dating. I'm not after a body to warm my bed," he explained. "I want somebody to share my dreams with, my children with, and most importantly, my love of God. You deserve to know this if we get together, because I've been celibate since my divorce. Sex is very important to me, and I'm going to save it for the next person I marry."

"I understand. Honestly, that's refreshing to hear. I've had too many men who were only after a warm body."

John paused as their waitress returned with the check, thanking her and pulling out his wallet. As he estimated the tip and started pulling out cash, he asked Selena, "Do you have a business plan written up or anything?"

"Yes. I have it on my Drive."

"Would you be willing to come to my place? We can pull up your plan and work out some other details."

"I would love to. I didn't have any other plans for today, and now I'm excited to get things running!"

Chapter 21

They spent the next several hours hunkered in John's living room with his laptop. Soft music crooned through his speakers, and glasses of ice tea perched on coasters. The brownstone was modestly decorated yet filled with light and plants. John wrote up a contract for their new partnership, and then he and Selena spent time going over her business plan and other documents before pricing trucks and browsing a few real estate sites. After taking a look at Selena's work schedule for the week, John called a friend of his who was a Realtor and set a day to look through commercial buildings.

They brainstormed slogans and merch, and John got in touch with one of his startups, a marketing agency, to commission help with slogans and branding. Selena showed him her current spreadsheet to track finances, and he added a few functions to automate certain processes. All the while, they talked about anything and everything. The pair felt like lifelong friends, possibly even soulmates. Being together, working together...It all just felt right. Eventually they slid the laptop away, curling with each other on the couch and just talking about life. Past, present, future. John talked about some of the other initiatives he had invested in, and Selena told stories from her time in Thailand.

Time slowly slipped past them. Rather than go back out, John cooked a simple dinner for them so they could continue talking. More and more, John found himself lost in Selena's voice. The conversation only started to lull when weariness crept into their bones.

"What time even is it?" Selena had asked while shielding a yawn behind her hand. John reached for his phone to check.

"You're not going to believe this. It's 2:22 in the morning."

Selena sat up a little straighter. "Wait, really?" She pulled out her own phone and sent a quick text.

"I'm serious. I'm sorry. Did you need to be somewhere tonight?"

"No, I just don't want Santos to worry. We're rooming together right now, though I've been hoping to save up for my own place. I know he's planning to propose to his girlfriend soon; he assures me I'm welcome to stay, but I would prefer to let them enjoy their own space, you know?"

"It's a bit late to be walking home. Would you like me to call you a cab? Or you could spend the night here. I know that's a pretty big ask for someone you just met, but I promise I have no ulterior motives. You can even sleep in the guest room if you would be more comfortable."

Selena smiled, but it was interrupted by another yawn. "I... would like to sleep with you, if that's alright?" She blushed slightly. "I want to be held."

John smiled. "Of course. Come on, before you fall asleep on the couch." He led the way to the master bedroom.

Moonlight filtered in through stained glass, painting the room in an array of colors. He had a fairly large four-poster bed, and the room was accented in natural colors like green and brown. All of his furniture was naturally-colored wood, and still more plants decorated the space.

"You really love nature, don't you?" Selena observed with a smile.

"I love surrounding myself with light and life," he confirmed. He moved over to his dresser and pulled out a pair of gray shorts and a tee shirt that read 'God is my plan, from A-Z and everything in between'. "Here. These might be a little big, but you can sleep in them."

"Do you always have ready-to-use sleepwear for impromptu guests?" she teased, and he laughed.

"No. Honestly, the only people to spend the night since I got divorced are my sons. Some people might be embarrassed to admit that, but I've just never wanted to invite anyone over."

"That's sweet. I feel special, now."

"You are special, with or without me."

"You make me feel special."

"God makes you special, not me. Speaking of, do you mind if we pray before we go to sleep?"

"Not at all," she assured him.

"Will you kneel with me?" He offered Selena his hand and then helped her lower next to the bed. Once he joined her, they folded their hands and lowered their heads on the bed like children often do.

"God, I want to thank You for this blessed day and the abundance You have given me and my family. I am grateful for the opportunity to help Felix, and even more grateful to have met Selena. Thank You for guiding us to each other and spurring our conversations." Selena smiled but blushed with the prayer. "I am grateful for my three boys and the young men they are growing to be. Please grant Liam the wisdom to find the right college, and protect Levi and Luke while they are away. I am grateful that You guide us to break generational curses and give us the means to help those in need. Thank You for blessing me with a healthy, strong body and mind, and please keep my soul pure. Continue to guide me along Your path. Amen."

"Amen. That was beautiful, John."

John smiled, standing and helping her to her feet. She slipped into the bathroom to change into the clothes he had provided; while she was out of the room, John slipped into his own pair of shorts and a shirt. Once Selena returned, they climbed into bed together. John wrapped an arm around Selena's shoulders, and she curled against him with her hand directly over his heart before falling into the deepest, most peaceful sleep she had experienced in a long time. At some point during the night, the pair turned on their sides. John continued to hold her tight.

2222: The Untold Stories

***

The next morning, John slept in past his usual 4:44 wake up. As he blinked over at the clock on his nightstand, he noticed it was 7:07. He didn't move right away, staring at the woman asleep in his arms. He couldn't remember the last time he had slept so deeply. He was tempted to stay in bed and savor the moment. Birdsong filled the air outside, and he glanced over Selena to see a red robin land on his windowsill to sing. Soon it was joined by a blue robin, as well, their shapes shimmering through the stained glass. John silently thanked God for the morning performance before slipping from bed and heading to the kitchen. He left a quick note for Selena.

Selena,

I went for a quick run. I'll be back somewhere around thirty minutes. If you read this, go back to sleep so I can surprise you with breakfast. If you need anything, feel free to call or shoot me a text.

He added his phone number to the bottom so she could reach him, especially if there was an emergency, before sliding his phone into his armband. Despite the beautiful morning, he kept to his word and returned home a little after 7:40. He moved into the bathroom for a quick shower. As he stood under the water, he closed his eyes and lifted his face to the sky.

"God, thank You for this blessed, beautiful day. Thank You for Selena. I know we have only known each other since yesterday, but she is from You. She is so different from the others I have crossed paths with. I am sad to hear of the wounds in her soul, but grateful that she trusts me with the knowledge. Please help us turn our wounds to Your glory together."

After he had washed and dressed, he moved into the kitchen and started pulling out ingredients to make a full breakfast. He put some oil in a skillet before adding in the potatoes and stirring them to heat. Once they were warm, he added in chopped onions, peppers, and spinach and sautéed them together. Once the vegetables were tender, he added Daiya mozzarella cheese and Just Eggs before topping the whole thing off with some Impossible sausage. While the skillet simmered, John pulled out a frozen triple berry mix and some dark chocolate almond milk for smoothies, adding in some chia seeds for an additional boost.

The upper floor of John's townhouse had a room that overlooked the street, and he often ate his meals there. Today, he set the table with meticulous care, arranging breakfast on his subtle yet elegant dishware. The scent of the fresh breakfast and the abundance of greenery in his home transformed the brownstone into a secret escape, a magical garden hidden away from the mayhem, disaster, and disarray of the world— if only temporarily.

As John looked over his work, he felt a stab of pain as he thought back to his previous marriage. He had been in a dark place, and his marriage had suffered as he and Susan drifted further apart. The final nail in the coffin had been when she cheated. But they both had spent the past few years working on themselves and focusing on their boys. While he occasionally regretted how things had turned out, he had learned to look forward. Now it felt like he was being given another chance. Despite how strongly he felt about Selena, he wouldn't be certain until she met his boys. John shook himself from his thoughts and moved to the bedroom; he needed to wake Selena before their food got cold, and yet he was nervous to start another day with her. He quietly walked up to the bed, leaning over to touch her shoulder.

"Selena? Good morning. Come on, I made us breakfast." She didn't respond, so he gently nudged her shoulder. Finally, he bent further to kiss the back of her neck. Selena hummed, rolling over to blink up at him and smile.

"That's one way to wake me up. Now you'll just have to learn all the others," she teased. They both laughed.

"Judging from your reaction to a kiss on the neck, I can only imagine how fun that will be. Now, come on, you. I've got breakfast ready." He winked at her as he straightened.

"That's very sweet. I'll be out in a moment." Selena rolled out of bed and moved for the restroom. After splashing some water on her face, she smiled at her reflection. "God? I know I don't pray to You a lot these days. So now You've put this guy in my life who invites me to join into his prayers. He must be from You. Every moment makes me more sure. I've never met anyone like him, and I'm sure I never will again even if I live a hundred lifetimes. I promise to cherish this gift You've given me. I know I don't deserve it. I'm a sinner, through and through. I've made some terrible decisions in the past. But You have helped me through everything, and now You're giving me another chance. Please help me proceed with wisdom. Cloak me in Your love, kindness, and protection. Amen."

Once Selena was finished in the restroom, she opened the door and called out for John. He let her know which room he was in, then stood as she entered and pulled out her chair.

"This looks and smells amazing!" she praised as she sat.

"Only the best for you," John replied with a smile.

"That's very sweet of you." She wouldn't admit that she had woken while he was out and then returned to bed with the biggest smile after reading his note. "No one has done anything like this for me before. Thank you."

"You're welcome anytime. What are your plans for today?"

"My morning is clear. I need to swing by my place before work this evening, but I've got plenty of time between now and then."

"Would you like to join me for a walk? I can take you by your place and then we can head to Washington Square Park. It's really nice there; I get a lot of inspiration for characters in my books. There are so many subcultures once you learn to spot them."

"All that talk yesterday, and you never mentioned that you write books," Selena teased. "But what do you mean by subcultures?"

"I've noticed the people there and those who live nearby look out for each other. They're not competing with anyone over a loaf of bread, but rather sharing what they have among friends. They're so grateful for what they have..."

"That's an interesting way to look at it. The park sounds like a good idea. I've gone there before to clear my head, but now I'll be looking with a different perspective." She took a sip of her smoothie. "Tell me about your books? I've always dreamed of writing one, but I never could decide where to start and where to go."

"My first book took a couple of years," John confessed with a chuckle. "I self-published it."

"First?" she prompted. "How many have you written?"

"Right now, I'm working on my sixth novel."

"What's it about?" She leaned her elbow on the table, intrigued, but John shook his head.

"I can't tell you. Too early to put it out into the world."

"What kind of books do you write?"

"Fiction."

Selena leaned back in her chair. "Now I'll have to look up your other books. Maybe I'll ask you for pointers and finally try to get some stories out there."

"Don't wait for tomorrow— time is a myth," John cautioned.

"What do you mean?"

"Tomorrow is never promised. We only have today. So you need to be present at every moment and ensure you use your energy wisely and sparingly."

"If you help me learn the discipline, I would love to take that advice. Your enthusiasm for life is contagious."

"As is your smile."

"You're sweet."

"You're blushing."

"I am not, stop." Selena smiled shyly, burying it beneath her smoothie glass.

They spent the rest of the morning together, swinging by Selena's apartment so she could change clothes and pack her work uniform. The day slipped past in the bliss they would come to know together over the next several weeks.

Chapter 22

From that warm July day, John and Selena were practically inseparable. She still had her job as a cashier, and she spent time with her brother. John had his time with his boys, as well. Eventually, they met each others' family. Santos was almost as in love with John as his sister was, and they were fast friends. The boys had been a little slower to warm up to the idea.

Liam took meeting his dad's new girlfriend the best. He was the oldest, and he understood that his parents deserved their own happiness. Levi and Luke had more of an adjustment period. They felt jealous and a little threatened that Selena's presence would change things with their father. Through it all, Selena had been amazingly patient. She was more than happy to let Levi and Luke have time with their father without her present, and she didn't push herself on them. John had also spoken with Susan, and they sat down with their sons together to talk over everyone's feelings and help create boundaries so the boys would be comfortable.

As everyone warmed up to each other, John and Selena decided to move in together. They kept to their word of no sex, though they spent many nights curled together as they had their first night together.

Outside of family time and work obligations, however, the couple were never apart. They had spent the past three months getting Plants off the ground. With John's connections and expertise and Selena's passion and skill, they started gaining ground quickly now that she had the funding she had been missing.

They found fast allies among the plant-based vendors of the city. They initially shared space with a vegan restaurant that John had helped get off the ground, storing their food together and using part of their kitchen area to start preparing meals. During down times, the kitchen staff often volunteered to help with the meals as well, fully behind Selena's mission. As more donations and partnerships poured in, John invested in a commercial building with an attached parking lot and an empty lot.

He paid good money to have solar panels installed over the roof of the car lot and the building. They updated the warehouse-style building to meet the code for food storage and food preparation, and John worked some of his connections to get good deals on energy-efficient appliances. His printing colleague had been more than happy to partner, only charging them cost for the staff shirts and cutting them a deal on promotional merchandise.

While they used the upper levels for food storage and prep, they opened the floor level to the community. With how quickly they were growing, they were able to open a food pantry and full-service kitchen. They also offered vegan cooking classes with a sliding payment scale. They had an initial charge, but people could apply for discount or scholarship. Some of their partners and students were so pleased with the courses that they offered 'scholarships' where they paid admission for a set amount of people and then let Plants choose who received the scholarships.

The empty lot beside the warehouse became the first of many urban gardens. Community leaders came together to help organize neighborhood gardeners, even working with nearby social workers to offer community service hours for juveniles and non-violent offenders. Once that idea took off, Selena also hired an employee to network with the local schools to go over vegan programs for their lunchrooms as well as educate teachers about their health-based curriculum for stretching and movement, as well as healthy cooking and eating. Soon they had grants for after-school programs to help kids in the community learn healthy habits.

Once word of their mission spread, they had an abundance of volunteers. John hired someone to update their website with all of their programs and classes, and he brought them on full time to manage their social media presence.

Even with all the admin work, John and Selena worked hands-on in the kitchen and with deliveries. They often ran the Washington Square Park deliveries. Being on the ground, working with people, seeing the light in their eyes when presented with a warm meal, filled their hearts with joy and drove them to continue.

Their program grew so quickly that it garnered attention from news stations desperate to share something positive for a change. While Selena wasn't comfortable on camera at first, having John with her helped calm her nerves and keep her clear-headed for interviews. Sometimes they would take the camera crews on tours of their facility or to run deliveries with them. The anchors were always so kind and enthusiastic, and occasionally they would come back outside of work to donate or pass on connections from other organizations they had covered.

Being out on the street, especially working closely with the homeless population, John and Selena kept a careful eye on any missing persons posters. They wouldn't immediately call the tipline; sometimes they found the person and sat them down for a conversation first. But they helped get several kids home, and they went even further to offer resources to their parents to help with anything they were struggling with. Many of the kids they helped would turn around and come volunteer for their program.

Keeping their eyes on the posters also meant they were inundated with advertisements, especially for bars and clubs throughout the city. It always seemed disconcerting, going from desperate pleas to find missing loved ones to vibrant advertisements for dancing, music, and parties. Generally they ignored the advertisements, not really interested in late nights or the party scene, but three months of non-stop grind had them both feeling tired and a bit worn out.

Selena had been browsing the missing posters when one of the clubs caught her eye. "Hey, look at this one, John," she called, pulling the poster away from the board for a closer look; she had some tape on hand to help re-secure missing posters that came loose, so she knew she could just tack it back up. The poster in her hand was full of vibrant colors splashed across a dark background, advertising a 'limited time only' club called The Unicorn. It appeared to only be in the city for a few weeks, hosting weekly Halloween parties through October. Unlike most clubs and parties, it didn't just list DJs or beer brands. Instead, it talked about live performances, international foods and drinks, games, and a costume contest. The entire party was going to be hosted under black light, and the dress code specified that it was a masquerade. Under admissions, the price list even offered an alcohol-free option, though you still had to be of legal drinking age to enter. John frowned at the poster.

"I wonder what kind of live performances. The way it's phrased seems like it's more than music," he mused, taking the poster to look over himself. He spied some small text on the bottom. "Hey, look. They're partnered with a costume company; if you shop at their store, you get a discount."

"It's not that expensive," Selena added. "Especially with the non-alcoholic option. If we don't like it, we could always leave. There's two dates left, why not go for the party on Halloween proper?"

John rubbed his chin. He had to admit, part of him was curious how The Unicorn planned to stand out. "Let's think on it." He pulled out his cell and took a picture of the poster. "For now, we have some deliveries to run."

***

Despite John's initial hesitation, neither he nor Selena could get the idea of the Halloween party out of their mind. After some discussion and then arranging workers to cover a few days of their shifts at Plants, they set a day to head to the costume shop and pre-registered for the party online.

They found the costume shop partnered with the club, and headed in with a code they had been sent after registering. In order to avoid any crowds, they chose to go in the middle of a workday.

Like the club, signs in the costume shop advertised that it was only there for the Halloween season that year. John recognized the address as one of the commercial buildings that had been empty since the pandemic lockdowns. He had loved the little vegan boutique that used to fill the space, but they hadn't survived the shut down and he hadn't known in time to offer them help. Too many people had suffered, and he had been unable to learn about them in time. He hoped to make up for what he viewed as his failure during such hard times, even though a small voice reminded him that he wasn't God— he had no way to know all things at all times.

True to their predictions, the shop was empty aside from a couple of workers dressed in costumes. There were advertisements for The Unicorn posted throughout the shop, and rows upon rows of costumes, accessories, wigs, and masks of all kinds. There were even some Halloween decorations and props for sale.

Both workers called a cheery 'hello' as they walked in. The one dressed as a zombie nun stayed at her task of straightening costumes on their hangers and fixing up displays, while the other young woman dressed as an anime schoolgirl came sashaying up to the front. "Welcome to Luci's Closet! Can I help you guys find anything?"

John and Selena exchanged glances, but Selena spoke up. "Well...Let's just say we're costume newbies. We're planning to go to the last Unicorn masquerade party, but we have no idea what to wear. We do want to make sure the costumes are vegan, though?"

"Oh, absolutely. Only the best for our clients. There are some textiles that aren't plant-based, but the hairs and furs are sheared from animals who live peacefully with their caretakers. Corporate has a partnership with some agricultural-based villages in places like Africa and somewhat isolated rural communities through North and South America. They're very strict to ensure the animals are well-cared for, but it's a way to help fund the communities out there. Also those costumes are well-marked, so if you're the type of vegan to avoid all animal-related products, you're all set."

John pulled a skeptical expression, but the dark lighting in the shop made it hard to see. He had seen too many examples of companies that claimed one thing and put on a good show only to be found out for their cruelty later. "No animal-products at all, please."

"You should also know that every costume in here is unique. They sometimes share a theme or subject, but no two are exactly alike. We have some of the softest, most magical fabrics. I can't tell you exactly what's in them, as it's a trade secret, but you can see the certifications stamped on their tags. We have QR codes to look up the companies that inspect our textiles, but they are under strict NDAs." She looked them both up and down. "You two are in amazing shape. How comfortable are you with a little skin?"

"Not very," John interjected. "Some is fine, but I'm not interested in looking like we're heading to a porn shoot."

The worker's smile broadened. "Man, the boss is gonna love you two. Delicious and modest."

"What do you mean?" Selena asked, but the worker was already moving further in and motioning them to follow her.

"Sometimes it's more like the costume chooses the wearer," the worker was explaining. "You might be surprised what catches your eye. Come on."

They spent the next several hours perusing costumes and chatting with the worker, Georgina, for ideas. They decided to do a couple's costume, so that narrowed down some of their choices. They were allowed to try on the costumes, though they needed to keep their clothes on underneath for sanitary reasons.

Selena seemed to be having fun, laughing and joking with Georgina as they looked at different costumes, but John mostly hung back and tried on what she asked. Some of the costumes were a bit more revealing than he would have liked, but Selena really seemed to enjoy how they looked on him— and he had to admit, she looked amazing in the matching outfit. A part of him wanted to show her off, make the others in the club jealous. But he was also worried about temptation. They had been following their promise to save themselves, and he didn't want to misstep. Finally he asked Georgina to let them talk for a couple of minutes, sharing his concerns with Selena.

"Oh, John, I'm sorry. I'm not trying to make you

uncomfortable! But it's just for the party, isn't it? And we can save the costumes back to have more fun when we're actually married. I know you won't let anyone make me uncomfortable or get too handsy. But you really are so stunning, I want to enjoy my handsome, healthy man."

After a little more talking, John felt more comfortable. Since he and Selena were on the same page, he started trying on a few of the more revealing outfits. Soon, the pair stood in front of the mirror, and Georgina was clapping in the background.

"That one is perfect," she proclaimed. "They fit amazingly, and you really have the forms to pull it off."

"I have to admit, it feels amazing," John confessed. "I think we have our winners." They spent a few more minutes finding masks that matched, and then they moved to pay.

"How much do we owe you, Georgina?"

"For both costumes, the mask, the body paint, and the face paint, you're looking at a thousand."

Selena visibly hesitated. "Oh, I wasn't paying attention. That's an awful lot, John."

"It's alright. It's our first night out in a while; I've got it," John assured her, kissing her temple before counting out the cash. He also pulled out an extra fifty for Georgina. "That's for you. Thanks for letting us take up so much of your time."

"Of course. You guys have a blast at the party! They get

crazy fun. I might attend this one myself, since the shop will be closing early." Georgina packed the costumes carefully and then slid them into a tote with the company's name scrawled across. "Just so you know, some people decide to go by different names at these parties. Some like to be called by their costumes, whereas others just want a chance to cut loose. So think about if you want to use you're real names while you're there." She slid a few papers into the bag. "There's a coupon card in there that will prove you bought your costumes here. Some of the workers will be able to tell, but others might not, so be sure to keep it on you for your discounts. And please, come back and see us next season! We might not be at the same address, but I'm sure you'll find us." She waved as they left, smiling brightly.

Man, the boss would eat those two right up. They would have so much fun.

Chapter 23

John's apprehensions slowly melted away the closer it came to Halloween. By the time the day arrived, he was just as excited for the party as Selena. Since it was their first night out to just relax, John surprised Selena with a hotel reservation. He treated her to a couple's package at the hotel's spa and salon so they could feel their absolute best when they put on their costumes that night.

"Oh my gosh, John, the fabric feels even more amazing than I imagined!" He heard her exclaim from the bathroom when they were getting changed that evening.

"You're not wrong. It's incredibly comfortable." He stood in front of the room's floor-length mirror, turning side to side. "Do you need help with the body paint?"

"A little. Let me finish up in here with the face."

When Selena joined him, she almost looked more like a floral goddess than Eve. Close knit fabric vines wrapped around her in the shape of shorts and a crop-top with a plunging neckline. The vines continued, looping down her legs in looser and looser spirals to show off her calla-lily legs. They traced up her sides while leaving her midsection bare, then wrapped up and over her right shoulder. The vines were decorated with leaves and flowers, and she had painted a few more leaves and flowers along her bare shoulder and face. She had dusted her entire skin with a soft golden powder that wouldn't rub off. Her mask also looked like vines twirling around the top half of her face.

John's Adam costume was made from the same vines. They wrapped around his legs in full but left his torso bare. Vine bracelets and a necklace of flowers completed the look. He didn't paint on any flowers, but he did let Selena dust him in some of the gold. He took the paints and carefully finished some of the flowers on her shoulder blade.

"You look absolutely fantastic," he confessed. They had purchased dark green shoes that would blend well with the ensemble while protecting their feet from any missteps among the crowd.

"You look even better," she teased, turning to kiss his cheek. "I'm really looking forward to tonight. We haven't had a chance to just have fun and enjoy each other in a while."

"If you decide the club is too much, just let me know. I won't mind, even with the costumes. We can find something else to do tonight, ok?"

"Of course, hun. And you're sure you're ok going by Adam and Eve?"

"I think I'd be embarrassed if someone recognized us," he admitted with a laugh. "I'm fine using the costume names. We can always 'come clean' if we make any friends while we're out."

Since they weren't sure what would be served to eat, they ordered in for dinner and lounged on the bed to watch the news. It was all rather dreary, so they slid through the channels until they landed on a show they both liked. They weren't worried about arriving at The Unicorn right when the party opened, as it lasted into the next morning. Once they had eaten and checked over their costumes, they slipped into some loose sweatpants and jackets and called a ride share.

* * *

They could feel the music as they waited in line outside. The deep bass thrummed through their feet and up into their bones. Signs were plastered along the walls, listing different rules or reminders like 'costume does not equal consent' and 'consent necessary.' John frowned at a couple of the signs. Was there that much trouble on their dance floor, or did they post all the signs to ensure there wasn't? There were signs about what wristband colors meant, and rules about not leaving the premises with drinks. He was surprised to see a few signs offering hotel rooms within the building. There were also signs with instructions to check tickets for code words guests could give staff if they felt unsafe. The code word was different on every ticket, so harassers wouldn't know the word was given until they were removed from the victim.

It all sounded surprisingly well thought-out for a pop-up club. Then again, Georgina had mentioned that Luci's Closet was seasonal but always came back in a different place. Perhaps this was something similar.

The lines led into three large sets of double doors, with bouncers at each entrance to scan tickets and hand out wristbands. Since John had paid for non-alcohol tickets, they both were given green wristbands.

"Lucky you. Wristbands don't always match costumes," the bouncer had joked. "That might score you some extra points in the contest." He wrote their chosen names on the wristband in sharpie. "There's a little basket just inside with a program," he explained. "It includes a little map of all the rooms in the building and different event times. Most of the staff are in costume except security, and we're all wearing silver wristbands like this." He showed his own as an example. "If you need anything, just look for the silver."

"Thank you!"

Selena reached over and grabbed a program as they walked inside. By now, the music was vibrating through their bones and into their souls. The rooms inside were dark, blacklights raining down to pop out every color. They stopped just inside to step into the bathrooms and slide out of their cover-ups. The venue had lockers in the bathroom, so they stashed the extra clothing for now and then met back outside. Selena had to stand on tiptoe and yell for John to hear her over the crowd. "There are little lights on the tables by the bar. Let's get some waters and take a look at the events?"

"Sounds good," he hollered back, twining his hand with hers and weaving through the crowd.

The place was absolutely packed. Costumes of all sizes and colors surrounded them, hundreds of faces hidden behind masks. The first room had a bar with several tables to one side, and an absolutely massive dance floor to the other. John hesitated when he noticed poles on stages and a couple of cages with dancers inside, but he shook off the pang of concern and moved for the bar. The counter was incredibly long, but there was also a policy not to crowd so people could get in their orders and receive their drinks. John suspected it was also so the bartenders could ensure nothing got slipped in a drink once it hit the counter.

There were several bartenders along the counter, but the one who caught their attention and waved them over was a drag queen in a flattering red sequin gown. She was on the huskier side, but the gown was tailored to flatter her broader figure. She wore a fiery red wig with two red horns rising out of it. Her face was covered by a blood-red mask carved like gaunt, monstrous flesh, with only her eyes and mouth visible. A six-inch spike jutted out from either side, and two more spikes curled down to frame her jawline. It was almost a travesty that employees couldn't enter the costume contest— she would have easily won. She knew how to walk in heels, too.

"Your costume looks absolutely amazing!" Selena gushed as they walked over. "I've never seen such a realistic mask!"

"Thank you!" The bartender beamed. "You two aren't too shabby, yourselves. I love that version of our Adam and Eve set, and it suits you perfectly."

"You must be the 'boss' Georgina mentioned."

"One and the same. Luci's Closet is part of the family business. What can I get you to drink?"

"Do you have alkaline waters?" John saw her gaze drop to check their wristbands, and she smiled.

"I sure do. One sec." She stepped away and scurried over to a special fridge. They could see a few of the glass-front appliances dotting down the bar. Soon she was back with their waters. "Do you want glasses?"

"The bottles are fine, thanks." John pulled out his wallet and slid some cash into the tip jar.

"Thanks, doll. Enjoy!" She handed over the bottles and moved to greet another customer. John walked with Selena over to a free table, where she set down the program to open her bottle. They could hear some rather embarrassing sounds coming from a nearby booth.

"Still good?" John asked, twisting open his bottle as well.

"There's a few more..." Selena gestured around the room. "Public displays than I expected. But it seems like they're keeping to themselves."

"Remember, just say the word. We'll be careful and stay aware of our surroundings."

"I know. I love you."

He held his bottle out. "To our lives together. To our love."

"To a fun night out. To staying true," Selena added. They

clinked the bottle tops together and then downed the drinks like they had been stranded in a desert. She glanced down at the program, but even with the table's light, she was having trouble reading it. "Let's just wing it tonight." She handed the brochure to John, and he slid it in his waistband.

"Perhaps some dancing, then we can explore the different rooms and look for the games?"

"That sounds great."

Selena twined her hand with his again, and they moved for the dance floor. Despite the large crowd, bodies weren't pressed together unless they wanted to be. Everyone was respectful of everyone else's space. Still, some of the couples and larger groups around them were right up in each other's space and putting on a bit of a show. John guided Selena away from such displays so they could enjoy their dance without the distraction.

The deep vibrations of the music and the strobing lights felt like they became a part of them as they started to dance. Selena felt amazingly light, almost like she was floating. She slid her hands up John's chest and around his neck as they gyrated with the beat. John couldn't deny the heat rising in his chest with the feel of her moving against him. He felt a little lightheaded from the music, but he kept his wits about him. He didn't become a complete bump on a log, still moving with Selena and enjoying the feel of her. He was a bit too aware of some of the other dancers watching them, but so far it seemed ok. He started to become less aware of the erotic displays peppered through the dance floor, the movements blending with the dancers. As the beat pulsed through them and Selena's movements drew him in, they started to lose themselves in the music. He wasn't sure how long they danced or when he started kissing her, but suddenly he felt hot and crowded.

"I think I need another drink," he finally hollered down, and he found her panting. She nodded, and he helped her leave the floor and move back to the bar. When had they started kissing so passionately? And why hadn't he noticed others in the crowd watching them?

"That was amazing," Selena gasped as they escaped the crowd. "But I feel so dehydrated."

"We'll need to pay more attention to our bodies," John agreed. "It's pretty warm in here with all the lights, and there were a lot of bodies out there." Surprisingly, the same bartender was available when they returned.

"Whoo, look at you two. Worn out already?"

"A bit more than we expected. Your waters were delicious, though; could we get two more."

"Coming right up." As she returned and handed over the bottles, she added, "Everyone loves our water. They say it's the most invigorating drink we have, even compared to the alcohol!"

"We could use some extra invigorating," Selena laughed as John opened their bottles.

"Is this your first time at a swinger party?"

"At a what?"

She gestured around them. "One of these parties. Though the answer is pretty obvious now." She grinned widely at Selena. "You really are in for a treat."

She glanced at their wristbands before holding up her own silver one. 'Angela' was scrawled in fading sharpie. Then she gestured them over to the bar, and held out her hand for John's program. She spread it open, unfolding the map inside. "At midnight we have a drag show, it's my favorite event. That will be in here." She pointed as she spoke. "Then we have a light bondage show here, which starts in about half an hour."

"Did you say bondage?" John asked.

"Easy, Adam. You don't have to watch if that's not your kink." She winked at him, then slid her finger to the next space. "There's a little mini-casino in here if you want to try your hands at some cards or roulette. The theme rooms are through this hall; you can close them off for privacy or open them up to give others a show."

John was drinking his water. This...was not what he expected. But Selena was listening to Angela with interest still. Perhaps it wasn't too much, so long as they avoided a few things. Angela went down the list of events, and the later they ran the more lustful they sounded.

"Well, I doubt we'll still be here by then," John noted with a laugh. "This old man will have to be in bed by then."

Angela flashed him a devilish smirk that fit her outfit

perfectly. "Oh, I'm sure you'll be in bed, but I doubt you'll have left," she joked. "You'd be surprised how time flies when you're having fun. There's something for everyone in my place. We have people from all walks of life coming here," she explained. "Surgeons, lawyers, politicians, business owners, celebrities, priests, rabbis, housewives- everyone. Think of this as an adult circus where there's no rules, no morals, and no regrets."

"I'm sure others here may enjoy that, but it's not really for us."

"That's what they all say, Adam. Until they taste the fruit for themselves."

"How long have you been working here, Angela?" Selena interjected. "You sound like this club has run for a while, but the poster was only for October."

"My family has been in this business for a long time. We never keep the clubs in one spot for long. It's better to have something be the next best thing for people to do, especially in New York City. Besides, landlords are much more generous when they negotiate short term leases, so we take advantage of that."

"Do you travel to different spots?" Selena asked.

"Oh yeah, we have pop ups all over the world throughout the year. We'll have another NYC location for December, and our biggest parties will be Christmas Eve and New Year's. Running the clubs this way has been incredibly lucrative." Angela grinned mischievously. "There are no days off for sin, so a business like mine will always win. It's like Disney World for adults, where the attractions are your wildest kinks. There are no kids here, no annoying spouse, no problems or responsibilities, just never-ending fun and games. You could never be bored at my spot because we have something for every desire. That's why everyone would rather be here than home."

"I like earning money the wholesome way, where I can sleep well at night knowing I'm doing something right," replied John.

"I make money any way I can," Angela shrugged. "I've found the best ways are always through people's little vices. They rarely change. I sleep great at night."

"You be you, and we will be us; I could never profit off of someone else's poor decisions," said John. "My grandad always said we should only invest in companies we believe in that help the planet, and I've done perfectly fine sticking with those principles."

Angela scoffed jokingly, shaking her head. "Well *my* grandfather always said to only invest in things you can control, which is everything. And I've come to find our family does just that. We'll leave it there, Adam."

Chapter 24

Selena tugged on John's hand and he took the hint, tilting his bottle in cheers towards Angela before escaping to a booth. He felt warm and flustered.

"It's getting pretty hot in here," he confessed. "And a bit humid. Are you holding up ok?"

"I'm not wearing much, but it's hot in here cause it's so crowded. There are way too many people here. It's a good thing I'm not claustrophobic."

John grimaced as he downed his water. "I'm not so sure about this place anymore, babe. I think we stumbled into something we didn't understand."

"Do we need to understand it, though?" she asked back after downing the rest of her water. "We know who we are, we know where we stand. And they already have our money. It's not like we're paying extra, since we won't be getting a hotel room or anything." She startled slightly when one of the other bartenders walked over and placed down a platter of succulent fruits.

"You two are looking a bit pale," he explained. "Make sure you keep your blood sugar up, ok? It's easy to lose track of the last time you ate."

"Thanks, man. Here, for looking out for us." John pulled out a few extra dollars and passed them over.

"Anytime, mate. You let us know if you need anything. And there's a first aid room next to that emergency exit sign." He pointed to one of the back corners. "If you start to feel lightheaded, you can always lay down in there."

As he walked away, Selena was already biting into a strawberry. "Oh, my God, Jo--er, Adam, these taste amazing!"

"They look amazing," he confessed, picking up a few grapes.

"Maybe we shouldn't judge this place on one bartender."

"One *owner*."

"One person," she corrected. "The other staff here seem pretty kind, and it's not like the kinkier guests are forcing everyone else to participate."

"She called this a swinger party. I could swear I've heard that term before." John reached for his water, surprised to find the bottle empty. He noticed Selena's was as well, so he lifted the bottle and caught one of the staff's attention. Before long, they carried over two more. "Thanks." He handed a water over to Selena. "This really is good water, though. And the fruit is divine."

"When Angela was pointing out the different rooms, I noticed there's another room for food and drinks. They probably have actual meals in there."

John nodded. He was starting to feel calmer, more relaxed now that they had sat down to eat something. "Alright. We can check out a few more things and see how we're feeling."

They polished off the fruits and returned the platter to the counter. They tossed their empty bottles into a nearby bin marked for recycling and kept the others on them. John offered Selena his arm, and they strolled from the main room to explore the rest of the building.

They found the casino first. The games really did look like a lot of fun, and a heavy pumpkin scent hung in the air. All of the tables had large bowls of candies with clear markings indicating which bowls were allergen friendly and which bowls had vegan treats. John pulled out a wad of cash for them both, their hard limit for any gambling, before they walked inside. Soon they were laughing and enjoying themselves again, the dark conversation with Angela forgotten.

They had a surprising amount of luck at the tables, which inspired them to play more. A crowd gathered to watch, people eager to see gambling pay off so they could bolster their own confidence to play longer. A few of the watchers looked the pair up and down, but no one pressed their luck beyond simple flirting since neither Adam nor Eve reciprocated.

When their luck at cards started to dwindle, they took a break for some roulette. John let Selena pick their bet, and they won big. He pulled her close, kissing her deeply in celebration. She slid her arms up and around his neck to reciprocate, temporarily forgetting the crowd despite a stream of whoops and whistles directed their way. When John became aware of the sounds, he pulled away with a deep blush. He gathered their winnings, grabbed Selena's hand, and quickly stepped from the room.

"Sorry. I don't know what came over me."

"Don't be. It was just a kiss. A really good kiss."

They wandered further and found another room with games, these ones more like what you might find at a Halloween carnival: bobbing for apples, tossing balls into jars, and the like. They laughed and played, feeling like kids again. They held hands as they moved between the attractions, held each other as they waited their turn, and enjoyed the sights and sounds. The room smelled like candy, filling their minds with sweetness.

They were surprised when an intercom came on to announce that seating for the drag show had started.

"Is it really midnight?" Selena asked in surprise.

"I guess we have been having fun."

Rather than go watch the show, they moved for the eatery Selena had seen on the map. True to Selena's prediction, the menu was full of meals and platters. There were tables and booths scattered around, and the wait staff was full service; no standing at a counter and shouting to order. It was cozy and quiet compared to the rest of the club, so John found them a booth.

They curled up with each other as they ate and laughed. Selena reached up to feed John a piece of her meal, and he hummed as she slid her finger along his lips as she pulled her hand free. She looked absolutely stunning in the lights, the gold causing her to glow even without the blacklights. He noticed the vines accentuated her shape well, sliding his fingers down her bicep. She lifted her large, chestnut eyes to meet his gaze.

"Adam. Kiss me?"

He obliged, closing what little distance was between them. He felt like a man starved, hungry for the delicious morsel beside him. He craved her so strongly that it started to scare him, but the concern melted away as she moaned in his arms. Her hands slid along his sides, and their tongues danced. He never wanted the moment to end. He wanted to feel her, touch her, everywhere. Yet as her hands dipped to his legs, he pulled away, clearing his throat.

"M-maybe we should go watch a show."

Selena's lower lip puckered slightly. "We could find somewhere more private. It's just kissing, but I know you don't like being watched."

"Just kissing," he murmured, sliding his gaze across the room to keep from hungrily staring at her. He was feeling warm again, the heavy scents of the room making him a little lightheaded. "I don't know, Eve. I'm...I'm starting to struggle. I haven't felt this tempted since we started dating. It's like there's something in the air. Or the water."

"Or we're just finally not distracted with work, so it's harder to ignore. The waters were sealed, hun. This is just us." She took his hands in hers, lifting them to kiss his palms. "I know...We weren't going to have sex. But what if we help each other relieve some tensions in other ways? We could make out, maybe I could give you a blowjob?"

"Maybe we should leave."

"Are we going to feel any different somewhere else?"

"I don't know." John shook his head. Three times now, he had started to slip in his restraint, twice among a crowd. Was he really just being paranoid? Was he overthinking things? Just because they didn't want to have sex, didn't mean they couldn't do other things. They had made out plenty of times, after all, just nowhere quite so public.

"Is there anything I can do to help you relax? Do you want to upgrade our tickets and have a Halloween shot?"

"You know I don't drink."

"Yeah, but it's a special occasion. And you seem like you're having a hard time letting yourself have fun." Selena slid up next to him, rubbing her hand along his back. "You work so hard, Adam. I want you to enjoy this place as much as I am. I want us to be able to enjoy our time together."

John sighed. "You're right. I'm sorry. I don't mean to drag our fun down. It's not you, or this place. It's me. I'm not controlling myself. I'm torn between wanting to keep our vow and wanting to let loose. I love you. I want to show you how much I love you. But I told you from the beginning

I wasn't after a warm body. I don't want you to think that's changed. I love the person you are; I don't want our relationship to become about sex."

Selena listened to him calmly. She slid a hand up to caress his face. "And I appreciated that assurance. I know you were real. We love each other as who we are. Maybe it's time we revisit that discussion. You and I both know we're soul bound. We've met each other's families, we've built a successful organization. We're doing good things. So maybe it's time we accept that we're a pair, and quit denying our full desires."

It made sense, really. The only reason John had yet to propose was because they didn't want to steal the spotlight from her brother and his fiancée. And the more she put the thoughts into words, the more John realized he had started feeling the same way for a while now. He slid a hand up to her chin and pulled her into a kiss. The heavy scent of the room faded as he allowed himself to truly taste her. She hummed as she returned the gesture, licking his lips. He slid his tongue to meet hers, and they danced.

"Alright. Let's explore one of the theme rooms."

Selena's expression split into a wide smile. She slid from the booth and backed away, holding both her hands towards him. He followed, reaching out to take one, and she spun and led him giddily down the hall.

***

They followed the map in the program to another large room. This space had been split into several smaller rooms.

Each little room had a door leading in and a large window with a curtain. The walls were pure black with vibrantly painted figures posing along them. Orange Amazonian women with large breasts and no clothing. Green reptilian aliens with large cocks on display. Humans of different idealistic shapes and sizes, monsters and aliens, all decorated the walls in vibrant colors.

People wandered the hall, sliding their hands along the velvety surfaces of the wall and giggling as they explored the painted figures. Some of the rooms were occupied, various erotic acts on display, while a couple more had their curtains pulled shut and doors locked.

"Pick a room, baby, but I don't want an audience."

Selena nodded in agreement, winding through the people to find an empty room. She pulled John inside and then backed against the door to close it. She leaned against the door and seductively slid her hand up to find the little chain. John grinned as he watched her, but he also moved to pull the curtain closed. "Are you absolutely sure this is what you want?"

"You are what I want," Selena purred. "I know what you mean, though. I do feel a bit wasted, even though we haven't had anything other than water and food."

"I almost feel like I'm high," John confessed. "But you sounded clear-headed in the booth."

Selena stepped away from the door, sliding her hand up his chest. "I want you, John," she whispered, dropping the fake names for now. "I want you so badly I can barely breathe." She slid a hand down to tease his cock through his costume. "I want this inside me," she whispered, rising up on her tiptoes to brush her lips against him. "I want to be all yours."

John closed the distance between their lips, devouring her in a kiss. He wrapped his arms around her waist and pulled her close, grinding his pelvis against hers. Selena's hands slid up and into his hair, and his own grasp slid down to cup her buttocks. He pressed against her to urge her to walk, backing her against the curtain and pressing her against the window. Their movements slid the cloth a little, but it also cast their shadows through the curtain for the watchers.

They no longer thought of windows or doors. They no longer thought about vows and chastity. They only thought of each other. They lost themselves to the movement, to the music, and to the night so thoroughly that they paid little mind when the curtain was askew. They didn't hear their costume announced across the loudspeaker. They didn't think about the curious, prying eyes or the devious, greedy bartender.

All that mattered was the pleasure.

Chapter 25

The day after Halloween, John woke to the sounds of Selena vomiting in the bathroom. He found that he had a splitting headache, as well, but he forced himself out of bed and moved to hold her hair.

"Fuck, John. I feel hungover. How is that possible?"

"I don't know," he confessed, rubbing at his eyes. "I feel pretty rotten myself. Probably all the strobing lights or something." He folded his arms, leaning against the bathroom counter while she washed her face. "Are you still...ok with what happened?"

Selena gave him a tired smile. "I don't regret sleeping with you, if that's what you mean. I think I just went a little overboard with the smells and the sounds and didn't eat enough food."

"Why don't you join me for a shower, and we'll order in for breakfast? We have another night here, so we don't need to worry about checking out today."

"That sound fantastic. Maybe we can get to know each other a little more once we're feeling better." Her big, beautiful lips curled up in a smile, and John couldn't help returning it.

After the night at the club, John and Selena had no qualms about sleeping with each other. They spoke at length about what they had enjoyed from that night, and they even started looking up new techniques for the bedroom. It was a couple of weeks before John remembered to look up the term 'swingers' in a slang dictionary. He found the information equal parts fascinating and disturbing. He did set a boundary with Selena— he was happy to sleep with her, and only her. And he was happy for her to sleep with him, and only him. He wasn't interested in an open relationship or swinging, even if they did start looking into more sex clubs.

Even so, it was like a lock had been released. They felt free to explore each other and be intimate more often. They started watching porn together and investigating things like bondage. They started taking more time away from Plants to go to new clubs and play with new toys. John stopped waking up at 4:44 in the mornings. He was attending his jiu-jitsu class, but he wasn't making it to the gym the rest of the week.

One morning after yet another foray into a new club, Selena found John sitting at the breakfast table, staring out over the street. He hadn't touched his food.

"Hey, handsome," she greeted, bending to kiss his cheek. She frowned at the serious expression on his face. "John?"

John sighed, gesturing to the other chair. "Selena…We need to talk."

"What's wrong, baby? Was I too rough last night?"

"No, that's not it at all." He frowned, trying to gather his thoughts. "I'm worried that we're going too far," he confessed after a few moments of silence. "I feel like we've never been closer physically, but emotionally we're falling apart. We haven't been connecting, but we've also been letting other things slip."

"What do you mean?"

"I haven't worked on my book in a month. We've turned down three interviews with bloggers interested in Plants to go to more clubs, have more sex. It just...It feels like we've opened Pandora's box, and I'm struggling to return the lid."

Selena reached across and touched his arm. "It's probably just the pendulum effect, babe. We held back for so long, now that we're finally free, we've swung all the way over. We just need to find our balance."

"And how should we do that?" John looked up to meet her gaze. "Selena...When's the last time we prayed together?"

She hesitated, blushing when she realized she didn't know the answer. She sighed, leaning back in her chair. "I suppose now isn't a good time to tell you that I found these at last night's club." She tossed the postcard she had been carrying in her other hand onto the table. It was for The Unicorn, listing a new address and December dates. "It's the big Christmas Eve party."

John hesitated. A part of him didn't want to go at all, but he could already see the disappointment building behind

Selena's gaze. He didn't want to become a controlling partner; he didn't want to disappoint the love of his life. And yet he didn't want to go. He reached for the postcard and picked it up. They were going with a winter theme now, which made sense. And they were advertising an indoor ice skating rink, hot cocoa flights, and more. It could be fun, if they could stick to their boundaries.

Selena could see the gears turning in his mind. As soon as he picked up the card, she knew he was tempted.

"I won't say 'no,'" he finally agreed, setting the postcard down. "But if we start to feel drunk after only drinking water, we're going home." She nodded. "And I think I want to set a few more boundaries. But most importantly, I want to scale back. Try to get into our routine again."

"I can agree to that. And if we go, and we don't have fun anymore, we'll leave."

***

As Christmas Eve drew closer, John was feeling more comfortable about their decisions. They had fallen into a routine of working in the warehouse three times a week and only going to one club each weekend. Selena had been incredibly understanding of his new boundaries, and she was working to help him wake up in the mornings again for his runs. They had started paying attention to missing posters again, but John had almost felt his heart stop when he saw a face he recognized. He reached for the poster of Ethan Bísólá and let out a slow breath.

"John?"

"This boy. I know him," he explained. Selena walked over and wrapped her arms around his shoulders. "He and Levi went to the same middle school. This should have been his last grade before moving to high school."

"That's a pretty hefty reward."

"His parents work at the embassy," John remarked absently. Did Levi know Ethan was missing? Another horrifying thought struck him, and he lifted his gaze to meet Selena's. "I might need to go talk to the police."

"What? Why?" Her gaze grew concerned.

"Last year...Last year, when Levi was in grade 8. He caught one of his teachers..." John cleared his throat. "*Eying* him. Checking him out."

"Oh, my God. Did you report him?"

"I tried. I went straight into the office and raised hell. But the asshole just stared at me and let me yell at him, and the dean said they couldn't really do anything without proof. We argued for a bit, and he agreed to move Levi out of the guy's class, but...it never sat right with me. After talking to Susan, I let my boys finish the year and then I pulled Luke out to a new school while Levi graduated to high school. And now a boy from their old school is missing?"

Selena nodded solemnly. "I understand. But you should probably talk to Levi first. I know he's a minor, but the police might want to talk to him about the incident."

John agreed. "I'm also worried if he's seen the posters. I'd rather he hear from me."

"Why don't you call Susan while we're in the truck and see if you can pick him up from school today? Let her know what's going on, too."

"What about you?"

"I can stay at the warehouse a little later than usual and then catch a ride back to the house. I'll be fine."

John kissed her cheek. "Thanks, love."

***

By the time John reached out the police station, he wasn't surprised to hear that the detective in charge of the case had been planning to call him. But his schedule was pretty tight with the search operations taking place and the upcoming holiday. John arranged to meet with him a few days after Christmas, and the detective asked him to bring Levi, as well.

After he had spoken with Susan, she had called Levi's school and spoken with the guidance counselor in case he needed a little extra support the next few days because his friend was missing.

John tried not to let the concern gnaw at him. Selena started helping distract him by planning their night at The Unicorn's Christmas Eve party. She convinced him to go shopping so he could watch her try on some beautiful dresses, and she helped him pick out a wintry tux to match. They ordered matching custom Venetian Colombina masks, and Selena chose a pair of opera gloves to match her gown. Once more, John made arrangements for them to stay at a fancy hotel and get dolled up before the party. They were dressed to impress, so John sprung for a white limo to add to the experience.

As they pulled up to the venue, all eyes were on them. One of the valets opened the door, and John stepped out first before turning to help Selena. They started for the main line, but were instead ushered to a much shorter, VIP line since they had made such a grand entrance. The wristbands were winter themed tonight, with staff wearing blue against their white outfits. John and Selena were presented with silver wristbands, on which they wrote 'Adam' and 'Eve' once more.

Inside was a winter wonderland. Beautiful crystal lights and dancing colors filled the air. Tables had full decor, including floor-length tablecloths and candelabras. The flames were LEDs, since open flames weren't permitted. The music was orchestral this time around, with several pairs of dancers currently waltzing through the room. A portion of the dance floor was cordoned off for a course on Regency dancing.

John smiled at Selena, offering her his arm. "This is much more my style," he confessed, and she smiled as she looped her arm with his. The room even smelled like Christmas, and there were multiple lavish trees decorated throughout. As they approached the bar area, Selena squeezed his arm. "Angela's working tonight," she alerted him. Tonight her costume was befitting an ice queen, with a lavish blonde wig and a full Volto mask. She lifted a hand in greeting as they approached.

"Adam! Eve! It's good to see you again!"

John couldn't mask his surprise. "Really?"

Angela chuckled behind her mask. "No hard feelings about last time," she assured him. "Everyone can be a little uncomfortable when they first visit, but they always come back— with or without their partners."

Selena gasped. "Is that true?"

Angela nodded. "Most people here, and in our other clubs, are married outside of swinger life. They party with us at night, then celebrate with their real families in the morning. We know more about them than their spouses do. Alkaline waters again?"

"Please," Selena answered, right as John responded,

"That must be awful for their families. I could never do that to someone I love."

Angela retrieved their waters before shrugging at John. "Everyone has their little secrets, but others are open with their families about their activities. We don't judge here; we just serve what they desire." She leaned her elbows on the bar. "I know you two always get the non-alcoholic bands, but how about a couple of shots with me? On the house."

John firmly shook his head. "I appreciate the offer, but I don't drink."

"Eve?"

"I support his decision by also not drinking."

"Suit yourself." She pulled out a glass and salted the rim before preparing a tequila. She lifted the bottom of her mask just enough to down the drink before shifting it back into place. "I see you have your programs. Just so you know, the layout here is set up the same as our Halloween location, with a few bonuses. The ice rink is out back in the courtyard, but we erected barriers to keep out any prying eyes. There are skates available to rent if you don't have your own. If you decide to try the hot cocoa flights, make sure you specify that you're vegan so you get the right milk. And if the fancy music isn't your style, we have an EDM dance room a couple floors higher."

"That sounds great, thanks, Angela!"

Angela winked at Selena. "Don't be strangers tonight. I'll be working the whole party, but I won't always be behind the bar."

John lifted his bottle in cheers before guiding Selena to a small table. "Drinks and then dancing?"

"I would love to try the Regency dances. I've read so many historical romances I think I could find ways to help you enjoy them immensely."

John laughed as he took a sip of his water, immediately feeling a rush of exhilaration. "EDM might be an experience in this get up," he joked, indicating his tux. Selena laughed.

"You look so sexy, baby. But I know what you mean. I still want to try ice skating."

"I won't promise to be any good at it."

Selena had pulled out the program to check the timing for the Regency dances, but her finger hesitated on the itinerary. "Do you want to watch any of the shows?" She glanced up at him. "I'm not sure how those fall with the new agreements."

John slid the program over to look at the list. "I don't mind if you want to watch, but I don't want to participate. You're the only one I want to touch, and I want to be the only one touching you."

They spent a few more minutes picking their poison for the night before they set about enjoying themselves. Like the Halloween party, they started with the more innocent fun. The rink attendants were trained to help guests in and out of the skates around their fancy outfits, and several staff were out on the ice to help beginners get a feel for the movement. Since John and Selena were already athletes with impeccable balance, they started picking it up pretty quickly. It was almost freezing outside, but the movement brought them warmth for a little while. They went inside, warming up with hot cocoa flights and a light snack.

John downed his first but then stopped, staring at the cup. "Hey, we got the non-alcoholic version, right?"

"Of course, baby. I made sure. No booze, all vegan. Why?"

"I feel a bit warm."

Selena laughed. "Adam." The name came more naturally now, smooth as silk. "We've just been out in the freezing winter air, and now you're drinking hot cocoa. Why does this surprise you?"

John cracked a smile. "Ok, fair. I guess I'm feeling a little paranoid after last time." He picked up the second tasting cup and tilted it towards hers. "To good, hot drinks, and an even hotter night."

"Hear, hear." She clinked her cup to his and downed it. "These are so creamy."

"The almond milk adds a nice, nutty undertone."

"A good appetizer for other nutty things."

Once they had warmed up, it was time for one of the Regency dances to start. Selena eagerly led him into the cordoned area on the dance floor. The instructor first taught them the steps in pairs, so they got to learn the dance as a couple. Selena really had been getting some good tips from her novels. Several hidden, furtive touches left him craving her, but then they were combined with other dances. Whenever they shifted partners, he lost her touch. More to his chagrin, he sometimes received touches from the other dancers. A glance or a shake of the head generally saw them leave off, and then he was with Selena again. He decided to draw the line at one dance to avoid any more advances, though he promised to make it up to her with an actual class since she had been enjoying the dance as much as the teasing.

Chapter 26

As the hour grew later, John and Selena climbed higher. In the upper floors, the vibes and the aesthetic started to change. Bass-heavy music thumped through the rooms, and the lighting grew darker. More colors of light joined the white, and the sounds of pleasure slid from several smaller rooms around them. The fuzzy feeling from the hot cocoa had been growing in the pit of their stomachs, and now their senses were assaulted by the mixed scents of Christmastime and sex.

They curled together in dark booths, toying with their flesh as they watched others act out erotic acts on stages. They celebrated success in the casino with passionate kisses, though they pulled away when too many eyes gathered. Through it all, John was starting to feel *wrong*. But unlike the night at the Halloween party, he couldn't ignore the growing feeling of discontent. The lightheadedness and loss of inhibitions. He tried to convince himself that it was his imagination, or that he was overthinking things, but he steadily started feeling nauseated.

"Hey, baby, I think I need a break. Let's have some food, ok?"

"Of course, Adam. Come on, I'll find us a seat."

With the solid food, he started to feel refreshed.

"This place really is a lot different from the other clubs," he observed, and Selena smiled.

"Isn't it great? There's so much more to do here, and the food is amazing. I can't believe they have so many things for different diets. They really must bring in a lot of money like Angela said."

"Yeah..."

Selena's smile slipped at his tone. "Adam, what's wrong?"

He shook his head. "I'm not feeling this place, Eve. I just can't shake this sour feeling in my stomach, though the food is helping a little. And yet every time we get something to eat or drink, every time we head up a floor, I start feeling nauseated. I lose myself in you for a while, and then the spell is broken and I'm miserable again." He lifted his gaze to meet hers. "Baby, why are we here?"

"Because there's so much to see and do. Haven't you been enjoying the dances, the shows? I feel like a kid in a candy store."

"Yeah, and I feel like a pig in a slaughterhouse."

They fell silent for a moment before Selena asked, "Do you want to leave?"

"I don't know," John sighed. "I feel like a wet blanket. I don't know what's wrong with me. I'm in a ritzy club dressed to the nines with the love of my life, and I just can't seem to relax. I constantly feel like we're being watched. I haven't felt this paranoid since I quit taking drugs."

"Let's finish our meal, at least. Maybe we can move to a room and just have the rest of the night to ourselves. We can make sure the curtain stays closed this time by staying away from the walls. How does that sound?" She reached out to touch his arm, and he took her hand in thanks.

"Ok. But if I start feeling any sicker, I'm not going to be up for much."

"Then we'll just leave. But let's get more food in you, first. Maybe we just went too long without eating."

"Can you go ask for a couple more waters, too? I'm starting to feel a bit warm."

"Yeah, it doesn't help that we're higher up in the building now. I'll be right back."

When Selena returned, she curled against him in the booth but didn't try to start anything. Instead they chatted while they ate, admiring the room around them and discussing what they had been enjoying from the evening. Steadily John felt himself calm, so he went with Selena to find the themed rooms. He still felt lightheaded, but he wanted to push through for her.

They decided to start light, moving to the bed and sitting on the edge. As they wrapped their arms around each other and tasted each others lips, John was reminded of being a kid in high school, hiding under the bleachers with his girlfriend to practice kissing. But this wasn't some schoolyard fling; this was Selena. And they had spent the past several weeks learning each other's bodies intimately.

Since making out was going well, she started to let her hands roam as well, slowly stripping off his jacket and then unbuttoning his waistcoat. The music from the EDM dance floor pounded through the hall and each room, and Selena's movements started timing themselves to the beat. John slid his hands around her waist to start unzipping her gown. They started slowly at first, sensually. But as more of their skin was exposed, their nerves lit on fire, they started moving faster. Soon they were ravenous for each other. John trailed kisses along Selena's smooth flesh, and she turned him over before sliding down the length of his body to take his cock in her mouth. The more she sucked and licked, the hotter he started to feel.

"Baby, I'm getting too hot," he panted, arching his hips slightly. "I need air. Please. Let's go ahead and crack the door open."

Selena lifted herself from him, frowning down. "Are you sure, hun? You didn't want an audience."

"I know. But I can't stop right now, and I'm going to be sick if we don't do something."

"Ok." She moved to the door, cracking it slightly and then chaining it. She hesitated when she locked eyes with a gorgeous blonde-headed woman. The woman's gaze slid past her to John on the bed. She stepped up to the room, placing a hand on the door.

"Hi, beautiful," she purred to Selena. "Can we come in?"

"That's up to my partner."

"We just want to watch. You two look absolutely delicious."

Selena glanced over her shoulder at John.

"Just watch?" he confirmed.

"Yeah, baby. Just the two of them."

"I guess that's ok. I just want you back over here baby, please. I'm so hard."

Selena opened the door for the blonde and her partner to enter before closing it again.

"I'm Sara. This is David."

"You can call us Adam and Eve."

Sara's lips curled into a smile. "The first soulmates. I love it." She stepped up to Selena and pecked her cheek. "Just a quick thank you. You two are yummy."

"You're not so bad looking yourself," Selena breathed. Sara smelled like sugar cookies, the scent filling Selena's nostrils from the woman's closeness.

Selena returned to the bed, wrapping her hand along John's cock to work him back up. Sara and David settled themselves on the bed nearby, stripping and teasing each other while they watched. Sara gasped when she caught sight of John's enlarged length.

"Your cock is so big," she purred, licking her lips.

"We said we'd just watch," David reminded her. "We don't want to make them uncomfortable."

"I know. But how can you see that and not want to touch it?"

John moaned as Selena slid over him and started rubbing her moist folds over his hardened cock. Sara and David's whispers were distracting; he just wanted to be encompassed. His hands slid up and down Selena's sides, and he saw her gaze drift back to the other pair.

"Fine. Touch. But just to help me get inside her," he murmured, barely aware of what he was saying. Sara giggled as she slid over to grasp his erection. She slid her other hand along Selena's folds and slipped a finger in long enough to determine where she needed to aim, and then she helped the two come together.

"God, you two fit together so well," she hummed appreciatively. She tossed her hair over her shoulder to look at David. "Take me from behind while I toy with them. I'm already so fucking wet."

As David rode her from behind and Selena rode John, Sara toyed with the couple in her hands. She massaged John's balls and tickled Selena's clit, heightening their pleasure. The sensations were so overwhelming that all four of the people in the room didn't notice the crowd gathering to peer through the ajar door to take in the show.

John slid his hands up to Selena's shoulders, and then his right went further behind her head and into her hair. He twined his fingers through the ebony strands and pulled her down, devouring her mouth. He arched into her for an extended moment, and Sara squeezed his cock as she felt him erupting inside Selena. Selena moaned and shook as she joined John in his orgasm, and the sight and feel of their connection set Sara into one as well.

As the two couples steadily came down from their highs, there was an awkward silence as they separated. David and Sara stepped away from the bed and wiped off with one of the provided towels in the room before starting to get dressed.

"If you thought that was special, you could really have some fun if you let us do more," Sara teased. "We host a monthly swingers club. You'd fit right in." She glanced back at David. "Normally we charge, but for the pleasure of teaching you two how to enjoy multiple partners? I'd let you in for free."

John was sitting up now, wiping his face down with another towel. "No thanks. I'm not really interested in swinging," he muttered.

"You sure about that?" David laughed. "You really enjoyed Sara's intervention there. And no one knows how to enhance a guy's pleasure like another guy getting in on the action."

"I'm sure. I don't plan on swinging ever again."

"No one plans on this Adam. It just...happens. First you're in a club, enjoying your partner. Then you decide to sample the other wares together. Then you decide you like the taste and come back to the counter for more." Sara laughed. "You really want to spend the rest of your life just fucking each other? Swinging together or even just having an open relationship can be so freeing. We can do whatever we want, whenever we want. Right, boo?"

"We have kids, but being open means we can still have an active sex life. One of us can stay with the kids while the other goes out to have some fun. It's not like we never play with each other or anything. But we also have other partners. Sara even spends part of the year in Europe to be with her other beau's polycule."

"I only made it three months this year, sadly. Next year I want to spend more time overseas."

"What part of Europe?" Selena asked.

"Oh, all over. We have houses in Greece, Italy, Spain, and Amsterdam. Well," Sara shrugged a shoulder. "My daddy has the houses right now. But they'll be mine, and he lets me use them whenever I want."

"You don't go with her?" John asked David.

"Nah, not often. The kids are a bit young to be jet-setting across the globe all year, you know? We do go on a few vacations together. Honestly, it's really helped our marriage, because we don't feel trapped together all the time."

"You're really ok just...leaving your kids for months on end?" John asked Sara. She leaned back into David's hold.

"It's not like they're with a stranger. I know David is taking good care of them, so I get to live however I want. And we don't give a fuck what anyone else thinks; it works for us, and we can afford it." She looked up at her partner and raise a hand to cup his cheek. "I adore David because he's not possessive, jealous, or clingy. And he's rich. He knows I have an insatiable appetite, and so does he. We let one another be. Besides, no one person can satisfy all of your needs, which is one of the reasons this arrangement works well for our family."

"But aren't you worried one of you will fall in love with someone else?" John's brow was furrowing further, and he looked a bit pale.

"Oh, Adam, you really are new to this, aren't you?" Sara's smile widened. "Love has nothing to do with it. Sex, hell, *life* is all about pleasure. It's our innate human right to give and get as much pleasure as possible."

"Are you ever jealous?" Selena asked.

"Baby, are you ever jealous?" Sara asked with a purr.

"Only at first. I was really resistant to the idea of having multiple people in bed for sex. But there's something really arousing about watching three other guys team up on your girl. Sometimes it's other girls, sometimes it's a mix. Sometimes we're just one big room full of people having sex, and you lose track of the numbers."

"That...sounds disgusting," John groaned into his towel, leaning over his knees.

"Eve, don't let him hold you back," Sara cautioned. "After our first group session, I was covered in cum. I wound up being so sore afterwards. But it was so cleansing. Other people have their church and their religion, but I do what I want for my mind and body. If I want to let go, no one can stop me. It's my body to treat as I please."

David turned to face the couple. "When we first met, Sara said I'd have to let her do whatever she wanted so she won't get bored and look for someone else. That's why we decided having an open relationship was the best alternative for us. Now, we've had hundreds of experiences and learned lots of techniques to pleasure others and ourselves. Every party just gets better and better."

"And we don't mind pushing the limits, right baby?" Sara giggled.

"Anything goes," David said with a smug smile. "We've been doing this for six years. Life has never been better. We like to try and live it to our fullest potential."

John shook his head. He stood, throwing on his pants and shirt. Selena had pulled on her gown when he started getting dressed, so even though the back was still undone he grabbed her hand and pulled her out of the room and down the hall. He didn't stop until they had found a bathroom, locking the door behind them. He let go of her hand, quickly moving to the toilet so he could throw up. "I can't do this, baby. I can't," he gasped, kneeling over the rim. "I don't want to." Selena came up behind him, kneeling and rubbing his back.

"I can't be like…all these people. I waited so long for you, baby, and we've been doing such amazing things. I can't lose all that we have to lust." He paused to throw up again, and then Selena helped him to the sink to wash his face. "I know some people would think I'm crazy, that this could be a great life, but I'm not them, Selena. I'm me. I can't do this anymore."

Selena pulled him into a hug, cradling into his neck. "No. No, you don't need to apologize. You're right. I'm sorry. I let myself get so caught up in the pleasure that I lost sight of what brought us together. How special our relationship is. But talking to them, seeing what we might become...I can't even imagine. That doesn't work for me."

"We need to leave, baby. We need to get out of this place, and get back into ourselves."

"Ok. Let's take a few minutes to clean up in case you get sick again, and then we'll leave."

They stood together for a while, just enjoying the embrace. Finally John stepped away and got a washrag to help clean them off. He helped Selena get back into her gown, and then she helped him with the tux. As they moved downstairs, they passed by the bar and saw Angela serving drinks. She smiled widely at them.

"Heading out, you two? Have a Merry Christmas! We have another party for New Year's coming up; I can't wait to see what you wear."

John shook his head. "Thanks for the sentiment and hospitality, Angela, but we're done. We won't be coming back to The Unicorn."

She laughed. "That's what they all say, Adam. And then they keep coming back, again and again. Sometimes they'll continue coming as a couple, other times we'll just see one of the pair. Usually it's the latter." She gave Selena a knowing glance. "No one here cares about your personal vows or hesitations. Eventually we'll see you on your knees."

"If you see me on my knees, it will be in prayer. We're returning to God's work, because this isn't it," Selena declared. Angela scoffed.

"God doesn't exist. Quit trying to let some magic sky daddy run your life for you and just be yourself."

"Think as you wish, but we know better," John replied.

"One day you'll realize you're wrong," she cautioned. "Evil will never die, no matter how much you pray. You're never going to stop mega corporations from posing as churches and convincing hard working people that if they just give enough money, they'll be saved. You're never going to stop pedophiles from preying on weak kids. People will continue to murder, lie, cheat, and steal. Wars will consume us and the planet will die beneath us, but at least we can go out in a blaze of glory and pleasure. No one can stop the corruption in politics or commerce."

John met her gaze steadily from beneath his mask. He stood up straight, squared his shoulders, and answered: "We can damn well try."

She laughed. "And just what do you hope to accomplish? The wealthy control the world and whatever truth the public sees. Monetary interests are going to kill humanity, and we'll only find comfort in our pleasures and vices. The gluttonous will remain gluttonous; the adulterous, adulterous. People are just going to keep killing each other, animals, and the very world beneath their feet. So ignore the darkness and escape into the wonderland we provide."

Selena squeezed John's hand. "Nothing will ever get better if we just roll over and prepare to die. Through the grace of God, we will prevail."

With that, they both turned their backs on the laughing woman and walked away.

"You'll fail!" she called after them. "People will hate each other. Kill each other. And you'll come crawling back to what little paradises we tuck away in the shadows!"

Chapter 27

Five Days After Christmas

Maria Alvarez had never been one for excess. Sure, she might enjoy a glass of wine during the day from time to time, but she followed a balanced diet. She admittedly enjoyed her husband's wealth to dress as she pleased, but she kept her closet to a reasonable size and donated things she no longer wore.

Since that disastrous Christmas dinner, however, she had taken to drinking more during the day.

She and Abraham had mostly stopped trying to talk, which was a small blessing. But she had to smell that damn slow cooker for several more days and endure the courier service coming and going as he continued putting on a show for everyone around them. She was also trying to find a decent lawyer. She knew the pre-nup had any divorce proceedings locked up pretty tight, but she wanted to do everything in her power to save her boys from being trapped with that monster and slowly becoming like him.

There was more than just the looming divorce weighing heavily in the air between them, but she couldn't figure out what. That dark feeling in the pit of her stomach was back. The more time passed, the more she was certain that seeing Ethan Bísólá hadn't been just her imagination—

though whether it was a revelation of past events or a premonition of her own danger, she wasn't sure. She kept looking up to find Abraham glaring at her or overheard him muttering to himself again. She knew where he hid at least some of his drugs, and the supply was dwindling faster. And then there were things she had called him out on or been caught off guard by the past few weeks. The odd cleaning spree. The misplaced dishes.

She did try and take steps to protect herself. She started leaving the home security cameras on. She let a few friends and Carlos know this fact so that if something happened to her and the cameras were off, eyes would turn to Abraham. She also had Esmeralda come over to help with the boys; not because she had a lot of appointments or errands to run, but so there was another adult in the house. Besides, she could use the help packing since she was preparing to move out.

Her mother Mary had pulled in a few favors and found a nice little brownstone in the city. It was a rental, and she would keep the lease up until the divorce was finalized and Maria knew where she could live with the boys. Mary was keeping her home in Rhode Island, but she would be at least temporarily moving to NYC to be with Maria and the kids.

So it was that Maria had started sorting through her belongings, working to downsize before her move. Esmeralda had first dibs on anything she decided not to keep, and then the rest would be donated to a local thrift store. She had discovered a wonderful little charity called Plant Love and Nourish the Soul that had connections to vegan-based charities and thrift stores, so she hoped to work with them to find new homes for all of her vegan clothing and accessories.

Maria had already cleaned out her area of the main closet upstairs. Now all she had were the coats and jackets in the closet by the door. She waited until Abraham left the house to be with the guys so that she wouldn't have to deal with his pointed looks or accusatory stares when she was near his items as well. She was very purposefully not touching his things so that he couldn't accuse her of anything, but that didn't stop him from glaring at her as if she was pulling out his things and throwing them away.

With how often they had been coming and going from the house lately, they had primarily been using the same coats and gloves, with the other hangars shoved to the side. And after Christmas, they had been compressed even further to make room for their guests' coats as well. Maria left the coat she had been wearing almost daily, and Abraham had taken his. She didn't bother the boy's current coats. But there was a collection of older jackets and coats that had simply been taking up space.

She broke her habit to pull out some of the boys' old things. They were too small, so there was no reason to keep them in the closet. Jesús's jackets went into the box to donate, while James's went into another box for storage in case Jesús wore them as he grew. She found a couple of Esmeralda's coats from days when she would send the girl home with something and she would forget the coat she had worn into work that day. And then...There was another coat. Maria frowned at the puffy material, pulling it further out. It was far too small for her or Esmeralda, but far too large for James. She checked the brand and plugged it into the internet. It was a popular clothing brand for youth-sized clothing.

"...Esme, I need to run an errand," Maria called, keeping her voice calm. "Can you take the boys to the park?" Esmeralda knew that Maria was trying to limit how much time Abraham was around them, and they didn't know when he would be back.

"Sure thing, Mrs. A. I'll just grab your keys really quick so I can grab the car seats."

A few minutes later, Maria was headed to the police department with the coat carefully wrapped in a plastic bag. She had called ahead to let them know she was coming, but she hadn't been willing to discuss why over the phone.

The precinct was a flurry of activity when she arrived, but she ignored it all and headed straight for the front desk to ask after Detective Jimenez. He had left instructions to take her straight to his office, though Officer Hope let her know he had stepped out for a quick phone call. Maria sat in the chair opposite his desk, the folded bag on her lap and her legs tapping nervously.

"Mrs.— Maria. Sorry to keep you waiting." Jimenez let himself in behind her, walking around his desk. He paused when he caught sight of her distressed expression. "What's wrong?"

"Shouldn't you be asking if you can record?" she asked in a thick voice.

"All right." He pulled out the little tape recorder and ran her through her rights. "Now will you tell me what's wrong?" He offered her some facial tissues from his desk, which she gratefully took.

"I think I was very, very wrong, Detective," she confessed in a soft voice.

"About what?"

"A great many things, but primarily my husband." She took a steadying breath. "After our trip to New England, I... started to notice some things. Just little, odd behaviors. When we had returned home, the place smelled like disinfectant; he told me that he spilled the pig feed."

"Pig feed?"

"I'll get there. Please."

He nodded for her to continue.

"Abraham has never cleaned a day in his life. He had recently started attempting dishes as part of his whole 'new man' shtick, though." She sniffled. "This is relevant, but it will sound like I'm rambling for a moment: our nanny has OCD. She helps me with a lot of the housework, so as she's learned to manage it, I've worked with her to create little systems around the house. This includes how the dishes are stored. I had noticed Abraham was using and attempting to wash more shot glasses, but I also...I found two sets of our special occasion dishware out of place while getting ready for our big Christmas dinner. He tried to convince me I was crazy, but those dishes haven't been used since Esmeralda and I had cleaned them after a fundraiser dinner in the fall. And there were two full sets out of place."

She used the tissues to dab at her eyes. "Then I noticed that some of our food was missing. Most people might assume Abraham had just pigged himself out even more while the family was out of town, but it was all *my* food. I thought maybe I had misremembered since he had started making me breakfast in the morning, but now I'm certain."

"Why are you certain now, Maria?"

"When we last spoke, I told you that Abraham and I had been in touch through the day, but that was only partially true." She reached into her purse, pulling out a text message log, including the photos he had sent her, and the call log from her phone statement. "I never had any reason to think he had someone over while I was gone, but..." Her gaze drifted down to the bag in her lap.

"What's in the bag, Maria?" Jimenez prompted. Instead of answer, she shakily handed it to him. Jimenez could feel the cloth inside. He gripped the item through the bag so that he wouldn't get any fingerprints on it, and rolled back the plastic.

"None of the kids who were at our place on Christmas wore that coat," she explained, her voice cracking. "I...I don't know where it came from, but..."

"You and I have the same suspicions." He carefully set the bag on his desk. "Maria, look at me. Do you think you are safe at your home right now? Assuming I can confirm where this coat came from, this will be enough to get a search warrant for your home. I don't want to alert Abraham to anything out of the ordinary, but I don't want you in danger."

"I'm moving out in three days. And I have our security cameras turned on. I should be ok, I just…I don't know how I'm going to sleep at night next to him."

"Does he know you're planning to move?"

"In abstract. He knows I'm planning to move and planning to serve him with divorce papers, but not when."

"Then here's my advice. I want you to call your real estate agent and see if you can bump your moving day to today or tomorrow, all right?"

She stifled a sob in her tissue, but nodded.

"Now. Tell me about this pig feed."

***

Mrs. Alvarez had been so distraught when she left the precinct that Detective Jimenez sent an unmarked car to follow her and make sure she stayed safe despite her assurances. He immediately sent the jacket off for processing so they could contact Ethan's parents for potential identification, and then he called The Happy Pig.

A few hours later, he was at the slaughterhouse with his partner. The main receptionist, Jessie O'Hara, met him outside. "Detective Jimenez, I presume? It's a pleasure."

"This is my partner, Detective Dawson," Jimenez introduced. "If it's alright with you, I'd like for one of your crew to show him to those bags while we talk."

"You've both got body cams on, yeah?" At their confirmation, Jessie nodded. "Then I'm happy to do so. I won't make you get a warrant or anything; we're happy to comply. Just making sure our bases are covered."

"Understandable, miss. Thank you."

He waited for her to call over a worker, sending Dawson off with the man while he followed Jessie into the office building. She had him join her in a small office room set up for meetings. He set up his recorder with her permission, listed off her rights and assurances, and began the interview.

"Miss O'Hara—"

"Missus."

"My apologies. Mrs. O'Hara, what can you tell me about your dealings with Abraham Alvarez?"

"The Alvarezes have been ordering with us for a long time. Multiple generations. They're generally our best customers, though they have a few odd quirks."

"Like what?"

"Mainly an insistence on using their own feed for final meals. We haven't found anything harmful in the stuff, but it's an unusual request."

"And what about Abraham?"

"I don't want to get in any trouble, detective."

"I guarantee you will not, especially since you are voluntarily cooperating. I can still ask for a search warrant, if you prefer?"

"No, no. I would feel bad having you drive all this way. And I'd rather talk to you now." She leaned back in her chair, folding her hands in her lap. "Abraham has always been a bit of an odd duck."

"Why do you say that?"

"He had certain requirements for his orders. There was the usual one about the feed, but then he also requested his pigs be kept in pen six when they were getting ready to be processed. He also insisted on receiving recordings of the slaughters."

Jimenez pulled a face, and Jessie shook her head.

"Some people like to ensure their meat is handled well, but normally they watch once or twice. Maybe the occasional random request. But Abraham wanted every slaughter. And he told me his oldest son had been getting interested in the family traditions, so he was letting him watch."

"Father of the year," Jimenez muttered.

"This year, there was more." At Jimenez raised eyebrow, she continued. "First off was the size of the order. I know he donates a lot of pork, but nowhere near this much. Then he decided to come and feed them himself rather than send the feed bags through a courier. That wouldn't have been too odd if he hadn't come at some God-awful hour in the morning, long before we even opened."

"You mentioned that he gets videos of the slaughters. Do you have cameras on the pens? Or outside?"

"Yes and no." Jessie grimaced. "They aren't very good quality. Frankly, they barely work. They got busted up in a hail storm last year and we haven't been able to get them fixed."

"Can you see anything from his visit?"

"A little, and that's another oddity." Jessie pulled up her laptop. The film was grainy, and there were large cracks across the image. But Jimenez could just make out a blurry shape that could be an SUV and a figure walking back and forth.

"Can you tell me what's unusual?"

"Three things. First off, the number of trips he takes in and out. Mr. A left the empty bags and a couple extras inside for us. I imagine he carried them in one at a time, man's not the most in shape. But the number of bags doesn't match the number of trips. Second is the time stamp." She pointed to the small numbers in one of the undamaged corners. "Here is the last time he goes in." She fast-forwarded a bit. "And here is when he leaves."

"What was he doing in there for so long?"

She shook her head. "That camera is completely down. I don't have any footage from the pens."

"All right. And what about the third concern?"

"What you've sent your partner to investigate. When my boys were cleaning up the garbage Alvarez left in the aisles, it got shoved into storage with the full bags 'cause we had too much work processing orders before Christmas. When they went to take care of them, they found some weird residue on them."

"Jimenez." The detective paused when his radio squawked, reaching to grab it from his coat.

"Go ahead?"

"Let admin know I'm calling the local precinct. We need to process the scene."

Jimenez lifted his gaze to Jessie. "Acknowledged." He turned off the radio and leaned back in his chair. "Have there been any pigs in pen six since Abraham's order?"

"Yeah, unfortunately. It's one of our busiest weeks, so we gotta keep the rotation going."

"Hell of a way to celebrate the holidays," Jimenez sighed, then hesitated. "Sorry."

"None taken. It's not a very glamorous job."

"Is there anyway you can send me that footage? And the footage you sent to Abraham?"

"Let me put it on a thumb drive for you." She left the room for a moment to retrieve the memory stick before clearing it off and transferring the files.

"Thanks. How many pigs would you say you process in a typical quarter?"

Jessie whistled. "It varies, but it can easily hit the hundreds and thousands. Those aren't records I have access to beyond the current quarter, though. I'd have to talk to the boss."

"Awful lot of killing."

"Luckily they don't feel it. We follow all procedures for humane slaughter here."

"Humane slaughter? What does that mean, they volunteer to die?"

"They never know what hit him. It's quick, and they're gone in a blink."

Jimenez sighed. *Poor damn pigs.* "Well, I think that's all the questions we have for now. If it's all right with you, I'd like to go join my partner and start processing what he's found."

"Of course, detective. Please let me know if you need anything from us."

"For now, let's keep pen six clear. I know it's not pristine, but we still might find something."

"Understood."

Detectives Jimenez and Dawson spent the next several hours working with the local police department to painstakingly search and document the slaughter pen, the storage area, and the place where Alvarez had parked. While they worked, Jimenez explained the investigation to the local deputy in charge of the scene so he would know what they were looking for.

"Did you say Alvarez?"

"Yeah, why?"

The man rubbed his chin. "We had trooper call in a traffic stop with that name. Pretty sure it was in the time frame you're talking."

"You serious?"

"Pretty sure it's the same name. Want me to have dispatch look it up?"

"Absolutely. And if it's my guy, have them send the info to my office."

"You bet."

Once the officers were up to speed and had the scene under control, Jimenez and Dawson headed back to New York City. At 3:33 that afternoon, Jimenez's phone rang. Dawson was driving, so he went ahead and answered.

"Jimenez speaking. What can I do for you, Lieutenant?"

"Jimenez, how's The Happy Pig?"

"Nothing like it's name. Dawson and I are about halfway back with some evidence. I don't think we're going to like what we find, but it needs to be found."

"I'm afraid I agree with you."

Jimenez frowned. "Oh?"

"We've got an interesting tie-in. You know those food poisoning cases EMS and the ERs were reporting today?"

"Yeah?"

"Well, they kept coming. A full-on outbreak. Tons of complaints from other precincts, the fire department, a few homeless shelters— even some private citizens."

Jimenez's eyes widened. "Alvarez's pork?"

"Bingo. We've got samples from the deliveries, and we're adding the information to that search warrant application of yours. I'm going to see if I can get that sped through."

"I appreciate it. And the head's up. We'll see you soon."

Chapter 28

Maria Alvarez did her best to act natural. The boys were fast asleep in their rooms, and she had just heard Abraham creep into the bathroom after being out all night again. She slid from the bed and moved down into the kitchen. She didn't bother to change out of her silky white camisole, just wrapping herself in a warm robe.

It was a little early, 5:55, but not unheard of for her to be awake. She mixed up a small breakfast for herself and then started a pot of coffee. She poured her own cup, stepped into the hall to make sure she could hear the shower running, and then returned to the kitchen. She took a small handful of pills, ground them into a powder, and quickly mixed them into the remaining coffee.

She was just pouring her oatmilk creamer when Abraham came downstairs. He didn't say anything to her, just grabbing the pot and pouring his own cup.

"I think the machine is on the fritz," she told him calmly. "Grounds got a bit burnt."

He grunted in response, but moved to get his own creamer in case it had a taste. He then made himself a plate of breakfast and went back upstairs. Maria bided her time. She rinsed out the coffee pot with searing hot water to make sure there was no residue in case she made herself more later. Then she sat in front of the panoramic windows and gazed out over the backyard to drink her coffee.

When she returned upstairs, Abraham had fallen fast asleep, losing the plate of eggs to the floor. She didn't care. She walked over to his nightstand, snatched up his phone, and held it to his face. Once the screen confirmed facial recognition, she grabbed his hand and pressed his thumb to the screen.

She wasn't worried about waking him up. She knew just how strong those sleeping pills were because she had been taking them to sleep while Jesús was in the NICU. And she had given him far more than her dose. Putting it in the coffee had been a risk, but she couldn't bring herself to make the man's disgusting breakfast.

She sat on the foot of the bed as she navigated to his photo gallery. There wasn't anything too interesting in the camera roll, but when she clicked over to his albums she was greeted with dozens of collections. Some of them just seemed to be porn, but others had names. The most recent file was called 'Ethan B'.

The more she scrolled through the photos and played the videos, first in Ethan's gallery and then in the others, the more she cried. By the third gallery, she was shaking hard enough that she could barely navigate the files. She saw the photos of Ethan in that obnoxious costume from her dream, lying on her bed with a bag duct-taped around his head. Ethan on the garage floor. Ethan ritualistically butchered. Ethan fed to pigs. Then there were more. Kids in awful situations with her husband, some alive and weeping in the camera, others looking like they were at least pretending to enjoy his attention. But their fates were all the same.

How many years? How many boys? She pulled out her own phone and started searching the names on the albums before adding 'missing'. She stood with more calm than she felt and retrieved a notepad and pen before doing her best to identify every single one of her husband's victims. She went back a few years, but then she couldn't look anymore. She set both of their phones and the notepad on the dresser, and moved to her night stand.

She had started keeping the marble cross her mother had gifted her a few years back by the bed to help comfort her at night. Now it would bring her a new kind of comfort. She took the cross in her hand and climbed into bed over Abraham. She lifted her right hand as high as she could reach, and then brought it smashing down across his temple. She didn't pay any mind to the sickening crunch, the splash of blood. All she could think of was those poor boys. Their families. How she had never realized the extent of her husband's depravity.

She gripped the base of the cross and pulled, unsheathing a hidden knife within. She gripped the knife in both hands and started stabbing him again and again and again. Blood flung from the blade, splattering across their bed and the wall of family photos nearby. The sheets beneath Abraham stained red as the blood poured out from his head. Maria drove the knife down one final time, into his heart, and then left the bed to retrieve her phone. She calmly unlocked the screen and dialed Detective Jimenez's direct line.

***

When Detective Jimenez arrived at the Alvarez house, he found the door unlocked. He held his pistol to his side and knocked loudly.

"Maria?" When she didn't answer, he eased the door open and called out again. "Maria!"

He nodded to the officers behind him, and they filed into the house and swept the bottom floor. He could hear one of the boys, likely the youngest, crying from the upstairs, but they had to move carefully. Jimenez eased his way upstairs, nodding his backup towards the room with the crying and moving towards another door that was slightly ajar.

As he entered the room, he froze. Abraham was lying in a bloody heap on the bed, blood still pouring from his wounds. Maria was sitting on the edge of the bed, rocking slightly and covered in blood. She had drawn several shaky crosses along her skin, and as Jimenez approached, he heard her muttering Hail Mary.

***

Detective Jimenez called his lieutenant, advising him to initiate the search warrant and send forensics and a medical examiner. He also called for an ambulance. He tried to get Maria to talk to him, but finally he managed to take her hand and unlock her phone. He searched through her emergency contacts to find the boys' nanny and called her to come meet with a social worker outside. He wanted to be sure the boys had someone familiar amidst all the chaos.

Luckily, the oldest was enthralled with the officers that had come to check on them. Two of the officers with Jimenez's initial team were parents, so they stayed in the playroom with the boys and kept them occupied. Jimenez asked Esmeralda to bring them some breakfast, as he assumed from the washed out coffee pot his officers found in the kitchen that they would need to canvas the room as part of their investigation.

While the medical and forensics teams labored feverishly to canvas the bedroom, Jimenez had a team cordon off both ends of the street. That didn't stop the Alvarezes' neighbors and random passers-by from congregating nearby, speculating what could be happening. News teams and paparazzi soon joined them, though the officers on duty did a good job of keeping them back and blocking their photos for now.

The precinct sent more officers down to canvas the neighbors, but they had little to add to the investigation aside from Carl, who had spoken with Abraham when he left for New England back before Christmas. Though there were still no details, the neighbors started to whisper about domestic violence or abuse, wondering if one or both of the Alvarezes were dead. They had seen the nanny arrive and collect the children, so they knew the little ones were safe, at least. But they didn't want to obsess; whatever happened would provide some good neighborhood gossip for a while, but they wouldn't dwell on the crime lest it affect their property values. Some were already considering selling, while others alerted their brokers to keep an eye out for the real estate listing so they could purchase the Alvarez home.

The large home had been in the Alvarez family for generations. Some of the neighbors speculated that if the current residents had perished, it would likely pass to another family member before going up for sale. The New York City Department of Buildings records only went back two hundred years, but tax records dating further back still placed the property in Alvarez control.

The home was exquisite, with all of the original ornate woodwork meticulously cared for throughout the years. Abraham's family was proud of that property as it stood for the resilience, perseverance, and tenacity of the family legacy. Only the men truly understood the sacrifices that were made to enable their family's wealth, and they dutifully ignored them.

The outside of the home was a lovely patio with ornate concrete pillars framing the door. As police walked in and out, a potted plant was knocked aside enough to reveal a detailed rendition of the devil's face. Records indicated that neighbors had sued in the past but lost, because the building was historical and the design could not be altered. It had been Maria's idea to set the plant there, as she couldn't stand the sight of the thing, either.

The inside boasted three sprawling floors, with several floor-to-ceiling windows offering a gorgeous view of the West Side River. The twenty-million-dollar home was a dream for anyone who had ever seen it, and the neighbors were already salivating over offers they might make to the family.

Now the home was documented in a far more grisly fashion. The forensics team took dozens of photos, including of Maria. She looked like someone from a horror film who had been doused in buckets of fake blood. Jimenez urged the team to work quickly so that he could get her out of the crime scene and to a hospital. They would help her clean up and then initiate a psychiatric evaluation.

Abraham's body was recovered face-up from their shared custom-made king-sized bed. Maria had stabbed him a total of sixty-six times before gutting him like a pig. The medical examiner, Richard Garcia, painstakingly documented and photographed each wound. He would later testify that of all the murders he had examined, especially involving wives and their cheating husbands, this was by far the most gruesome. Monstrous. The inflicted wounds carried a special, specific, severe sense of vengeance, rage, and punishment.

As Jimenez spoke with another officer outside, he couldn't help noticing the dissonance of the sunny winter's day contrasting the bloodcurdling scene inside. There wasn't a cloud in the sky, and several birds dotted through the neighborhood called together in perfect harmony, an orchestra to oversee Abraham's demise.

Finally, they were ready to remove Abraham's body. Even with the evisceration, the man was so large that the two medical examiner office workers needed extra hands to get the gurney downstairs. They had covered Abraham in a white sheet in an effort to prevent any of the news crews from catching a glimpse. Just as they made their way from the patio to the extra ambulance, six identical black drones descended from the sky.

One of the neighbors had pointed them out first, but soon everyone was looking. The paramedics scrambled to find extra sheets to put over Abraham's corpse in case there were cameras, while one of the police officers procured a megaphone and tried to order them away.

The six black drones were completely in sync; even their red and green lights blinked in tandem.

Everyone's gaze was so focused on the drones, no one noticed Abraham's bloodied left arm slip from the gurney. As more blood dripped and slid down his hand, the diamond-and-ruby gold ring loosened and dropped from his hand. Six small laser pinpricks immediately lit up on the gold, and the ring disintegrated.

***

Jimenez had tried to read Maria her rights, but the woman was completely non-responsive. She wouldn't say a word until she was being interviewed by the intake assessor in the psychiatric ward. Then it was like a dam had burst.

"Abraham was a demon. A demon. I always knew he was a liar and a cheater, but this...this...He was working as a schoolteacher for God's sake! How many of those kids were his students?!" she had wailed. "And now I find out he was dressing in drag for these creepy sex clubs? That motherfucker got exactly what he deserved! I wish he were alive so I could kill him over and over." She sniffled, wiping at her eyes as best she could; they had kept her handcuffed in fear of a violent outburst.

"You know, even before we had James, he loved kids. I always thought he was going to make a great dad. Now I see what's really on his phone, and I'm sorry I ever pulled children into this hell hole." She sobbed again. "Oh my boys, my boys, I'm so sorry, Mommy's so sorry. You'll be ok now. Surely you'll be ok." She rocked in her chair, but her expression shifted to a scowl. "I carved him open like he did the pigs on Christmas, used his damn tools to rip open his chest." She lifted her gaze to the assessor, eyes wide.

"Did you know? He had a heart after all. I was beginning to wonder. He went through the motions of trying to be a good role model, husband, and provider, but the truth is he was none of those things. He was a fucking monster. When I saw the videos of all of those terrified boys on his phone, I knew he was the Devil himself. There's no other explanation for being so...so barbaric." She buried her face in her hands and cried. "I'm tired. I'm so tired. But I'm relieved." The cries mixed with laughter, and she fell silent again aside from those hysterical sounds.

Chapter 29

John and Selena had taken the first few days after Christmas off to fast and pray. They had journaled their thoughts privately, spending time first with themselves before coming together again to discuss what happened. They had even spent the first two nights after in separate rooms. On the third morning, John sat with his journal in the living room and invited Selena to come sit with him. He turned to face her, taking her hands in his.

"Selena. I need to apologize to you. I'm ashamed of myself for the lack of discipline I showed, for giving in so thoroughly to temptation."

"John, it's not just your fault. It's mine, too. I fell into old habits far too easily. I'm not my past, and I shouldn't let it control me. I don't want to live that way."

"I'm grateful you feel the same way. If we hadn't landed on the same page after this, I don't think our relationship would have survived."

She squeezed his hands. "You're my soulmate. I'm so glad God brought us together. The world tried to break us apart, and we overcame it together."

"And you're mine," he agreed, lifting her hands to kiss them.

"It's so strange…" she started, trailing off for a moment before continuing. "In those clubs I felt both empowered and completely out of control. We got to play dress up, roleplay, and enjoy our bodies however we desired, but… In the real world, it seems quite lonely, doesn't it? I keep thinking back to Sara, going on and on about leaving her kids for months and going to orgies. I don't understand what keeps her and David together. He even admitted she threatened to leave if he wouldn't let her have her fun, and now she's pulled him into the same empty life. They sounded so sure of themselves, tried so hard to convince us their life was perfect, yet all I heard in their words is desperation."

"I know what you mean."

"I don't want that kind of empty existence, John."

"Me either. I wouldn't trade 'us' for anything in the world. So please, let's keep our energy on things that raise our vibration. Let's cut off the clubs completely, and go back to who we were before we ever found those awful places."

"Yes, let's." Selena smiled. "Let's dedicate ourself to Plants again, and really live up to the name."

"What did you have in mind?"

"After the year turns over, I want to start hosting a church. But we won't run on tithes; instead, we'll keep pouring into the community. I just want to offer a space for God's Children to come together without all the pressure."

John smiled. "I love it."

2222: The Untold Stories

***

As they entered the third night of their fast, John invited Selena to pray with him next to the bed as they had their first night together.

"Dear God, we cannot thank You enough for the clarity of mind and wisdom You have granted us to escape the pit we had fallen into. I am so very thankful to You for so many things: Selena and our love; my boys, and the difference they will make in the universe. My wealth, and all the things I can use it for in Your name."

He took a deep breath. "Lord, we failed You. We failed ourselves. But with Your blessings, we will come back from this darkness with a renewed vigor to spread Your light. We will spread Your love through the streets of New York City, sweep it across the continent, and inspire a revival throughout the world. We will turn Angela's words into concrete falsehoods, one step at a time. From those poor souls digging through garbage cans for a bite to eat, to the invisible people sleeping outside on the streets." His eyes started to water. He felt vulnerable but refreshed.

"Our bodies are Yours, Lord. Our wealth is Yours. Our minds, our spirits, all Yours."

"Please give us the strength and guidance necessary to continue Your work," Selena chimed in. "Help us keep at bay the demons who would drag us from Your purpose. You have provided us with beautiful minds, spirits, and bodies that are meant to be loved, not used."

"We love You, Father," John continued. "Now please help us learn to love ourselves again, so we may pour that love into others. We pray for all this in Your name. Amen." As Selena echoed his amen, John stood and offered her his hand. They curled together on top of the bed, with Selena resting her head on his chest. As they savored the moment of peace, both of their stomachs suddenly growled. John laughed.

"Selena, maybe I was overzealous with 72 hours. Especially after the party."

"No. I think it's the perfect time to fast. We've got this without the distractions of food, sex, or social media. Just us, giving ourselves the chance to reflect, empathize, and feel the hunger plaguing so many around us. We can never truly understand their pain without being homeless ourselves, but we can learn to empathize and better serve their needs."

"I couldn't have said it better myself. All right. We'll keep going." He craned his neck to kiss the top of her head. "That will be easier with sleep. I love you."

"I love you, too." Selena curled into John's hold, feeling truly safe again for the first time in weeks. They fell asleep in each other's arms, intertwined in body and spirit.

***

John and Selena knelt on the ground, surrounded by a brilliant white light. God stood before them dressed in a white robe, His face shining like the sun.

"Behold. I am the Lord, your God, the Architect of all existence. It was by My will that your paths intertwined in eons past and have come together again.

Faith in my omnipotence must ardently burn within your hearts, My Adam and Eve. For you have passed the tests I laid before you. I name you the heirs-apparent, king and queen of this Earth; the first man and woman since the Fall to be free from the curse.

Be wary of Our adversary the Devil. He shall wear myriad guises— kin, friend, partner. His essence is deception, bringing forth temptation through vices such as lust, inebriation, dependency, and more. In this era, his reach has been magnified through dominion over digital expanses and popular distractions that divert your gaze from your sacred mission.

Humanity extols praise for leisure and downtime, but many of these things I have deemed as deviations. You must dedicate yourselves to the downtrodden, laboring tirelessly to serve those in need. You must remain the best versions of yourselves, ever-striving to reach the potential I have bestowed upon you.

Acknowledge the divine spark I have granted you and be liberated; you shall neither fear nor falter. Your lives shall be free of disease, hunger, and the specter of mortality.

Together, as a testament to peace and eternal love, your existence shall be a beacon of everlasting life. You are to remain ever-present, omnipotent, dependent solely on your steadfast belief in your divine essence.

To guide your path, I present these commandments and urge you to spread My Word through all your days:

- Do not eat of animal's flesh, that you may gain the gift of eternal life.
- Pass not by your brethren in need, but extend your hand with generosity.
- Mock not the less fortunate.
- In all interactions, act with the compassion you wish bestowed upon you.
- Forsake the sin of adultery.
- Shun the grievous act of murder.
- Covet not your neighbor's spouse.
- Avoid gluttony; honor your body as a sacred temple, not an object of fleshly desires.
- Turn away from lust, whether of the body or through covetous eyes.
- Trust not blindly in the flawed words of news and leaders; deceit often lies within eloquence.

Remain vigilant against the Adversary's allurements, for he seeks to seduce you into tasting once more from the tree of knowledge, as in the age-old tale. You epitomize humanity's potential, and thus I have never forsaken you. Should you embrace this divine mandate, life shall extend for centuries, proving My existence through your reign.

But be forewarned— in the year 2029, Adam and Eve will die. You shall soon be brought back to life for the world to see that I am real and ever-present. Do not be afraid. Let not doubt deter you, for skeptics thrive where miracle descends. Stand unwavering, for you are indeed My children, destined for greatness.

When Selena woke, she found that she was crying. She lifted her gaze to John, finding him awake and weeping as well.

"John...?"

"Did you...see what I saw?" he asked breathlessly.

"God appeared before us, and gifted us new commandments. He...He said we were Adam and Eve reborn?"

"He did. Oh, thank you, Father." He held her tightly. "He hasn't forsaken us! He trusts us, even after all that we did." He nuzzled into her hair. "Never again, please baby."

"Never, ever. I don't want us to be distracted again. That's what the Devil wants, just like we were warned in our vision. He doesn't want us serving food or spreading the gospel, which means we need to make sure we keep doing so."

"I couldn't agree more, baby. Never again will I doubt our mission and purpose. We have been anointed." He rubbed her arm before sitting up. "And from the sounds of things, we have a lot of work cut out for us. With the minor inconvenience of death in five years."

"That's not funny, John," Selena chided. "Either you believe or you don't. There is no in-between. I'm not afraid, so long as He takes us together; I know we'll be back stronger than ever before."

Chapter 30

John and Selena spent the first part of their morning worshiping God before moving to end their fast. While they were wary of what the news sources of the world would tell them, they wanted to stay abreast of what was being said so they could connect to those around them. John settled on Channel Six news, and Sofia Guzman appeared in the midst of the morning headlines.

"— more confusion and speculation regarding recent drone sightings. The strange flying objects match no design currently on the market, and now NASA scientists warn that scans of the items do not return materials known to Earth. The drones have been spotted outside of churches as well as government buildings, the World Health Organization, and more. Each drone appears to be equipped with a camera, and can be recognized by it's seamless design and synchronous red and green lights." As she tapped her notes on the desk and looked at a new camera, John and Selena exchanged looks of disbelief.

"In local news, Father Peter Johnson of the West Side parish was arrested today for allegations of child pornography and sexual assault, stemming from incidents that allegedly occurred inside the church. Officers led him from the cathedral in handcuffs, while authorities seized several computers, at least one phone, and multiple external hard drives. A spokesman for the church had no comment when asked questions regarding the allegations. Meanwhile, Channel Six investigative teams have found that the priest had been transferred between different parishes at least six times over the past six years, though the sources did not state why. Online court documents confirm that he has faced accusations before, with some cases settled outside of court."

As the headline story finished, the camera switched to Guzman's co-anchor, Marcus Brown. "Another story tonight tears through the hearts of local communities. Activist Javier Nunez, known for his commitment to bringing child predators to justice, has been found dead in his home. Nunez received the NYC Child Humanitarian Award three years in a row for his tireless efforts. His resilience and perseverance have created a safer place for our children to live and grow peacefully. He will be greatly missed. In a shocking turn of events, he was found with his lower half mutilated and a message written in blood that read: 'You will never stop us. For every six hundred you arrest, six hundred more shall rise.' Forensic teams are currently analyzing the message."

The camera switched to Ms. Guzman again, who's stoic expression seemed much more practiced than it had before. "Viewer discretion is advised for this next story." She paused to allow parents time to ferry away their children. "Abraham Alvarez, a local teacher and philanthropist, has been found dead in his home."

John sat up straighter, staring at the screen.

"In what has been described as a gruesome, vengeful scene, Alvarez was found in his bedroom with sixty-six stab wounds and severe mutilations. His wife Maria is currently hospitalized in police custody. No further details regarding the death have been reported. Ironically, sources indicate that both the FBI and local police had been attempting to serve a search warrant at the Alvarezes' home relating to the disappearance of Ethan Bísólá."

Guzman paused, composing herself. "Police have confirmed Ethan Bísólá has perished. Our condolences to his family at this time. The Nigerian embassy has requested privacy on their behalf while they grieve the loss of their son."

She continued, "Neighbors of the Alvarezes are shocked to learn of both the allegations and Abraham Alvarez's demise, claiming that there had been no signs of difficulties between the young couple or a potential darker side to Abraham. Friends of the couple, however, painted a different picture. One friend, who wished to remain anonymous, claimed their relationship had many problems, including infidelity."

As Guzman continued to discuss what information was publicly available, Selena caught John's arm. "John. Look at his eyes." John frowned at her and then looked back up at the image of Abraham on the screen.

Together, they realized: "That's Angela!"

Author's Notes

My co-author and I began writing this tale nearly three years ago. The process has altered our lives in surprising ways. Working on the book was more difficult than we anticipated, especially when juggling everyday life. We visited multiple parks throughout New York City because we felt a sense of peace when sitting to write.

Washington Square Park was an ideal place to sit, write, and contemplate life. The characters from our book were given life and power there while we saw those powerless rummaging through garbage cans for food. They were young and old, of all ethnicities, and the common denominator was they needed help.

The pivotal time came in May 2023 when we took a hiatus from writing to start a non-profit called Plants on Wheels, in New York City.

Neither of us had any proficiency in running a non-profit, nor did we have much money. But we did have a profound yearning to help people, coupled with a common desire to make a difference in the universe we're part of. We reached out to dozens of vegan food vendors and received numerous food donations, as most companies empathized with our cause.

Once we started receiving donations, we began cooking vegan food and distributing it to homeless people throughout Washington Square Park. Never have we experienced such gratitude and humility as when we looked into the eyes of people who had thought they were forgotten. Suddenly, our needs, wants, and desires seemed meaningless compared to people without food, water, or any place to live.

We sent hundreds of emails to local pantries and now continue to partner with them to provide healthier plant-based foods. We also contacted teachers, principals, and school administrators throughout NYC to bring in plant-based taste tests; so far we have presented vegan comfort food to middle and high school students with resounding success.

Plants on Wheels began a mobile food pantry that delivers to people in need. Our pantry will expand to all five boroughs by 2026. While we haven't yet achieved a shared dream with Selena to wrap our trucks in plant-based messaging, it is one of our many goals.

Plants on Wheels set a mission goal of feeding ten thousand people in 2024; by this writing, we have far surpassed that. Our goal for 2025 is to feed a million. For every purchase of this book, we plan to donate a plant-based meal to someone in need. This book is the first in a series of two. We hope to release the sequel in early 2025, with a goal to feed five million people with the proceeds.

Running a non-profit is a lot of work, and there is no monetary reward. It requires a substantial amount of time, effort, and energy. However, it is also the most rewarding thing we've ever done. When you look into the eyes of a stranger thanking you for a hot meal, you understand your purpose in life.

We are blessed with an opportunity to make a difference in the world and help radiate light. Please visit us at plantsonwheels.net and help us with our goals of feeding millions of meals to people who desperately need our help. Plants on Wheels thanks you for being part of our movement, where we envision a world where nobody is hungry or without a place to live. We envision a world where animals' lives are respected, and people spend time in nature enjoying the sunlight and a good conversation. We envision a world where our children are not indoctrinated, nor taken advantage of. We envision a world of love, peace, and harmony.

Milton Keynes UK
Ingram Content Group UK Ltd.
UKHW041736231124
451587UK00027B/78